THE LANGLEY IRREGULARS

FIRST MISSION

HOMELAND INSECURITY

Shawn M. Warner

Black Rose Writing | Texas

ISBN: 978-1-68513-428-0 (Paperback); 978-1-68513-470-9 (Hardcover)
PUBLISHED BY BLACK ROSE WRITING
www.blackrosewriting.com

Printed in the United States of America
Suggested Retail Price (SRP) $21.95 (Paperback); $26.95 (Hardcover)

First Mission is printed in Garamond

*As a planet-friendly publisher, Black Rose Writing does its best to eliminate unnecessary waste to reduce paper usage and energy costs, while never compromising the reading experience. As a result, the final word count vs. page count may not meet common expectations.

HOMELAND INSECURITY

For Chris and Elin,

We had a spectacular time in your beautiful home.

Peace and happiness!

CHAPTER 1

Something collided with Jack's back. His shoulder thrust forward sending his books skidding across the pavement.

"Out of the way, fish."

Fish: slang for Freshman.

Hazing: another word for stupid.

Jack took in a deep breath for calm's sake. Squatting to gather his scattered papers and school supplies before a summer's end breeze could scatter them across the schoolyard, he felt his face burn. His cheeks, he knew, were so flushed his dusting of freckles were nearly invisible. Head low, Jack rolled his eyeballs up towards his red-silk eyebrows to keep tabs on the bully.

Jack recognized him as a Junior. Paul Ackerman. He was a big, burly customer, but his overweight appearance belied colossal strength and surprising speed. Jack's sister, Grace, once talked about Paul with her best friend Kelly, oblivious to the fact Jack was in the same room. From what he overheard, Paul was the star player on the football team, which was his one saving grace. Off the field, according to both girls, he was a jerk.

Jack tucked his books back beneath his arm and stood, whispering to himself, "Gossip confirmed."

Ahead of him, Paul targeted another victim. "What are you looking at?"

A thin and pale boy whose name Jack knew from middle school, but nothing more, stammered a frightened, "N-n-nothing."

Paul loomed over poor, skinny Oliver like a falcon over a field mouse. "I saw you eyeing me. You trying to start something?"

Without warning, Paul's meaty fist shot out and punched Oliver in the face.

Jack's books hit the ground the same instant as did Oliver's body. "That's enough."

Paul turned slow and menacing. "You going to be the hero here?"

Jack took a step forward. "He's not even half your size. Leave him alone."

Paul lumbered forward. "I'll leave him alone. Long enough to pound you."

A circle formed around the two. The chant, "Fight! Fight! Fight!" roiled like water coming to a boil.

A huge arm swung towards Jack's head.

Jack ducked, allowing the blow to whiz over his head. Slipping in and to the side, his foot darted out, making a jab at the back of Paul's leg.

Paul dropped to one knee, throwing his hands against the concrete to keep from landing flat on his face.

Spinning, Jack landed a back kick on Paul's nose. It burst like a red-dye water balloon.

A teacher wedged herself between Jack and Paul. "Stop this at once. Office. Both of you."

Paul staggered to his feet, gingerly tapped at his nose, and stared at his blood-stained fingertips. He growled at Jack.

"Don't!" the teacher shouted. "You're in enough trouble already."

Jack turned and retrieved his fallen books before making his way to the office. Out of the corner of his eye, he watched Paul do the same. Behind them, the teacher bellowed, "The rest of you get to class!" before trailing them into school.

Moving towards the school building, Jack caught sight of Kelly buried in the crowd gathered around the door. Her eyes weren't bright and gleeful over having just witnessed a spectacle. They were studying. Calculating.

Feeling like a fly being summed-up by a spider, his feet stuttered under the power of her gaze, but he was in too much trouble to stop. Unnerved, he plodded into school and went straight to the office. A secretary shook her head in dismay, sending the clear plastic beads of her glasses' tether swaying. "Three days into the first week? This has to be some kind of record."

She scowled at Jack and pointed to a line of tan, wooden chairs beside the principal's door. "Take a seat over there."

She turned her sour face to Paul. "You. Go see the nurse, then come join your friend. And no more foolishness, or it'll be the police you're talking to and not Principal Kohl."

Jack

BriNLee

CHAPTER 2

Jack's eyes darted over to Paul who, returning, took up a seat three away from him. The beefy teen glared back with twists of blood-stained gauze stuffed up his nose.

Inside Principal Kohl's office, wimpy Oliver was giving his version of what happened. Jack squirmed knowing soon it would be his turn. Despite having right on his side — being scrawny doesn't give anyone the right to slug you — Jack's throat was too tight and dry to gulp down the nervous lump lodged in it.

When the principal's door opened, Jack flicked his eyes over, trying to get some indication of how Oliver's interview went. Pale-faced, except for a bruise that was starting to tint his cheek, Oliver shuffled out. Jack returned the half smile Oliver flashed him. His smile faded when he saw Oliver bow his head in shame as he scampered past Paul. The memory of what happened would haunt him for a very long time.

Thinking about it made Jack's blood boil. Principal Kohl, scowling at both him and Paul, was all that kept him from telling Paul exactly what he thought of him and starting their fight all over again. Instead, he tilted his head and looked his principal in the eyes.

Principal Kohl was a black man who, like Paul, was a football star in his day — first college, then pro — until a knee injury ended his career. Muscles bulged beneath his crisp-starched shirt. A powerful, scarlet tie added to the intimidation factor.

"We're waiting for your parents to arrive," he said in a baritone grumble before returning to his office, snapping the door shut.

Jack drew his fingertips across his clammy palms, pulling them into fists. From kindergarten to eighth-grade, Jack was the model student. Smart. Quiet. Helpful. Now that he'd made it to high school, he was sitting in the office for first time ever.

He chewed his bottom lip. The urge to stand and pace made him fidget but, he knew, as soon as his rear-end left its chair, he'd be shouted down, making matters worse. Grinding his teeth, he forced himself to stay put.

Trying to take his mind off the trouble he'd landed himself in, he studied the small team of gray-haired office secretaries as they shuttled between their desks, filing cabinets, and various other offices. The phones rang incessantly. A steady trickle of students dropped in, running some errand or another. Jack's ears burned whenever one of them caught sight of him, sitting outside the principal's office with a dejected pout marring his face, and struggled not to laugh at him.

Soaking in the office hubbub, Jack watched a dumpy-looking man in an unimaginative gray and black uniform emerge from the bowels of the administrative offices. A tin shield, the word 'Security' pressed into the metal, was pinned to the front of his shirt at a crooked angle. Jack choked on an unpleasant whiff of grocery-store-after-shave as the security guard bustled past and gave a light rap on the principal's door.

While the security guard and the principal conferred, Jack noticed a woman who looked very much like Oliver, slip into the office and stand meek and unassertive in line alongside the students. Being so unassuming, it took several minutes for the office staff to notice her.

"Parents don't have to wait in line, dear," a secretary stationed at the front counter called out. "How may I help you?"

The woman whispered something.

"Sorry. Missed that," the secretary said, leaning in.

"I'm Oliver Massey's mother," the lady said again.

"Oh, yes," the secretary shouted over the din. "Please come around and take a seat. There's coffee at the back, if you'd like a cup."

Oliver's mother refused the offer with a titter and settled onto a chrome and polyester couch on the side of the office farthest away from Jack and Paul. Seconds later, the security guard emerged from the principal's office and Principal Kohl invited her in.

With nothing else to do, Jack went back to watching his classmates come and go, to picking at his fingernails, to counting the number of times Paul rocked between sitting back in his chair and leaning forward with his elbows on his knees. Closing his eyes, he day-dreamed he was an undercover operative shackled outside some evil villain's torture chamber awaiting interrogation. A sly smile crept onto his face as he wondered how he was going to get himself out of this mess.

Paul flinched when Principal Kohl's door opened, pulling Jack back into reality.

"Your son is waiting in the nurse's office," Principal Kohl said to Oliver's mom, who was standing next to him. "It's your call whether Oliver finishes the day or if you want to take him home. Just let one of the secretaries know which you decide."

Oliver's mom mumbled something and held her hand out to Principal Kohl. His massive hand covered hers like a blanket.

Like her son, she smiled at Jack and whispered, "Thank you," as she scurried by.

Passing Paul, she gave a derisive sniff, but kept her head up, eyes locked ahead of her. Jack and Paul got another frigid glare from their principal. Jack's anxiety flooded back into him.

Time ticked on and all Jack could do was to sit, simmering in nervous uncertainty. Over the following forty-five minutes, that anxiety ebbed away and was replaced once more with fidgety boredom. When his mother arrived his heart rate roared back up, perspiration misting out every pore, making him itch.

Paul's father arrived at the same time. Jack watched as Mr. Ackerman held the office door open for his mother. Mr. Ackerman was as red in the face as a carnival balloon and his lips not so much as twitched in response to the smile of thanks his mom flashed him.

They sat on the same couch Oliver's mother had used. Jack mouthed the word, "Sorry," at his mom from across the room.

Her lips were a grim line as she shook her head in disappointment, but her eyes remained kind.

The tension Jack's body was clinging to vanished. Letting his weight relax onto the seat of his chair, a slow breath crept out of his lungs. His mind flew back to the time when he was four, sitting in her lap with that same disappointed look gazing down as she rocked him. He'd swallowed a penny and the ensuing stomachache kept him awake. He was too old to be held like that now, but his face burned as he admitted part of him still wanted to be.

Squeezing his eyes shut, Jack winced in embarrassment over his memories. Slouching forward, he rubbed the back of his neck. To distract himself, he shifted his focus off thoughts of his mom and onto Paul's dad.

Mr. Ackerman looked furious. His jaws knotted and Jack thought he could hear the man's teeth grinding from across the room. Paul, Jack noticed, kept his head down and sulked. Out of the corner of his eye, Jack watched a tiny runnel of sweat roll over the heavy jowls Paul inherited from the man sitting next to his mom.

Lost in thought, Jack jerked his head up when Principal Kohl popped open his door. "Mrs. Straw? Jack. Please step inside."

Jack waited for his mother to enter, then followed her in. As he always did, Jack scanned every detail. The office had three chairs — two rather uncomfortable looking, armless, wooden ones facing the desk, and Principal Kohl's large office chair. The desk was loaded with files and papers, but everything was neatly stacked, not cluttered. On the wall beside the desk was an enormous laminated calendar with dry-erase notes covering it. Behind the desk was a low file cabinet on top of which were potted plants that could do with some sun and individual pictures of three children and one woman. In front of the woman's picture was a rectangular, wrapped, gift-box.

"Take a seat," Principal Kohl said, easing into his swivel chair behind the desk. "Mrs. Straw, you need to know that the district has a zero-tolerance policy for fighting at school . The consequences could be as severe as permanent expulsion and reassignment to the district's alternative school."

Jack's mother blanched. "Is that what you intend to do to Jack?"

"That is up to him," Principal Kohl said, turning to Jack. "I want you to tell me what happened. I am letting you know up front: if you lie, the consequences will be far worse than if you stick to the truth."

"I understand," Jack said. "I don't have anything to lie about."

Jack's next words tumbled out as he explained to the principal and his mother what took place. Reliving the ordeal, Jack's adrenaline shot up again.

He took a moment to breathe.

Forcing himself to keep calm, he again picked up the story and didn't embellish or downplay any part of it. Despite having taken down one of the strongest athletes in the school, he kept his report humble and gave no details of the actual fight, sticking to the events leading up to it.

When he was done, he and his mother were sent to wait back outside the principal's office as Paul and his dad were called in. Principal Kohl's door closed with a crisp snap.

"Mom, I'm sorry you had to come down here and everything," Jack said.

She mothered his fiery bangs away from his eyes. "Your dad and I will always come to you when you need us, Jack. I don't know what's going to happen but, after hearing the circumstances, you aren't in trouble at home."

"You mean you're not mad?"

"Of course I am! But at the situation, not you. Jack, you made your choice and choices have consequences. We can't protect you from that. But I understand why you did what you did. I'm sure your father will, too."

Jack sat pressing his shoulder against his mother's arm, trying not to be too obvious about it. Her half-closed lids and faint smile let him know he failed, but he didn't care.

Principal Kohl's conference with Paul and his dad ran much longer than Jack's. When, after what felt to Jack to be an eternity, Principal Kohl opened his door and stepped into the hallway, Jack flinched.

"Mrs. Straw," Principal Kohl said, "if you and Jack would join us, please?"

Paul and his dad were seated in the two armless chairs until Paul was given a rough jab from his father's elbow. Paul shot to his feet and moved to stand against the back wall, making room for Jack's mom.

"Thank you," she said, giving Paul a smile Jack didn't feel he deserved.

Jack took his place standing beside Paul, who scooted over to make room, his lip quivering away from his teeth. Jack smirked. He was indifferent to Paul's bluster, but he kept his eyes on Paul's dad. The man was flushed in the face when he first arrived. Now, he was the crimson color of a circus clown's nose. It made Jack nervous. He didn't like his mother sitting so close to someone that angry.

"Jack," Principal Kohl said, breaking his train of thought, "it isn't your job to enforce school rules or to protect the other students. I understand you felt you had to act, to do something, but you made the wrong choice. You should have found a faculty member to deal with the situation, not try to handle it on your own."

Jack's muscles tightened and his nostrils flared. "I understand."

"But you don't agree?"

"Honestly? I don't know. I mean, I let him knock my books out of my hands and didn't do anything. But when he went and hit Oliver ..."

Jack clenched his teeth together. He was standing in the principal's office for fighting. His mother had to leave work and come to his school. And here he was, admitting he would do the same thing all over again. Choking down words of justification, he raised his hands in a shrug of surrender.

"Well," Principal Kohl sighed, "I have no choice but to suspend you. The remainder of this week will be spent in Room One-oh-Four. You'll do your course work there. You will eat lunch there. Before and after school, you will be dropped off and picked up from that room. It goes without saying, you are not to attend any extra-curricular activities. At the end of the week, we'll talk again."

Paul's dad hissed out a sigh of relief. "A few days In-School Suspension? That isn't too bad. And I'm sure Paul will have learned his lesson."

Slow and deliberate, Principal Kohl turned his head and gave him a far less gentle glare than the look he bestowed on Jack.

"Jack will be spending the remainder of this week in ISS, Mr. Ackerman. Paul will have ISS for three weeks and…"

Paul shoved himself off the wall. "Three weeks! That's not fair!"

"…AND," Principal Kohl continued, now staring Paul down, "you will not be allowed to take the field for any game for the remainder of the year."

"Now hold on just a minute," Mr. Ackerman objected in a growl. "Paul is a junior. Talent scouts and college recruiters will want to see him play. You can't do this!"

Principal Kohl rested his elbows on the armrests of his chair and intertwined his fingers over his stomach. "Trust me, I am being lenient. Given what I saw on the security footage and the fact that Paul was more than willing to lie about events until he was confronted with that video evidence, I have more than enough justification to re-assign him to the district's alternative school which has *no* athletics program. He can still be on the team, but he will not play."

Paul's dad shot to his feet.

Jack's mother flinched.

Jack's back flew off the wall.

"We'll just see about that," Mr. Ackerman snarled. "Come on, Paul. We're going home."

Jerking the door open with one hand while grabbing Paul with the other, Mr. Ackerman steered his son out of the office.

"That poor boy," Mrs. Straw said after they left.

"We'll keep an eye on him," Principal Kohl promised as he moved to the door and watched Paul and his dad leave the school. "I'm sure everything'll be fine after they calm down."

"I hope you're right," Mrs. Straw said. "Can Jack walk me to my car before he begins this, what is it? ISS?"

"I think that'll be okay. Jack? You look like you want to say something."

"Huh? Oh! I just wanted to wish you a happy anniversary. Twenty-eight years is a long time."

Principal Kohl's eyes widened. "Why thank you, Jack. But how did you know my wedding anniversary is today?"

"There's a present on the cabinet behind you. Can't say for sure, but it is about the right size for jewelry of some kind. Plus, it's in front of your wife's picture, not one of your kids. Also, that paper — it isn't birthday wrapping so the gift must be for some other occasion. Then, on your calendar, today's date is circled with the note 'A equals twenty-eight'."

Jack shrugged. "It's kinda obvious."

"That's pretty impressive, Jack," Principal Kohl said.

Jack felt a playful swat on his arm. "The man's private life is none of your business, mister."

To Principal Kohl she said, "He's always doing things like that. Let me tell you it's pretty annoying come Christmas."

She held her hand out. "Thank you for being so understanding, given the circumstances."

Jack led his mom through the front office and out of the building. The sun was a refreshing change to the stuffy, artificial lighting inside. Jack walked with his face lifted, his eyes playing in the clouds. His hands trembled with nervous relief as he opened the car door for her.

"See?" she soothed. "That wasn't so bad. Now, come on, you owe me a hug for this one."

Jack stepped into her open arms. Looking over her shoulder, back toward the school, he saw his three best friends; a gorgeous, caramel-skinned girl named Phil, the muscular athlete Peter, and the young school prodigy Collin, standing in a huddle, sarcasm screaming loud and clear out of their postures.

"It's about to get worse," Jack groaned.

CHAPTER 3

After school, Jack found himself sitting in the same school-office chair he sat in that morning. His mother was standing at the long desk students used when talking to the secretaries. Her jaw was working like she was chewing on a great wad of gum. She never chewed gum.

Jack knew it wasn't him she was mad at, but he still felt like a worm. Principal Kohl wouldn't let him go out to meet her. She had to come inside the school, in person, to collect him from the office. While there, Principal Kohl felt it necessary to go over the rules and restrictions of being on ISS in painful detail. Now that he was finished, his mom was working her way through a stack of forms, signing them, saying that she understood it all.

When finally released, the march to the car was brisk and filled with tension. Jack knew better than to say anything.

"All I wanted to do," his mom ranted as they were pulling out of the school parking lot, "was pick you up and get home to take my meeting. For the love of mercy! What was all that about? Completely unnecessary. Now, I'm going to be late!"

Jack spent the rest of the drive stewing in a silence thick with tension. He jerked forward, then rebounded against the back seat when his mom stopped the car in their driveway. Peering out the backseat window he saw his friends, who were sitting on the sky-blue steps of his front porch, their backpacks dumped in the grass. Grace and Kelly had their school bags still slung over their shoulders, telling Jack they just arrived. They stood talking to Phil, Peter, and Collin. Jack's stomach knotted, knowing they were talking about him.

Without saying a word, his mom scrambled out of the driver's seat and dashed around the front of the car to pull open the passenger side door. Her body drooped as the weight of her laptop bag struck her arm. Giving the car door a firm slam, she trotted toward the house.

From inside the car, Jack heard her say, "I'm working from home this afternoon. Stay off the wi-fi," as she passed the group on the steps. The screen door slapped shut behind her.

Turning his gaze back to his friends, he saw Phil staring back at him, grinning her silent dare for him to get out of the car. Unless he planned to sleep in the back seat, he had no choice. Surrendering to being heckled by his friends, he crawled out of the car and shuffled over to them.

With his head hanging down, Jack moaned, "Hey."

"Oh! I'm so late for my meeting!" his mom's voice grumbled from inside.

They all heard her continue to mutter to herself as she set up a workstation at the kitchen table.

Phil's eyes glimmered with mischief as her lips rose in a sneer. "Now look at what you've done."

"Criminal," Peter said, shaking his head in disgust. He had the same teasing glow in his eyes as Phil.

"I'm not a criminal," Jack murmured.

Jack's eyes darted to Grace, waiting. To his surprise, she didn't take the opportunity to pile on and rub his nose into the mess he made for himself and their mom. Instead, she tip-toed up the stairs and went inside. A gentle hand patting his back, brought his attention back to the group.

"It's all right, Jack," Kelly said. "Everyone knows you did the right thing. This isn't your fault."

"Thanks, Kelly. Do you know my friends?"

"I know Phil." Kelly smiled at Phil. "You spend as much time over here as I do."

"More," said Phil. She leaned her shoulder into Peter's knee. "This is Peter."

"Hi, Peter," Kelly said. "You're on one of the sports teams, aren't you?"

Peter's body stiffened with self-consciousness. "I'm on the swim team. Not what you could call the top of the athletic food chain."

Kelly giggled and said, "I'm sure that's not true."

Put at ease, Peter slid back into his slouch. "Yeah," he laughed, "it is. This geek is Collin."

"Haven't I seen you on the second-floor at school?" Kelly asked Collin. "Freshmen are supposed to stay on the first-floor."

Collin stood up and held out his hand to Kelly. She took it, smiling at him. Peter and Phil cast sidelong glances at each other and sniggered.

"Ignore the savages," Collin said, even though his cheeks burned pink. "To answer your question, I'm taking a couple of senior classes."

Phil made a derisive snort. "Don't be shy, Collin."

She looked at Kelly. "He's taking Honors Physics, Honors Computer Science, and Honors Calculus."

Kelly's eyes widened. "Wow! You must be smart."

"I told you," Peter said, "he's a geek."

Phil's face took on a mawkish expression. "But we wuvs our wittle geekykins."

The pink tint in Collin's cheeks crept down his neck and disappeared beneath his shirt collar. "I love you, too, Philomela."

Phil lunged across Peter in a half-hearted attempt to slug Collin. Peter caught her and, lifting her as if she were a toddler, dumped her back onto her butt beside him.

Sounding like it was an apology, Jack said, "And those are my friends."

Grace bounded out of the house, car keys dangling off her finger. "Let's go Kel."

"Mom gave you her keys?" Jack asked.

"Yeah. I mean, I asked her, and she sort of waved a hand at me, letting me know it was okay."

"Pretty sure she was sayin', 'go away'," Jack said.

Grace scowled at him. It was her way of telling him she was well aware of their mother's true intentions.

"Go on," Phil encouraged, "before your mom figures out what happened, comes out, and takes her keys back."

"As long as she thinks it was her fault for not paying attention, you're forgiven. Make the most of it!" Peter chimed in.

"You guys are awful," Kelly said, but she was smiling, too. "What do you think, Collin? You seem to be the brightest bulb on this particular string."

Collin sat and pretended to think. "If you're back before dinner, Grace's mom might not even notice you've gone. If she does, Peter's right, Grace can say she misunderstood what her mom was telling her. It's worth the risk."

Kelly made an exaggerated 'O' with her lips. "You're as bad as they are!"

"Worse," Phil said. "He's sneakier than the rest of us combined, and smart enough to know how not to get caught."

Grace smiled. "Is that right? Back before dinner, Collin?"

Collin nodded.

"C'mon Kel!"

Grace and Kelly jumped into the car and pulled out of the drive.

"What's up with those two?" Peter asked as the car sped off.

"Nothing," Jack said. "Why?"

Phil answered for Peter. "She and your sister were arguing about something after school. I mean, Kelly seems okay now, but she didn't look so okay on the walk home."

"Kelly has been a bit flakey," Jack said, as if it required deep concentration to realize it. "She and Grace seem to be arguing more and, whenever she's over, and Grace isn't around, she looks, I don't know... Sad?

"Then, and I know this sounds weird, but it feels like they've been hanging around me a lot more, too. And Grace is being nice to me! Did you see how she *didn't* give me a hard time about this ISS thing? Something's up, but it's none of my business."

In his toneless voice, Collin said, "Because that's how you wind up in ISS — by minding your own business."

Jack gave him a wry grin. "So maybe I don't always mind my own business, but I stay well out of Grace's. And she keeps out of mine, which is how we like it."

"Pitiful," Phil said, shaking her head.

Peter heaved a sigh. "Whatever! I don't care about Jack's sister or her goofy friend. What I do care about is sitting out here on this porch with nothing to drink."

Phil and Collin turned to look at Jack expectantly.

"Fine," he groaned.

Jack went inside and up to his room to drop off his book bag. Coming back downstairs, he passed his mother at the kitchen table, surrounded by her work —papers, folders, a calculator; all in disarray, spread across the table. Keeping quiet, both to not disturb his mom and to not draw attention to himself, Jack opened the refrigerator.

There were no sodas of any kind inside, as he expected. Sodas in his home were reserved for special occasions or holidays. He did find a large jug fitted with a spigot that was filled with water and lime slices. At the bottom were the remnants of undissolved sugar.

Grabbing the jug by its handle, he went to the pantry and pulled out a bag of plastic cups left over from some party Jack didn't care enough about to remember and scurried back to his friends. They poured and gulped glasses of limeade, no one complaining they'd rather have sodas. As they sat, Jack recounted for them the events that led to his In-School Suspension.

"What a tool," Peter said, referring to Paul Ackerman.

Phil wobbled her head with arrogance. "Lucky for him I wasn't the one who saw him picking on people."

"Lucky for you. You'd be in Juvie, not ISS," said Peter.

Phil straightened with pride. "Darn right I would."

"I'd have thought, being a football hero and all, he'd have put up a better fight," Collin said.

"I guess if I was carrying a football and running away from him, he would have. It was obvious he had no idea how to defend himself," Jack said.

"Be fair, Jack. You've been in karate for as long as he's been playing football."

Phil looked at Collin with disgust. "Bullies don't deserve fair."

"Doesn't matter. It's over and done. Well, except for the ISS bit," Peter said.

Collin's face turned grave. "Not too sure it is over. Ackerman's popular, and the team isn't going to be too happy their star player is benched for the season."

Peter shrugged with indifference. "Anyone interested in tackle-tag?"

"I'm in," Phil said immediately.

"If I must," said Collin sounding disinterested, but Jack knew better.

"You guys sure you don't mind playing with a 'criminal'?" Jack asked.

Phil darted off the porch shouting, "Criminals are 'It' first!"

Peter and Collin leapt up and ran close on her heels.

"You're on," Jack yelled.

For the next thirty minutes they chased each other around Jack's yard, taking turns tossing or being tossed to the ground. Peter was near impossible to tackle without slamming him down. Thing was, the harder Peter was hit, the more he enjoyed the game and tackled harder himself.

Collin was an easy takedown but was so nimble he was difficult to catch. Still, when he was caught, Jack tackled him more gently than he did his other two friends who, Jack knew, did the same. For whatever reason, being the least athletic, the smartest, or the youngest, Collin was cherished.

Phil was a bit of both, hard to catch and difficult to bring down. She thrilled with the game and, as always, competed more against herself than any of them. Her laughter filled the neighborhood.

"Peter Jeremiah Rochelle," Mrs. Straw scolded from the porch, "tell me I did not just see you dump a girl onto the ground!"

Jack turned, hearing his mother's voice. With a wild holler, Phil wrapped her arms around him, lifted him off his feet, and drove him into the grass. She rolled off his body and trotted away to give Collin a high-five.

"Never mind," Mrs. Straw drawled. "Jack, where's Grace?"

"You told her she could take Kelly to the mall."

"I never!"

"She seemed to think you did."

"Well, I didn't. Did she say when she'd be back?"

Jack bit his lip to keep from laughing. "I'm sure it'll be before dinner."

"It better be," his mother said before going back inside.

Phil cooed, "That was so sweet of you, sticking up for your sister like that."

"I wasn't. Look, when you got a sister, or, I suppose a brother, too, and one of you gets into trouble, the other one's turn isn't far behind."

"Yeah, right," Peter scoffed.

"It's true. I can't tell you why it is, but it is. So, if I can keep Grace out of trouble, I keep me out of trouble."

"But you're already in trouble," Collin said. "You've got ISS."

Jack shook his head. "Different kind of trouble. Mom and Dad, the ones who matter because they can make my life miserable, twenty-four-seven? They aren't mad at me."

"Dude," Peter said, "that makes no sense."

"Doesn't mean it isn't true," Jack answered.

"What's true," Phil said, leading the way to the porch, "is that I want another drink."

They each poured another glass of limeade before sitting on the porch steps. Phil, Peter, and Collin had no brothers or sisters. Life with a sibling fascinated them. Phil had romantic notions of a live-in best friend. Peter wanted a puppy that doubled as a servant. Collin wanted someone to be bored with; play chess, talk about books, that sort of thing. Jack envied their singleness. As they were arguing the pros and cons of having a brother or sister, Grace and Kelly returned.

"Mom wants to talk to you," Jack said as soon as Grace reached the porch.

"She mad?"

"A bit, but if you don't say anything stupid, I think you'll be okay."

"I better go and get this over with. Kelly? Why don't you hang out here till it blows over."

Jack noticed Grace giving Kelly a raised-eyebrow look and a tilt of her head in his direction.

That simple nod left Jack with the impression that Kelly talking to him and his friends was more the point than staying out of harm's way while she got chewed out by their mom. It was just a hunch, a quirky feeling in his gut, but his hunches were, more often than not, right.

"What was that all about?" Jack asked Kelly once Grace was inside.

"What was what all about?" Kelly asked. She sounded defensive.

"Grace's up to something and she's dragged you in on it."

"No. It's just that, well, we're all going to the same school now, Grace and me, and you four. She thought it a good idea I get to know you."

"Hah," Peter barked. "We've been Jack's friends for years and I don't think she even knows our names."

"That's not true," Kelly protested.

Eyebrows raised, Phil's head warbled. "Uh, yeah it is!"

"Look, I'll go inside if I'm bugging you."

"You're not bothering us," Jack said. "We're just hanging out. But I know Grace is cooking up one of her schemes and if it involves us, we want to know."

"Honestly," Kelly said, "Grace just thought it a good idea I get to know you."

"Kel?" Grace called from inside. "Coast is clear. Come on up to my room."

With a hasty chirrup, Kelly said, "See ya," and left.

"See what I meant earlier?" Jack asked. "Something is definitely up with those two and I'm being dragged into whatever it is."

CHAPTER 4

Peter's fist hurtled towards Jack like an artillery shell. Jack's first inclination was to throw up a hard block with his right arm while ramming his own left fist into Peter's diaphragm.

Instead, he forced his right arm to relax. When Peter's punch made contact, Jack bent his elbow, pushing upwards so that the blow was redirected over his head. Darting under Peter's arm and to the side, Jack grabbed the wrist and pressed his elbow down across Peter's, driving him to the floor. If Jack continued forcing the elbow down while lifting the wrist, Peter's arm would snap.

"Ow! Ow! Okay!" Peter wailed.

Jack let go of the pin and helped his friend to his feet.

"Man!" Peter said. "I can't believe that worked. And you didn't have to use a ton of strength?"

"Strength isn't everything in a fight," a firm voice said from behind them.

The two boys snapped to attention.

"You're very strong, Peter, but there will always be someone out there who's stronger. When outmatched in power, someone well trained in technique can still win."

"Yes, Sensei!" both boys barked.

"Take, for example," Sensei continued, "Jack's misfortune that led to his being sentenced to In-School Suspension."

Jack's spine sagged.

"Yes, Mr. Straw. I know about it. Speak with me after class."

Jack snapped his shoulders back. "Yes, Sensei."

"Now, Peter," Sensei went on, "Let's see if you can do that move as well as Jack."

Jack and Peter both bowed before turning to face each other. Jack knew better than to let his concern over what was going to be an awkward chat with his karate instructor affect his performance.

Peter's movements were flawless. It was Jack's turn to lie face down on the mat, wincing and begging to be released from the pin. Sensei grunted in stoic approval before wandering off to critique other students.

After taking several turns attacking each other, Jack swapped partners with other students in the class and spent the next hour and a half working on throws and takedowns that required very little strength, but relied on delicate movement and timing.

At the end of class, several white-belt students, under the direction of those with higher ranked belts, started mopping the mats and putting away equipment. Jack, being a junior black-belt, no longer was expected to perform these duties. He shuffled over to where his Sensei was talking to a group of students and waited to be acknowledged.

"You know how I feel about fighting outside of the dojo, Jack," Sensei said when they were alone.

Jack lowered his eyes. "Yes, Sensei."

"Explain yourself."

Just as he'd done in his principal's office, Jack recounted the events with humility. This time, his stomach quaked and his voice cracked. He'd accepted his principal's authority to pass judgment and assign punishment. In Jack's mind, that was how a command structure worked, but that was all there was to it. Sensei's opinion mattered to him. This felt personal.

As he talked, he could hear Collin, Peter, and Phil's hushed voices as they waited for him, trying to eavesdrop without getting caught.

"That was different," Collin was saying about the class when Jack, having bowed to Sensei, joined their huddle.

"It was," Phil agreed, "but I liked it."

"You would," Peter teased her.

Phil folded her arms across her chest and jutted her hip out to the side. "Just what is that supposed to mean?"

In a nervous rush Peter stammered, "I only meant that, you know, you're so much better at those tricky kinds of moves. That's all."

"That better be all," she said, wobbling her head with sass, "or I'll prove to you I can thrash and pound just as good as you. Better, even!"

Phil winked at Collin.

"What was that all about?" she asked Jack, nodding her head toward Sensei's back.

Jack knew Peter filled the other two in, but answered anyway. "He wanted to talk about my fight at school."

Collin winced. "Bet that was fun."

Jack didn't answer.

"So, what'd he say?" Peter pressed.

"Stuff about being certain the cause you're fighting for is worth the consequences, because violence always has its price."

Phil's lip curled. "Leave it to Sensei to talk in riddles."

"Makes sense to me," Collin objected.

"Of course it does," Phil teased as she moved toward the girls' dressing room. Jack and Peter chuckled and started for the boys'.

"Well, it did," Collin said, falling in behind them.

After changing, they stood squinting in the white sunlight of late summer. A big SUV pulled over to the curb with Collin's mom behind the wheel.

"Hey Jack!" Collin called out as he, Peter, and Phil climbed in. "You want a ride home? We can put your bike in the back."

"That's okay. It's nice out. Besides, after spending all week stuck in ISS, I want to spend my Saturday outside. I'll pedal."

"Good," Phil teased, "because I don't want to be seen with no ISS criminals! Besides, you stink. Probably went for a run this morning and didn't shower before coming here."

"Why would I shower if I was coming here to get all sweaty again?"

She eyed him with pity. "You can take more than one shower a day, Jack."

"That right there, is crazy talk!"

"You're right," Phil said through a toothy grin. "It is! We'll call you later. See what you're up to."

Summer was in full swing, which suited Jack. He liked it hot. Today, the bright sunshine, offset by a gentle breeze, drew his neighbors out of their homes. They were tending flowerbeds, walking their dogs, jogging, and biking. He sped past a group of children wearing their most tattered clothes. Their dad was walking down the drive with a ladder over his shoulder. Jack made a quick study of the faded beige house and decided the family was turning painting their home into a family-bonding project.

Knowing his neighborhood as well as he did, Jack didn't need to concentrate on where he was going. Being out, riding fast, taking the corners in steep leans, was heaven to him. Pulling into his driveway, he flung his leg over the bike's seat and stood on one pedal, allowing his bike to coast into the garage. He was on autopilot.

"Back, Mom," he shouted as he entered the kitchen.

Pulling open the door leading to the basement, he bounded down the stairs. Without untying them, Jack pressed the toe of one foot against the heel of the other and pried his feet out of his sneakers. The full stench of his run and bike ride poured out of them. He chucked his martial arts uniform on top of his battered shoes. With sweaty, over-stretched socks bunching around his ankles, he plopped down onto his favorite beanbag and began playing the latest video game to captivate his attention.

As it always did when he was gaming, the real world turned into background noise. Time, which always seemed to drag on and on when sitting in Biology class, flew by.

"Oh! My! Gosh!" Grace barked over an hour later.

Jack twisted around in his beanbag and scowled at his sister, who stood at the bottom of the basement steps, still in her sleepwear, with her forefinger pressed horizontally under her nose while making a big performance out of how badly the room reeked. Kelly, who spent the night, was standing beside Grace, rolling her eyes at the melodramatics.

Glowering at his sister, Jack felt like he was staring himself down in a mirror. Even the small dimple on her chin was twitching like his did when he was mad.

A strand of strawberry hair fell in front of Grace's eyes. With a whip of her head, she slung it back into place.

Jack smirked just to goad her.

Biting his tongue to keep from starting an argument, he spun around and returned to his video game. The styrofoam beads inside his beanbag crunched as he moved. Muttering something foul under his breath, the beans crunched again as he squirmed deeper still into the bag. He had allowed his sister to distract him for too long and now his avatar was surrounded, taking fire from all sides. Nothing he could do would prevent it from bursting into flames.

"Oh, come on Gracie," Kelly said behind him. "It isn't that bad. You should smell our house after my brothers get home from playing soccer!"

Hearing Kelly take his side made a self-satisfied smile tickle Jack's lips. Kelly was okay in his book. Her dusky skin and flowing black hair caught the eye of all the boys at school. Jack knew they paid a lot of extra attention to her, but she never acted stuck up or snooty. Instead, she was kind and had a quirky down-to-earth sense of humor he appreciated.

Not that it mattered. She was seventeen and he was still two weeks shy of turning fourteen. The possibility of his going out with her never occurred to him. At least not seriously. All he could ever be was her best friend's little brother and she, the only one of his sister's friends he didn't despise.

As his game started up again, he wondered, not for the first time, what secret bound the two girls together. Their friendship was a mystery to him. Kelly and his sister were nothing alike. Kelly was cool. His sister? Not so much. If it were anyone but Grace, he'd snoop around until he found out what their secret was. Since it was his sister, he could not have cared less.

The two girls crossed the room and flopped down on the couch behind him, causing the fake leather to make rude noises. The girls giggled.

Jack groaned and put all his effort into pretending they weren't there. Knotting his brows and gritting his teeth, he tried to engross himself in his game. The girls made that impossible. The game room wasn't cramped, and there always seemed to be more than enough space when his friends were over. Somehow, Grace had a way of making him feel smothered.

Five feet of rust-colored shag carpet separated him from the hushed voices behind him. It felt like less than one. His teeth clenched as he fidgeted, unable to get into a comfortable position.

Behind him, Grace and Kelly whispered about whatever it is high school girls talk about. Jack couldn't keep himself from thinking they were talking about him. Wiggling deeper still into his seat, he retreated into his game, but found he couldn't concentrate. As his avatar exploded on the screen again, he made one final effort at distraction.

Jack and his friends were all going to be spies when they grew up. The actual title was Intelligence Officers, but Jack liked Spy better. Intelligence Officer sounded boring. He planned to be a man of action and couldn't imagine doing anything else with his life.

As he sat waiting for his game to restart, he fantasized he was in a crowded arcade. The place was noisy, but it was his mission to collect intelligence by eavesdropping on the saboteurs behind him. To make himself blend in, he pretended to be absorbed in a video game. The fact that his 'targets' were gossiping about who was making-out with whom at school ruined the fantasy.

Grace erupted in gleeful indignation over some piece of juicy gossip. Her over-the-top scorn put the final bullet into his daydream's corpse. Thinking they were ridiculing him, he ducked his head and, trying to be inconspicuous about it, pinched the front of his shirt and lifted it to his nose.

Sniffing his shirt, he wondered, *Do I stink that bad?*

Grace pushed herself off the couch.

In an embarrassed rush, Jack dropped the collar of his shirt. He turned to look at the two girls to see if he was caught smelling himself.

"I'm grabbing a cup of coffee," Grace announced. "You want me to bring you one Kel?"

"Sure," Kelly answered. The broad smile that was stretching her features a second ago melted away. "Milk. No Sugar. Thanks."

Just before climbing the stairs, Jack noticed his sister giving him an odd glance over her shoulder. He was expecting to see disgust on her face, like she was staring at a wad of gum, or worse, stuck to the bottom of her shoe. Instead, her eyebrows drooped and her shoulders sagged. It left him with the impression she felt sorry for him. That glance, such a small thing, planted an unsettling feeling inside him.

"She's being weird," Jack said after Grace climbed the stairs and closed the kitchen door behind her. "And she's showing off. She never drinks coffee unless one of her friends is over."

Kelly began picking at the corner of a couch pillow and turned her eyes anywhere but at him. "Maybe she just likes drinking coffee with company. You know, someone to talk to?"

He doubted that, but wasn't interested in arguing over it.

Catching him by surprise, Jack had toes thrust into his armpit and grinding into his ribs.

"Hey! Cut it out!" he shouted while laughing.

Kelly ignored his pleas and kept tickling him with her toes. Without warning, she hopped off the couch and plopped down to sit cross-legged next to him on the floor. She snatched the game controller out of his hand. To his surprise, while he struggled on the level he was playing, she breezed through it.

"Wow!" he said in surprise. "You're good!"

Her brow wrinkled in concentration as she threw her shoulders left and right in response to the on-screen action. "Brothers," she mumbled.

Grace yelled from upstairs, "Hey, Kel! Ashley just texted! She and Becky are going to the mall to do some window-shopping. Want to go?"

"Sure," Kelly called back.

She paused the game, rolled over her calves so that she was sitting on her heels, and handed the controller back to him. Without warning, she pressed her cheek against his so that her lips were right next to his ear.

"Take a shower," she said in a gentle whisper.

Then, to his complete amazement, she pressed her lips against his cheek and gave him a quick peck before dashing upstairs. He watched her go, rubbing his cheek and feeling his face flush hot-rod red.

CHAPTER 5

Jack's eyes fluttered open. Turning his head, he squinted at the alarm clock he'd set up on the far side of his room to force himself out of bed in order to shut it off. It read six o'clock in the morning. Any other day of the week it would be screaming at him. Habit nudged him awake this morning but, being Sunday, he could ignore the world and go back to sleep.

Snuggling deeper into his sheets, he thought of Phil's hatred for mornings. Every Saturday she showed up for karate late for the bow-in with crazy hair, yawning, and rubbing sleep out of her eyes. The same was true for first period at school, except her hair was tame...most of the time.

His mind turned to Peter and Collin. They were already up, he knew, and were getting ready for church. Rolling over to go back to sleep, Jack pictured Peter sitting in church and grinned. Mischievous energy beamed out of Peter like sunshine. He was one fidget short of being diagnosed hyperactive. With his devilish onyx eyes, black hair and, for as long as Jack could remember, a faint, dark shadow of a pre-mustache under his nose, the thought of him squirming in a pew for an hour-long service seemed ridiculous. Jack faded into unconsciousness, chuckling over Peter's wiggly plight.

It was early-afternoon when he scraped himself out of bed. Rummaging through multiple heaps of clothes on his floor, he picked out those he deemed to be the cleanest and, once dressed, grabbed a slice of cold pizza from the fridge before taking off to meet up with his friends at the park.

Most kids went to the downtown park with its skating area, swimming pool, and playground equipment. Jack, however, made his way to the massive green space at the edge of town. There, he and his friends explored the woods, played games, or just chilled.

"'Bout time," Phil said through a yawn as Jack joined them at the playground equipment.

She was sitting in a heap at the top of the slide, feet pointing down its shiny silver length. Her hair was pulled back into a shaggy ponytail and her eyelids drooped in sleepy squints.

"Don't pay any attention to her," Peter said. "You know it takes her a good hour to wake up. Collin and I haven't been waiting that long and we were here first."

Phil smiled. "If I wasn't still half asleep, I'd smack you."

"Then we'd better go before you wake up," Jack said as he led the way to the densest part of the forest. By the time they reached the spot on the creek's bank where they built a semi-permanent fire ring out of salvaged cinderblocks, they were laughing so hard their voices echoed into the distance.

With a sense of complete security, Jack and the others sat on old plastic milk crates Collin swiped from behind a nearby convenience store. Collin dismissed the exploit as nothing more than sneaking out of his house one morning at three AM, making two trips behind the convenience store and, voilà! They each had their own seat.

From out of his backpack, Jack produced a package of hotdogs. Collin pulled four bottles of water from his while Peter dug out matches and lighter fluid from his own. Phil conjured a bag of jumbo marshmallows.

Grabbing sticks suitable for cooking, they settled in to have a small feast. As they roasted this and burned that they talked about school, their family lives, and their shared passion — spies.

"Somebody is going to have to be the first girl super-spy," Phil said. "Might as well be me."

"You've got to get through high school first," Peter teased. "Keep sleeping in Biology and that's not going to happen."

"I don't sleep in Biology."

Jack gave a derisive snort. "You snore."

"Do not!" Her face fell with worry. "Do I?"

"Yeah," Peter chuckled, "you do."

"Whatever," Phil said, her cheeks reddening.

"So, Collin" Phil teased to shift focus off of herself, "I saw you talking to Casey on Friday before English."

Collin shifted his lanky frame on his milk crate. "So?"

Despite being the youngest of the group, he was miles ahead of them intellectually. When it came to social savvy, however, he was every bit as awkward as any other twelve-year-old. A wiry kid with white-blond hair that was always neat and trimmed, who preferred button-down shirts over Polos and t-shirts, Collin was an easy target.

Eyes twinkling and with a devilish grin, Phil kept the pressure on him. "So, we all know you like her. What did she say?"

"Too much. I never really talked to her before. I still think she is good-looking and all but, after talking to her, I'm not so sure I like her as much."

"Why? She find out you were still a baby and didn't want anything to do with you?" Peter jibed.

They all erupted in laughter.

"She suffers from an acute brain-cell deficiency!" Collin groaned.

They laughed all the harder. Compared to Collin, everyone at their school was brain-cell deficient, and that included the teachers.

"I tried to warn you!" Phil said.

"Yeah," agreed Collin. He flashed a rare grin at her. "You did."

"Now, if you are ready to listen to me, I think my friend Anne might like you."

Jack, Peter, and Collin shot each other smirking glances.

"What?" Phil asked.

Jack lost control, filling the forest with laughter.

"What!" she demanded.

Peter and Collin busted up, too.

"We always thought…" started Collin before another laughing fit got the better of him.

"What? Tell me!"

Peter was laughing so hard he started coughing on his hotdog but managed to get out, "We all thought she was interested in you!"

Phil hurled her half-eaten hotdog at him, hitting him between the eyes.

Jack and Collin fell off their crates, clutching their sides and squealing with laughter. She looked at them in disgust. "So who else at school thinks that? Is that what everyone thinks about me?"

"No," Jack said. He was still chuckling but saw how this could turn nasty. "It's just kind of a joke we three have. Honestly, I've never heard anyone say anything bad about you."

"They're all too scared to," Peter said with a smile, picking bits of hotdog out of his hair.

"Good!" grumped Phil.

"Seriously, kids at school think you're great," Jack said. "I mean, out of all of us, you are the only one that actually has other friends."

He was trying to be consoling, but his giggles ruined the effect.

"Yeah, Phil. Besides," Collin blurted out, "on Tuesday I heard…" He shut his mouth and stared into the flames.

Phil glared at him, eyes narrow with anger. "Heard what?"

"You promise not to throw anything at me?"

"I promise," Phil snarled through gritted teeth.

"Or hit me?"

"Prrrrromise."

Collin blinked rapidly, glancing toward Jack and Peter. "I was going to tell you privately."

"Out with it," Phil snapped, her patience at its end.

"It's just that I overheard Bobby Finn telling Kevin Mouser that he, Bobby, thinks you're hot."

They all fell silent. She looked at Collin, stunned, then at Peter and Jack. This was the first time any of them had reason to suspect someone outside of their own circle had any interest in them. The boys stared back at Phil. Her mouth was hanging open. Slowly, she closed it. No one knew what to say.

Phil broke the spell by asking, "Does anyone have a coin?"

"What'd'ya need a coin for?" asked Peter.

"I need to decide. Heads'll be Bobby and tails...Anne."

They all roared. Phil loudest of all.

"What about you, Jack?" asked Peter. "Got your eye on anyone at school?"

"No! Girls are too weird. Present company excepted, Phil."

"Gee, thanks," she said flatly, "but we are not weird."

"Oh yeah? Listen to this!" Jack told them the story about Kelly kissing his cheek in the basement.

"Jack," Phil asked when he had finished, "you don't think she was, like, flirting with you, do you?"

"Of course not!" Jack lied.

"Good! Because that would make you stoo-piiid!"

"That's the point, Phil. It was just...I don't know...weird!"

"She was toying with you, dude!" Peter sneered.

In an abrupt change of direction, Collin asked Jack, "How do you plan to deal with the football team?"

"I don't. I mean," Jack shrugged, "why would I need to?"

"You did get their star player benched for the season," Phil pointed out.

Jack jammed another hotdog onto his stick and dangled it over the fire. "He got himself benched. I doubt any of the other players are going to risk the same. Besides, Principal Kohl said he'd keep an eye on it."

"I hope so," Collin said. "I'm getting some pretty nasty looks at school."

Jack's spine jerked taut. He glared into the fire, grinding his teeth. He knew Collin could handle himself, but he shouldn't have to. Not for something he had no part in. Not for just being his friend.

Sensei's words came back to him. "Violence always has its price." Perhaps this was the price of his actions.

Jack shook his head and forced himself to relax. "We'll do what we've always done. Lay low and watch each other's backs."

His friends muttered in agreement, but the reality of their situation made the conversation lag. Even Peter was still. Jack, hypnotized by the shimmering, red coals, let his mind empty of worry. It felt good to be with his friends and that was more than enough for the moment.

"It's getting late," he murmured. "We should kill the fire and head home."

Jack's breaking the silence loosened Peter's tongue. "I was just thinking. Saturday. My place. Sleepover and spy movie binge?"

Jack thought about the first time he watched that kind of movie. It was years ago, on a rare moment his dad let him stay up super late and watch a classic spy flick with him. After that, playing pretend spy became one of his, and therefor Phil's, staple games. When Peter and Collin trickled into their friend network, they picked it up, too. Now older, it was more than a game. It was their shared career goal.

"I'm in!" he crowed.

Collin nodded his agreement, aided with a grunt, and followed Peter into the surrounding brush. Jack held back to kick some extra dirt on the coals. Phil stood waiting at the forest's edge for him. "You okay, Jack?"

"Sure. Why wouldn't I be?"

"Well, if you, you know, like Kelly, and she didn't know and was teasing you and stuff."

"I don't like her like that. It was just kinda creepy."

"Yeah," Phil drawled.

Shifting the focus off himself, Jack asked, "What about you and Bobby?"

Phil lowered her eyes and used her fingers to pin a wayward lock of hair behind her caramel ear. "I can't believe he thinks I'm hot!"

Jack swore. "Don't get all girly on us, Phil! You know, saying you're not pretty when you know good and well you are. Why are girls weird like that?"

Phil's head popped up. "You guys all think I'm hot, too? What the heck!"

"Jeez, Phil! If it weren't for us being friends since before forever, we'd be fighting with each other to go out with you! Of course, I'd win," he finished with an arrogant grin.

She smiled at the playful boast. "In your dreams, Jack Straw!"

"Oh yeah!" he drawled while nodding his head suggestively.

She threw a feeble punch towards his face. "Boys are so gross!"

Jack knew he could dodge the blow and knew Phil knew it, too. His stomach turned a quick summersault as he wondered if he could dodge an entire football team, or whatever it was Grace and Kelly were cooking up for him. Forcing himself to not think about any of it, he darted into the forest with Phil racing after him.

CHAPTER 6

Jack's life soon became regulated by his school schedule. The high school workload shattered what he believed to be "studying hard" while in middle school. With ISS now behind him, he went to his classes, took tests, and was supposed to be in bed by ten-thirty, which he never was as he struggled to keep up.

Rain or shine, he ran every morning. Collin joined him on Mondays and Phil on Thursdays. Peter never ran during the school year because the swim team practiced both before and after school.

The unusual thing was that his Thursday runs became all he saw of Phil outside of classes. She was spending more time with Bobby Finn and his friends. Jack didn't feel hurt by this, and he was sure Collin and Peter didn't either. The truth was, he missed hanging out with her. Not surprised when she joined them, clustered around Peter's locker on Friday afternoon, Jack was still glad to see her.

"We still on for movie night tomorrow?" she asked.

"Sure are!" Peter confirmed.

"Great! See you there!"

Jack watched as she trotted off to catch up with her new boyfriend. His eyes popped when she slipped her hand into Bobby's.

It seemed to knock Bobby off balance, too, because he threw a cautious look over his shoulder. He wasn't smirking or being cocky. His face was the color of oatmeal as he waited for Jack's reaction.

Jack forced a smile onto his face and gave a half-hearted wave. Phil, turning to see what Bobby was staring at, waved back. Still holding onto Bobby's hand, she tugged him down the hall and they left school together.

The next morning, when they were together for their karate class, Jack tingled with nosey curiosity. He wanted to know what happened between Phil and Bobby after school yesterday.

With a shake of his head to rattle his suspicions out, he straightened his uniform and cinched his black-belt's knot tighter. It was none of his business. Besides, she'd tell him whatever she felt like telling him that evening. Until then, he determined not to pry. Straightening his shoulders, he joined the line-up for the start of class. His mind was made up and he wouldn't press the topic, letting her bring it up first when she was ready.

"Let her enjoy her moment," he said aloud to himself.

Phil pounced into line beside him. "Let who enjoy what?"

Jack didn't look her in the eyes. Instead, he focused on a light pink bruise on the side of her neck, centered between her collarbone and ear, which she was pretending to hide beneath her crazy hair, but was doing such a poor job of it Jack suspected she wanted it to be seen.

"Nothing," he said, an enormous grin on his face, just as Sensei called the class to attention.

After class, Jack, Peter, and Collin dashed to change into their street clothes. Phil joined them outside the dojo when Peter broke the bad news. "Guys, tonight's off."

They all groaned.

"I know! Right? Mom got called out of town for some emergency meeting and Dad doesn't want a house full of kids. He's doing some kind of paperwork all weekend."

Jack thought for a minute then pulled out his phone.

"Hey, Mom? You know that sleep-over we were *gonna* have at Peter's?"

"Gonna have, huh?" his mom asked. She chuckled in his ear. "Well, you can have your friends over if you want."

"Thanks, Mom. You're the best."

"You will have to share the house with Grace and Kelly. They'll be there, too."

"Mom! Kelly spent the night last Saturday!"

"Is that too much to cope with? Because if it is, you can do without your friends spending the night."

From her tone, he knew it was pointless to argue.

"No ma'am. It won't be a problem. But can you ask them to stay out of the game room please?"

"They usually do, but I'll tell your sister to give you your space. Look, I've got to run. See you at home. Love you."

"Love you, too, Mom."

Turning to his friends, he smiled from ear to ear. "Back on!"

Jack spent the rest of the day preparing for the sleepover. Being short notice, they all agreed to come over after dinner, relieving him or, if he was being honest, his parents, from that last-minute burden. All he had to do was make sure the game room's mini-fridge was stocked with plenty of sports drinks. After that, he spread a couple of blankets out on the floor and tossed as many pillows as he could find on top of them, making a small nest.

Peter and Collin arrived together and laid claim to the piece of floor they wanted to sleep on by rolling out their sleeping bags. They always reserved the couch for Phil if she wanted it. She never did, preferring to flop down on the floor with the boys, but they still left it for her anyway.

After Phil showed up, late, they lounged through the first movie with just a hint of jostling. When the movie ended, Jack moved to swap that movie for the next one. Behind him a wrestling match began. Not wanting to miss out, he hit pause and, making an exuberant "whoop", slid into the pack.

If anyone got the upper hand on another, someone always intervened, destined to be betrayed by the one they rescued seconds earlier. They thundered, rolled, and hooted until the basement door opened and Jack's mom called down, "Phil? Are those boys being too rough?"

Jack rolled across the floor, laughing too hard to answer.

Collin breathed out, "I think she is being too rough on us."

"Good for you, Philomela," Jack's mom said.

Jack heard the note of pride in her voice. Phil must have tuned in on it too, because even in the dim light from the TV, Jack could tell she was beaming.

As his mom closed the door Collin tried to needle Phil. "Yeah! Good for you...."

"Collin Jensen! If you say it, I'll knock those teeth straight out of your head!" Phil threatened, knowing he was about to use her full name.

"You don't mind Bobby Finn using it," teased Peter. "I heard him after school on Thursday."

"Well, I tell you what, Petey-boy. When I start kissing you, that's when you can start calling me by my full name."

That shut everyone up.

"I think I'll just start the next movie now," said Jack in a mock, over-stressed voice, adding a forced chuckle to the end.

They were a third of the way into the film when Jack heard the kitchen door open, then slam. He checked his watch. 23:22. He assumed the racket was his sister and Kelly, back from their double date. Ten minutes after that, the basement door opened and Kelly crept down the stairs. Quiet as a timid mouse, she eased herself onto the couch.

"What's going on, Kelly?" Jack asked without taking his eyes off the screen.

He didn't want her there, but didn't want to be a brat and yell at her to get out, either. Besides, if Grace wasn't with her, something must have happened.

"Sorry," Kelly whispered. "Your sister's boyfriend is a real jerk! They spent the whole night fighting. They're on the phone now, still going at it. I didn't want to sit there having to listen to it so I snuck down here. Hope you don't mind?"

Peter, Collin, and Phil grumbled their lack of interest back at her. Her presence didn't bother them. Her talking did.

Jack did his best to resettle and get back into the movie's action. He shoved a stack of pillows under him and rested his head on top like a cherry on an ice-cream sundae but found no comfort in that position. Kelly's remark about Grace's boyfriend being a jerk gnawed at him.

The movie turned into Jack's history class. He was present. His senses took in everything that was going on. None of it penetrated his brain. He couldn't stop puzzling over what might have gone wrong on his sister's date. Irked by caring about Grace when he'd rather not, he stared at the screen and fumed.

Giving in to the fact he was too distracted to concentrate on the movie he asked, "He didn't hurt her, or anything, did he?"

The timbre of his voice worked like ice water being poured over them all. Collin picked up the remote and paused the movie. He, along with Phil and Peter, twisted around and stared at Kelly, eyes wide and dark, waiting for more. Jack remained where he was, his eyes glued to the frozen scene on the TV.

"No," Kelly said.

Jack's skin prickled as if the air was filled with static electricity.

Kelly repeated herself more forcefully. "No! Holy cow! You little beasts are intense, aren't you?"

Jack rolled over and sat up. He joined the others in staring at her with naïve eyes, forcing Kelly to explain, "He didn't...hurt her. Not like you're thinking."

Jack blinked, wordlessly badgering for a better explanation. He studied Kelly as she squirmed in frustration over his, along with his friends', inexperience. She cried out, "It's a high school romance, kiddies. They pretty much thrive on drama! He doesn't deserve a beat down or anything like that. I mean...."

She looked at Jack as if seeing him for the first time. When she picked up again, her voice warbled with notes of fear. "That's what you'd do? All of you. Isn't it?"

"What do you mean?" asked Collin, feigning innocence.

Her eyes narrowed as she glared at him. "I mean you guys are a little scary."

"I want a PBJ. Anyone else want a sandwich?" Phil blurted out.

The tension broke.

"I'll take one, please," Collin said, rolling over to lie back down on his pillows.

"Me too," chimed in Peter, "as long as you're making them."

"Jack?" Phil asked.

"No thanks, but let's take an intermission. We'll start back up after you come down with the sandwiches."

"Sure! Kelly?"

"Huh?" Kelly grunted, still not caught up with the abrupt change in direction.

Phil annunciated her words as if speaking to a small child. "Want a sandwich?"

"No thanks."

Out of the corner of his eye, Jack saw Phil raise an eyebrow at Kelly.

"Well, maybe half?" Kelly asked, searching for the answer Phil was fishing for. "If you don't mind splitting yours with me."

"Great!" Phil beamed. "Be sweet and help me make them?"

Without waiting for her answer, Phil headed for the stairs.

Kelly sat on the couch with her mouth hanging open. Jack rolled away from her, joining in roughhousing with his friends. He went on pretending to be oblivious until Kelly heaved herself to her feet and followed Phil upstairs.

Once Kelly was out of the basement, he separated himself from the pile. He could not for the life of him figure out why Phil was acting like a ditz, but he knew her well enough to know she was up to something. He also knew a way to find out what that something was.

"I need to use the toilet," he told Peter and Collin.

When the basement was converted into a game room, the heating, air conditioning, and plumbing was spliced into the first-floor's systems. The lower-level toilet was right below the first-floor guest bathroom which butted up against the kitchen. All three tied into the same pipes and ductwork. Standing inside, Jack could eavesdrop on every word that passed between Phil and Kelly.

"How're things between you and Bobby?" Kelly asked above him.

"We're fine. How'd you know we were going out?"

"My Physics Lab partner is Jake Finn. Bobby is his little brother and Jake was boasting all about how his brother had his first girlfriend. Jake said you were kinda pretty."

"Kinda? That's an odd way of putting it."

"Well, he said you were a bit tomboyish."

"Nothing wrong with that," Phil said. Jack thought he caught a hint of hurt in her voice.

"No," drawled Kelly. "Not if you are aware of it and don't care. If you aren't aware, then maybe there is."

Silence.

"Look," Phil said, "when Jack asked about his sister, he was just concerned. You know, like a brother should be?"

"I get concerned. I also get that you all were deadly serious, too. That was not just some baby-brother-looking-out-for-his-big-sister trash talk. Jack was making a real threat to do real harm. And don't pretend you weren't in on it, Phil."

"I'm glad you picked up on that. See, Jack told us about last weekend."

Jack heard feet scuffing on the floor, shifting nervously, as Kelly said, "Last weekend? You mean when I was teasing him?"

"That's right," Phil said, her voice like frost. "When you were teasing him."

"Does Jack think I was flirting with him?"

"He says no, but you know boys. They do the dumbest things to prove their bravery to each other but are total chickens when it comes to feelings."

Kelly ignored Phil's insights.

"Doesn't matter," Phil went on. "All that matters is that I think of Jack as a brother. I'd look after him same as he would his sister."

Her meaning was clear, both to Kelly and to Jack. He heard angry footsteps cross over his head. He had known Phil for most of his life—knew her well enough to know those weren't her footfalls. In his mind, he pictured Kelly closing in on Phil and jabbing a finger at her.

"Don't you threaten me, Philomela!"

Oh no! Jack thought. Phil's gonna kill her!

Still very much alive, Kelly continued, "You've no idea what my life's been like, but let me just say, I am not that easy to intimidate."

Seconds ticked past. Jack heard nothing. He flinched when a knife rattled inside a jelly jar, sounding like an alarm clock.

When the clanging stopped Phil said casually, "This knife is too dull to cut these sandwiches without destroying them. Mind grabbing a sharp knife from the block over by the fridge?"

"Don't do it, Phil," Jack whispered.

A loud staccato pop echoed down the vents. Then two more.

Jack squeezed his eyes shut in dread.

"Phil! What are you doing?" he heard Kelly exclaim.

Two more pops barked out like gunfire.

Kelly's voice rose. "Cut it out!"

Above him, pops started to rattle off like popcorn ricocheting off a kettle's lid.

"Stop it!" Kelly said louder still.

A long, steady stream of pops trickled down into Jack's ears in rapid-fire succession. Out in the game room he heard Peter's singsong voice, "Phil's showing off."

Jack had seen Phil do this trick before. She spent years working on it. Eyes still closed, he imagined the events taking place above him. Phil was standing at the kitchen counter with her left palm pressed down on top of a cutting board. She held a knife in her right hand and was tapping its point crazy fast between her widespread fingers.

The popping stopped, leaving a naked silence in its wake.

Cabinets rattled opened and shut. The sink tap started to run. His imagination shifted to watching Phil clean up the mess made by making the sandwiches. He also pictured what Kelly must have looked like — standing motionless, mouth gaping open, too stunned to speak.

"I've got Peter's and Collin's sandwiches. Be a dear," Phil simpered sarcastically, "and bring those other two plates when you come."

Kelly's reply was soft and unsteady. "Sure. I'll be down in a sec."

Jack bolted into action. He slapped the toilet paper roll, counted to ten, then slapped it again. He flushed the toilet then ran some water into the sink. Turning the water off, he tousled the hand towel on its rack. Finally, he lit the strong scented candle to cover the fact no stink needed to be covered up. He came out of the toilet just as Phil cleared the bottom step.

"Been in there this whole time?" she sneered at him.

He was busted.

Pretending to be a spy was one thing. Spying on Phil in real life left a sick feeling deep in his guts. She gave him a wink and a pitying half-smile. Knowing that she'd already forgiven him made him feel worse.

Peter and Collin grabbed their sandwiches. In either feigned or legitimate cluelessness, always impossible to tell which with Collin, he asked if they should start the movie or wait for Kelly.

Phil's face glowed with a triumphant grin. "I don't think she is interested in the movie."

Giving a shrug of his shoulders, Collin restarted the movie and nestled down on the floor between Phil and Peter. The hero was right where they had left him, outnumbered with guns a'blazing. Jack was the only one who noticed Kelly when she returned, balancing two plates on top of what looked like a fishing tackle box.

"Phil?" Kelly called over the increased volume of the shoot-out. "I've got our sandwiches."

Phil, surprise playing across her face, rose off the floor and went to the couch. The action-loud soundtrack died just in time for Jack to hear Kelly whisper, "My turn to make you uncomfortable. Sit your butt down."

He never heard anyone talk to Phil like that without getting a smack in reply. Stunned, he watched Phil sit on the couch as she was told. Angling himself on the carpet so that eyes-right allowed him to watch the movie while eyes-left gave him view of what was going on at the couch, he tried to do both.

A bright light flashed and all three boys jerked their heads toward the girls. Phil had her back against the arm of the sofa. Her knees were drawn up and crossed so that her right knee rested on top of her left. She was shining the light from her phone onto her elevated foot.

Kelly sat cross-legged at the other end holding the heel of Phil's foot in one hand while wedging some sort of sponge device in between each of Phil's toes. The box Kelly had brought down with her was open on the floor and Jack could see a mishmash of makeup, a variety of brushes, and nail polish.

Jack looked into Phil's eyes. She stared back like a soggy puppy who was being scolded. He had to avert his face to hide his sniggering.

He tried to get back into watching the film but curiosity kept getting the better of him. Giving up, he pushed himself off the floor and switched on the overhead light. Stopping the movie, he squatted on the floor at Kelly's end of the couch, well out of Phil's reach. He was soon joined by Collin and Peter.

"I've never seen this done before," Jack said.

"Then you can be next," snarled Phil.

Everyone laughed. Everyone except Phil. "Seriously, Straw. You. Are. Next. Or so help me…"

"Chill out, Phil. Wow!" exclaimed Kelly.

Phil whipped her head around and glared at her until Kelly added a playful, "Of course Jack's next."

Phil grinned wickedly.

Jack swallowed hard.

"What is it with you guys, anyway?" Kelly asked, breaking the tension.

"What are you talking about?" Peter asked.

"The spy obsession. What's that all about?"

"Everybody's got to be something when they grow up," Phil explained. "We decided that's what we want to be — super-secret-agents. How about you? Don't you have a dream job?"

"Of course I do, and it has nothing to do with violence or governments or anything like that. What I want to be is a make-up artist for the movie industry."

"That doesn't sound very exciting," Peter commented.

"If it's what you want, it's very exciting," Kelly countered.

"Can I ask a personal question?" Collin said to her.

"Sure! I'll either answer, or I won't. But you can always ask."

"I can't place your heritage. I mean your nationality. You don't talk with much of an accent, but I am picking up enough of one to think you weren't born in America."

"My real name is Kalila. It's Arabic. I was born in a tiny town called Wahat Jamila in Afghanistan. We left soon after the U. S. arrived, but I saw enough violence before NATO and American forces got there to know I want nothing to do with it. Now that those troops are supposed to leave, I worry the past will catch up with my family and me; that someone will come after us. So you see, a boring life is just fine with me."

"You're Muslim?" Jack asked.

"Christian. But we sometimes had to pretend to be Muslims. That's part of why we had to leave."

"Whoa!" groaned Collin. "Sounds awful."

"It was. But I moved here when I was small. I don't remember too much. None of us, Mother, brothers, we don't talk about it. We've moved on."

"And your dad?" asked Peter.

Kelly paused and lifted the nailbrush off the toe she was working on. She dipped it into a bottle and adjusted Phil's legs so that her left knee was now balanced on her right, leaving her left foot dangling in the air.

"He didn't make it out. He was supposed to join us, but never did. Now that NATO forces are leaving…well…we gave up all hope a long time ago."

"I'm sorry," said Peter sadly.

"Don't be." Kelly smiled at him and paraphrased the Bible. "There's no greater expression of love than to give up your life for the people you love."

"John 15:13," Peter mumbled.

Kelly nodded. "Every day since has been one more day proving how much he loved us. It is sad. But in a way, it is beautiful, too."

Kelly had just finished separating Phil's toes in a companion sponge when the basement door opened.

Grace called out, "Kel? You down there?"

"Uh-huh," Kelly grunted, concentrating on applying paint to Phil's toenails.

"What are you doing?" Grace asked, still on the top stair.

"Phil's toenails."

"Well, Blake and I are done on the phone now. Actually, we are done, done. Wait! You're doing what?"

"She's painting my toes," Phil chirruped happily. "Jack's next!"

Grace's eyebrows shot up toward her scalp as she crept down the stairs.

"Jack? You agreed to that?"

"Yeah!" Jack said with a laugh. "It was part of the deal. I'd let Kelly ruin my feet, and Phil would tell us all about her new boyfriend giving her a hickey!"

"I said no such thing, Jack Straw!"

"I heard you," lied Collin.

Peter piled on. "Me too!"

"Fine," spat Phil.

Kelly laughed one of her belly laughs and winked at Phil. "The rest of the deal was that these other two clowns have to get their toes done as well. Come down and give me a hand!"

Grace reached the bottom of the stairs and crossed the room. As she entered the better light, Jack saw her face was now twisted with disgust. She looked like she had just been ordered to scrub all the toilets at school.

"This had better be some juicy gossip," she said.

Turning towards Peter and Collin she asked, "When was the last time you washed those?" while gesturing with little flicks of her fingertips towards their feet.

"Let me think," said Collin, wearing his best deadpan face. "Wednesday is bath day and today is..."

Grace groaned.

CHAPTER 7

Fearing their actions would blow back onto Paul while he was in ISS, the football team limited their revenge to icy stares and snarling lips. Now that Paul was free, just as Collin predicted, they took every opportunity to make Jack's school life difficult. They blocked his path, jeered at him, and made nuisances of themselves, staying one step shy of physical violence.

"Hey look," they'd taunt. "There's that crybaby, Jack Straw."

"Yeah, we'd better not do anything or he'll run and tattle on us," others would say.

They always ended with, "Season's winding down, Straw. After that, it won't matter who gets benched, and we're going to make you pay for what you did to Ackerman."

Jack thought the whole situation childish and did his best to take it in stride. Meanwhile, Bobby and Phil were accepted at school as being an item. Their classmates buzzed about the new romance for a day or two before losing interest. Jack noticed Phil was spending more time with Bobby's circle of friends and less with Peter, Collin, and him. She was his best friend and he felt her absence keenly. As the year plodded along, Jack could see the inequality of time spent with her new friends versus her old ones begin to wear her down.

He wanted to help and tried to befriend Bobby, but it didn't work out. It wasn't that he disliked Bobby, they just didn't gel. In the end, Jack felt his efforts made things worse for Phil, not better. As helpless to stop it as he was the changing of the seasons, turning all the leaves in his neighborhood a gorgeous golden color, all he could do was watch as the sparkle over having a boyfriend faded from Phil's eyes.

October arrived bringing dreary thunderstorms with it. When the storms cleared out, more leaves were on the ground than remained on the trees. Every Halloween, Collin's family threw an amazing party where all the guests, even the adults, wore costumes. For the first time since the fourth grade, Phil missed that party. A few days later, she and Bobby were finished. Since Bobby didn't have two black eyes and a screaming need for emergency dental work, Jack figured the relationship ended on friendly enough terms.

Just like when she and Bobby started dating, he was willing to wait for her to talk about it in her own time. Phil, however, didn't seem as eager to discuss the break-up as she was the blossoming of her relationship. Peter and Collin let it go at that. Jack couldn't.

Whenever he caught the sad, furtive glances Phil made towards Bobby, he'd give her a smile or a nudge. She always smiled back and for the moment, that was enough for him. It wasn't until he heard her catch her breath at seeing Casey and Bobby holding hands at lunch that he braved asking if she wanted him to talk to Bobby.

"I don't need you to look out for me, Jack Straw," she snapped.

Jack jerked away, startled by her anger. From the look on her face, it surprised her, too.

The corners of her mouth rose in a weary smile as she breathed out, "Thanks, Jack, but if I wanted him dead, he'd be dead. Besides, Collin already stuck his big, fat nose in where it doesn't belong."

"What? Collin said something to Bobby? When? What did he say?"

"The day after we broke up. According to Kevin Mouser's girlfriend, Beth Mills, Collin told Bobby that whatever happened between me and Bobby was no one else's business and that it would stay that way unless rumors and trash talk started floating around."

Jack's lips pressed into a grimace. He was hoping for something a little more intimidating. "That's it?"

Phil chuckled. "You know Collin. It isn't what he said, it was how he said it. Beth told me Bobby was pretty freaked out over it. Collin didn't smile. Didn't blink. Wasn't angry. Wasn't anything. He just said what he said and walked off, like some kind of zombie."

Jack and Phil looked at each other, trying to suppress their giggles and, failing, burst out laughing. Collin and Peter came alongside and asked what was so funny.

"Phil just cracked a zombie joke," Jack said.

"I want to hear it," said Collin.

"You *are* it," Phil said.

Collin looked confused and turned to Jack, then back at Phil.

Still laughing, Phil dodged the topic. "We're going to be late for class."

Like a fever breaking, that laugh marked Phil's return to being more like her old self. After school, Jack and his friends walked home together and Phil took it in turns to tease each of them. The wind gusted bitter and damp in their faces. Jack's dad told him it was going to be a wet and cold winter this year and, although still autumn, Jack sensed his dad would be right.

One by one, they split apart to hustle to their respective homes to work on schoolwork. After pulling off his jacket, knit cap, and scarf, Jack headed straight for the basement. He had an English paper due that he'd left to the last minute to get started on and was looking forward to a long evening of seclusion to get it done.

Passing through the kitchen, he stopped to grab an apple out of the wooden bowl his mother kept stocked with fruit on the breakfast table. As he tried to decide which of the shiny red fruit he wanted, he heard voices in the basement rising through the air ducts. His shoulders drooped and his chin fell to his chest. Grace and Kelly were already down there.

Lately, they seemed to be everywhere — at least everywhere he was. They never tried to join in with whatever he was doing, but they cluttered his personal space like unwanted furniture. That was intrusion enough as far as he was concerned. Their tittering and gossiping burned like an ant biting him between his shoulder blades in a spot he could never quite reach. The longer it went on, the harder he found it to keep from hurling rude and sarcastic insults at them.

Turning on his heels to storm off, curiosity stabbed deep and pinned him where he stood. This opportunity to gather intelligence as to why Grace and Kelly were acting so bizarre lately was too tempting for a future spy to pass up. Cocking his ear toward the vent, he strained to catch what they were saying.

"It has nothing to do with you," he heard Grace tell Kelly. "I mean, I know it was your home and all, but that was a long time ago. You said yourself you don't have family there anymore. You live here now."

"You don't understand," Kelly said. "We made enemies before we left. We were given refugee status in this country because my father provided information. He named names!"

"He named Al Qaeda names. The Taliban are the ones in control of your hometown now," Grace argued.

"I somehow doubt the Taliban would concern themselves with the difference. I know they wouldn't if it were pointed out by an apostate family."

"Apostate?"

Kelly sounded desperate. "Yes! Leaving one religion for another is called apostasy. Mom and Dad were born Muslims. They converted to Christianity. According to Al Qaeda, and ISIS, and the Taliban, that is punishable by death."

Grace's voice brimmed with surprise and revulsion. "Do people really think like that?"

"Most Muslims don't," Kelly said in a sorrowful voice, "but enough do to make it a touchy subject. And a dangerous one, to the wrong people."

After a long silence Grace started over. "But you live here now. Changing religions isn't a crime here. You are safe."

Kelly scoffed, "Do you think the extremists don't have followers here? In this country?"

Jack had heard enough. He went back to his room and shoved his books into his backpack. There was no way he could pitch a fit over Grace and Kelly being in the game room. Not after what he overheard. That left one option. He had to be the one to make himself scarce. Taking off was the right thing to do, but he didn't have to like doing it.

Telling his mom that he was going to study over at Peter's, he left the house slamming the front door harder than he intended. As he marched over to Peter's, he muttered to himself so that, by the time he arrived, he'd worked his temper to the boiling point.

He pressed the doorbell at Peter's house so hard he heard the wood creak. Seconds later, the porch light popped on. Peter stood in the doorway with wide, questioning eyes. "Hey, Jack. What are you doing here?"

Behind him Peter's mother called out, "Who is it, sweetheart?"

Jack flashed a devilish grin.

"Bite me," Peter snarled softly. Louder he added, "It's Jack."

"Well, invite him in or go outside," Peter's dad grumbled. "Either way, shut the door!"

Jack bustled past Peter and caught sight of his friend's mom coming out of the kitchen to stand in the hallway wearing an apron. "We just finished dinner. There's some left-over stew, if you're hungry?"

"Thanks, but I ate before coming over," Jack said. "Peter and I have a paper due soon and I thought we could work on it together."

"Good idea," Peter's dad said, keeping his eyes glued to the TV. "Maybe having a study-buddy will help pull Peter's grades up."

"Dad!" Peter shouted. Quietly, he said to Jack, "Let's get outta here before I say something I'll regret."

Jack followed Peter to his room, which looked like a tornado had ripped through it. Peter pounced onto his unmade bed and crossed his legs on the rebound. "So, why *are* you here?"

Jack gave Peter a frustrated look. "To work on that paper."

Peter's eyes drooped. "Oh."

Jack shucked his jacket and pressed his back against the wall. Riding it down, he stretched his legs out across the floor in front of him, ankles crossed, and started pulling his schoolwork into his lap.

"Kelly and your sister still invading your space?" Peter asked.

"Always! I can't even turn around anymore without bumping into them. I was just about to settle down in the basement to work on this paper, but they got there first. It was like they were waiting for me!"

"Why are they being so...whatever?"

Jack's brows knit as he considered his answer in light of what he overheard. "You remember what Kelly told all of us? About how there's bad things happening in her home country? How she thinks she might be in danger or something?"

"I remember," Peter said. "Harsh. But what's that got to do with them crowding you?"

"I think Kelly's been hanging around so much because she is frightened. Maybe Grace put her up to it. I don't know. But, think about what she said about us. That we were intense? Scary even? Maybe she finds that reassuring now that she's scared. Like we would protect her if she needed us to."

"Well, we would. Wouldn't we?"

"Of course we would!" It was the stupidest question Jack ever heard. "But it'll never come to that. Kelly is over-reacting. Not surprising, after what she told us about losing her father and everything."

"So, what do we do?"

Jack laughed at the idea. "There's nothing to do." He didn't want to talk about Kelly anymore. "Come on," he said. "This stupid essay isn't going to write itself."

Peter mumbled his resentment over having to work on the paper, but soon enough settled down to the task. Jack grinned at the artistic flow of profanity Peter used as he wrote, then scratched out, three equally lame opening sentences. Beside Jack was a paltry stack of library books that he wasn't about to read, but was skimming for quotes and references for his paper. He was just thinking that he'd never been so bored in his life when his phone buzzed in his pocket.

"Hey, Mom."

She didn't return his greeting — a bad omen. "You planning on coming home tonight?"

Pulling his phone away from his ear, he checked the time: 22:30.

Jack swore.

"I'm going to pretend I didn't hear that, mister," his mother scolded as Jack's ear reconnected with the phone's speaker.

"Sorry, Mom. I'm doing homework at Peter's and lost track of time. I'll be right home."

His mother hung up on him. Another bad sign.

"You in trouble?" Peter asked, half grinning but not looking up.

"Nah," Jack grunted as he started shoving his things into his backpack.

His insides fluttered and he began making excuses. "Not really. I mean, I *was* doing homework. Mom's just mad I didn't call. I'll see you tomorrow."

"I better walk you out," said Peter, "or I'll be in trouble, too."

Jack started hurrying home. The cold nipped at him, stinging his cheeks and causing his nose to drip. The misting blanket of afternoon clouds was gone. Stars were free to shine in beautiful white pinpricks, but what feeble temperature the clouds kept netted beneath them was just as free to escape.

As he grew accustomed to the cold, the crisp clearness of the night refreshed him. He came to a full stop and tilted his head up to admire the skies, pulling in air in through his nose until his lungs ached from the cold. Exhaling, he watched his steamy breath fold around the moonlight. Above him, he picked out the three lined-up stars of Orion's Belt, then pulled his focus farther out to take in the whole constellation.

Across the street a door banged open, filling the dark street with its loud crack. A boy ran from the house. The porch light burst on, blinding Jack. A heavy man lumbered out the door behind the fleeing boy.

"Get back in this house," the man yelled.

The boy kept running.

Jack recognized the man from earlier in the year. It was Mr. Ackerman, and he was yelling at his youngest son, using some of the filthiest language Jack ever heard.

Headlights popped over a small crest in the road.

Jack's heart leapt into his throat. He darted into the street and rammed his crossed arms into the boy, sending him flying back onto the soggy grass. The impact of their two bodies stopped Jack dead in his tracks.

The car slammed on its breaks, but the wet roads made brakes useless and the rear of the car fish-tailed back and forth.

Jack dove for the curb.

The car swerved sideways missing the bulk of his body, but clipped Jack's legs.

Intense pain shot like lightning through Jack's body. He was in the air moving parallel to the curb, no longer toward it. Reflexes formed over years of taking falls in his karate class kicked in.

Tucking his chin tight to his chest, he tried to roll with it, but the force he felt as he struck the ground was unbelievable. He found it impossible to keep his head tucked and it slammed against the strip of grass beside the curb.

The cold was gone. The stars were gone. Jack lay motionless as the world turned black.

CHAPTER 8

Light began to trickle back into Jack's eyes. Straps bit as he struggled to sit up. Feeling the restraints made him fight harder.

"Cut it out, kid," a man beside him shouted. "You're going to make us drop you."

Jack's mind felt shrouded in a foggy dew. "What are you doing to me?"

"Just relax," a woman on the other side of the gurney cooed. "You were hit by a car. Do you remember?"

Jack squeezed his eyes shut. He remembered stars. He remembered two very large and bright ones coming straight at him. He remembered flying.

"No," Jack said.

He tried to sit up again after the wheeled bed was rolled into the back of the ambulance. "I need to go home. I'm already in trouble for being out so late."

"I think you're off the hook," the man chuckled, patting him down with a firm hand on his chest. "From what I've been told, you just saved another boy's life."

Relief hitched a feeble grin onto Jack's face.

"Lies," Jack whispered.

Jack's parents were at the hospital before the ambulance arrived. His dad was still wearing his slippers. They clutched his hands on either side of the gurney after he was offloaded from the ambulance and didn't let go until he was wheeled into an examination room and needed to be lifted onto a proper hospital bed. A nurse entered and squeezed past the exiting EMTs.

"I understand you did something very brave," she led off with.

"I don't remember," Jack lied, "but if I did, I'd rather you didn't spread it around."

She smiled at him. "Heroic and humble."

Turning to his parents she said, "We do, of course, have several forms that need signing. And Jack'll need to get out of those clothes and into a hospital gown."

"What for?" Jack protested as his dad signed everywhere the nurse pointed out an X. "It was my head that got cracked. Nothing else hurts. Well, my leg does, but I don't think it's broken or anything."

"We will still need to do a full examination. That will include blood work."

Facing his mother, the nurse asked, "Do you have a copy of his insurance card?"

Jack's mom began digging through her purse.

"Needles?" Jack winced. "I busted my head. I'm not sick."

"All part of the service. Now, I need to get your blood pressure, temperature, and pulse. After that, you need to change into a hospital gown."

She slipped a cuff over Jack's wrist and folded his arm across his chest. While she waited for the cuff to beep, she swiped a small wand across his forehead.

"I'll help with the gown," Jack's mother offered after the nurse left.

"No you won't!" Jack snapped.

"Don't be silly, Jack."

His dad rested a gentle hand on her arm before pulling the curtain around the bed and himself, leaving her outside.

Jack gave him a frustrated glare. "I don't need help."

Without responding, his dad began untying Jack's shoes.

"Dad! I said ..."

Removing each shoe and slipping off Jack's socks, his dad asked in hushed tones, "Why did you save that boy?"

"He would have been killed if I didn't!"

"I know. But was it for him? Or for you?"

"Dad! What is this? For him!"

"Then prove it. Swallow your pride and give me the courtesy of helping you when you need it, just like you helped that boy when he needed it."

"Fine," Jack groaned, "but I can manage my own zipper, thank you very much!"

Their eyes met and they both laughed.

As Jack lifted his hips, his dad pulled at the jeans' legs. Though his dad was being as gentle as possible, an incredible pain in his left thigh zapped through him. A warm rush flooded his head and he felt woozy.

"Okay. So maybe I needed more help than I was willing to admit," he whispered. "Thanks, Dad."

Between the two of them, they managed to get him undressed. Jack's muscles were far more stiff and sluggish than he expected. He noticed that his fingers were an odd purple hue and they refused to bend properly.

Bloodstains were everywhere; on his shirt, pants, shoes, even socks. His dad shoved the lot into a bag marked "Bio-Hazard." Jack left his underpants on and determined there would be a knock-down, drag-out fight if anyone tried to take them from him.

The gown was a puzzle. Neither of them could decide if it went on over the back, like a coat, or over the front, like an apron. Jack chose over the front, "... because it makes the least sense, so that must be the right way."

Only after he was beneath the bed's blanket did his dad re-open the curtain.

Then, the waiting started.

An hour passed before he was wheeled down to x-ray. After his return to the examination room, he waited another hour and a half for a doctor to show up.

"Mr. and Mrs. Straw. Jack. I'm Doctor Lloyd."

Jack's dad sounded like a soap opera actor. "How bad is it?"

"Surprisingly, not so terrible. Jack was very lucky his head hit the grass and not concrete. He did get a concussion and a pretty severe subperiosteal hematoma."

"What's that?" Jack interrupted.

"You probably have heard it called a bone bruise. You got smacked pretty hard in the femur. That's the big bone running down your thigh. Blood is collecting beneath the membrane that covers the bone, just like blood collecting under your skin forms a normal bruise."

"Is it serious?" his mother asked.

"Usually not. Jack's young and in excellent health, so I don't think there's too much to worry about from the leg injury."

Doctor Lloyd turned to Jack. "I bet it hurts a lot though and you'll need to take it easy for about a month."

"A month!" Jack couldn't keep from whining.

"Jack!" his mother admonished.

"It's okay, Mrs. Straw. A month can seem like a very long time to a youngster."

"So, when can we leave?" Jack's father asked.

"We'd like to admit him for observation. I don't think there's anything serious to worry about, but whenever a child gets knocked out, we like to err on the side of caution."

"I see," his mother said.

Jack was unimpressed. He knew he wasn't at one hundred percent, but he didn't need to stay in the hospital either.

"And he's also going to need stitches. Just three, I think, but..."

"...but you're going to have to shave my head," Jack finished for him, making a grimace.

The doctor's smile broadened. "Just a small patch."

Jack turned to look at his parents. They looked back with sympathetic eyes, but Jack could tell they weren't going to object.

The nurse who took his vital signs returned with a tray. Her eyes flashed at the doctor. Blinking, her cheeks coloring a rose pink, she looked away.

The doctor began explaining to the entire room, "Iris will clean Jack up a bit before we start with the stitches. She will be giving him a local anesthetic, that is, some pain killer," he tossed over to Jack as if he was too stupid to know what an anesthetic was, "so the wash and stitches won't be felt at all. Any questions?"

Dr. Lloyd's explanation was simple enough and nobody spoke as the sewing was done. Afterwards, Jack convinced his parents to go home. Iris came back after they left and announced he was going to be moved into a room shortly.

"When's the wedding?" Jack asked out of boredom.

"What wedding," Iris asked, looking flustered.

"Yours and that doctor's," Jack said, inclining his head toward the nurse's station and wishing he hadn't.

"You have a tan line where an engagement ring would be, and he couldn't bring himself to look at you when you walked in before, but you kept glancing over at him."

"You're an observant little guy, aren't you? August. We're getting married in August. And I promise I won't say a word about your being a hero if you don't mention our engagement. It's not against the rules or anything, but doctor/nurse relationships are looked down on around here."

"I won't say a word."

"Thank you. Now, try and get some sleep. I'm not sure when they'll show up to move you."

Nurse Iris dimmed the lights for him. Jack had just drifted off when the sound of the sliding door of his exam room woke him.

"You here to move me to my room?" Jack asked.

"I'm not taking you anywhere," an unfriendly voice said.

Jack snatched up the remote at his bedside and pressed for the light. Paul Ackerman was standing in the doorway.

"What are you doing here?" Jack demanded.

"My brother's here. Next hall over. You cracked a couple of his ribs when you hit him."

"I didn't hit him," Jack protested. "I pushed him out of the way of an oncoming car!"

Paul lifted his hands in an effort to calm Jack. "Bad choice of words. I saw you get hit by the car instead of him. If that car had hit my brother like that, it would have killed him."

Jack didn't answer. He knew Paul was right — knew it before he darted into the street to shove the kid in the first place.

"Did you know he was my brother? Before, I mean?"

Jack exhaled loudly. "You are such a dick! Yeah, I knew. So what? It was the right thing to do no matter who he was."

"That's what I thought," Paul said.

Paul and Jack eyed each other for a long time. Something was changing between them. Jack could feel it like the sudden warmth that heralded the end of a summer deluge.

Paul turned to leave. "See you around, Straw. And...thanks."

CHAPTER 9

Phil's bedroom was cramped and cluttered. Jack would never have suspected the room belonged to a girl if not for the bubblegum pink walls Phil's mother thought she'd love.

"What that means," Phil once explained to him, "is that Mom loved them."

Toeing aside a pile of clothes on the floor, unsure of whether they were clean or dirty, Jack cleared a path, giving himself room to pace.

"Would you sit down?" she snapped. "You're making me wiggy. Aren't you supposed to be recovering or something?"

"I was hit by that car two weeks ago. I'm fine."

He kept pacing Phil's room, building up steam.

"You don't get it, Phil!" Jack finally vented. "I can't keep this up! Everywhere I go," he threw up his arms, "Grace and Kelly are always there."

"Jack," Phil said, not pulling her face out of her textbook, "I already told you, either call them on it or live with it."

For the past several days he'd been living with it, doing his best to be patient and failing miserably. He felt like a tiger trapped in a low-budget zoo when at home, and like a snowman in the tropics when hiding out at Phil's, Peter's, or Collin's.

By his estimate, more than enough time had passed for Kelly to get a grip on her fears, see them as being irrational, and calm down. But she was more uneasy, not less and he, in turn, anxious and grouchy.

Sighing an obscenity, he sank onto a corner of Phil's mattress. "Grace and I used to have an arrangement. I'd ignore her, she'd ignore me, and we'd try to remember each other's birthdays."

He picked at the threads of her blanket. "You know the worst part?"

Phil grunted to show she was still listening.

"I know how scared Kelly is, but all I can think about is me. How lame is that?"

Phil scoffed at him. "I imagine it is difficult, lugging around everyone else's problems while ignoring your own."

The following day, Jack had to flee his home again to escape Grace and Kelly. This time, he took refuge at Peter's house as soon as he was sure Peter would be home from swimming. Aside from being royal blue, Peter's room was identical to Phil's. Clothes littered the floor. A petrified slice of pizza from the dawn of time, stuck to a paper towel beneath it, sat on Peter's dresser, the drawers of which hung at awkward angles.

"Dude," Peter said, "I don't get why you don't tell them to get lost. I mean, why do you always have to be the one to bug-out?"

The day after that, it was Collin's turn. His room was the complete opposite to the others. It looked more a monk's cell. The bed, its sheets tight and crisp, was long and narrow. Books lined the walls. Not so much as a sock desecrated the wood floor and dust gremlins were too terrified to gather in the corners.

"You have to talk to them. You know that, right?" Collin said without preamble.

"You think they don't know what they are doing?" snapped Jack.

Collin flinched.

"Sorry," Jack muttered. He wasn't mad at Collin. He was mad at the world.

Collin waved off the unnecessary apology. "I think they know what they're doing. I'm not so sure they're aware of what it's doing to you."

"Kelly's just scared," Jack said.

The tightness in his head, irritability, and anxiousness started to drift away, soothed for the moment by Collin's direct insightfulness.

Sitting on the floor didn't seem appropriate in Collin's room, so Jack dropped onto one of the hard-wood chairs and sighed. "I can hold out for a while longer if I need to. If Kelly and Grace are still a thorn in my side after Thanksgiving, I'll talk to them then. Okay?"

"I don't see the point in waiting," Collin said with a shrug, "but that's up to you."

Jack spent the afternoon studying at Collin's. When dinner time rolled around, Jack packed his books and went home not feeling very hopeful that his would be a pleasant evening. Over dinner, his mom explained that Grace and Kelly went out for burgers with friends and was relieved to discover they weren't waiting in the basement to ambush him.

After dinner, he lugged his books down to the basement to study in peace. Wriggling his shoulders deep into his beanbag, he prepared to go over definitions for an up-coming science exam when the basement door opened. His stomach plummeted. Grace and Kelly came down the stairs and dropped onto the couch. Their presence was a pain in his neck but worse, their new tendency to argue with each other like he wasn't there, made him sick.

Kelly's fear wasn't taking its toll on him alone. Her anxiety was grinding Grace down, too. Their friendship was starting to unravel. Never far from him, he was forced to watch it rot, powerless to stop it.

He knew he should collect his things and leave. That would be the wisest move. Defying his voice of reason, he gripped his textbook in his hands. A brick of stubbornness dropped into his guts and he refused to be driven off. Scrunching down into his beanbag, he tried to remain focused on studying, to ignore the chattering pair behind him, and above all, to keep a lid on his rising temper.

Grace propped herself against one arm of the fake-leather couch and flipped open a spiral notebook. "Okay, Kel, let's start putting our presentation together."

Kelly, who sat curled against the other arm, seemed not to have heard.

Jack wiggled deeper into his beanbag, hoping the crunching beans would remind them he did, in fact, exist. His concentration was so thrown off he had to restart the section of his Biology book covering the function of the mitochondria from the beginning.

Jack clenched his teeth. Every snap of binder rings or slapping of pages in a spiral notebook landed on him like a punch. Unable to control his reactions, he blinked at every sound.

Once again, the thought came to him that he should evacuate the area before he exploded, but he had waited too long. He was too mad and too proud to give in now. Not this time.

Beans crunched as he pressed his hips deeper still into his bag.

"Get out your notes, Kelly," Grace insisted. "We have to start putting this together."

Kelly's voice was a soft whisper. "I don't have them."

"You left them at home? Really? We were supposed to spend tonight working on our presentation!"

Jack flicked his eyes in their direction and watched as Kelly hugged her knees and looked miserable.

Jack started over, re-reading his paragraph for a third time.

"Kelly!" His sister sounded like she was making an accusation.

Kelly didn't answer.

Jack hunkered down. "Mitochondria function as the powerhouse of cells," Jack read, this time whispering the words.

"Well," Grace persisted, "can you go get them real fast? I mean, this presentation is due at the end of the week!"

Jack read louder, "They take in nutrients from the cell, break it down, and turn it into the energy the cell needs to function."

"I don't mean I don't have them with me," Kelly said. "I mean I don't have them. I didn't do it."

"The action of the mitochondria turning nutrients into energy to be used by the cell is called cellular respiration," read Jack in a loud growl.

"Didn't do it? Kelly!"

"Grace!"

Jack was gripping his textbook so tight the pages wrinkled. Angry perspiration seeped out of his back, producing an icky film between him and the beanbag. With a groan, he started over again, this time much louder. "Mitochondria function as the powerhouse of cells…"

"It's worth half of this quarter's grade!" snapped Grace. "We can't pass the semester without doing well on this presentation!"

"When did you start caring about grades?"

Jack slammed his book against the floor and sprang to his feet. "Would the two of you shut up! It's bad enough I run into you every time I turn around. But to have to listen to you yipping at each like tiny Poodles? It's too much!"

Jack stormed out of the basement. Jamming his bare feet into untied shoes, he rushed out of the house.

Before he reached the end of his driveway he realized how rash he was being. Running out of his house on a blustery autumn evening without any protection from the cold was stupid. Still, he was too angry — too proud — to go back inside now, even if only to reach in and grab his coat and hat.

He racked his brain for some place of shelter. Immediately, he thought of Phil and ordered his angry feet to carry him to her house.

"What the heck were you thinking?" Phil asked after letting him in, shivering and hugging himself for warmth.

"I wa-wa-wasn't."

"Clearly," she snarked with a shake of her head. "Go up to my room and wrap a blanket around you. I'll make us some hot chocolate. Then, you can explain to me what made you do such a dumb thing."

He made his way upstairs and draped Phil's crumpled duvet over his shoulders, waiting for her to come up with the hot drink. After a few sips of steaming chocolate, he let all his frustrations flow out of him.

Phil listened without interrupting, nodding her head in agreement and understanding. Even when he confided about being confused by Kelly's flirting, if that what it was, she kept silent. Her eyes widened and she pulled a sour face, but she didn't utter a word.

When he had finished, she sat chewing over everything he told her. "You can't keep doing this."

"I know, but what am I supposed to do? I mean, Kelly is totally freaked out."

"I'm not talking about Kelly. I'm talking about you. You can't go on pretending it isn't happening. You have to deal with it."

"I've been dealing with it," Jack snapped.

Phil kept her cool, despite him shouting. "No, you haven't. You have been putting up with it. That's not the same thing."

While talking, she pulled out her phone and her thumbs worked furiously.

"What are you doing?" Jack demanded.

"Duh! Texting."

"I can see that, Phil. I meant what and to who?"

"Peter and Collin. I'm telling them to meet us at your place. Grace and Kelly will still be there. We're going to get this out into the open once and for all."

"Phil! No! It will all blow over in a few more days. There's no need to make a mess of things now."

She locked her eyes on him, seeing him as no one but a best friend could, looking deep inside, beyond flesh, blood, and bone, down into the emotional stew that simmered underneath.

Feeling exposed, he wondered what she saw, looking at him like that, but couldn't bring himself to ask. The accusation, "What are you staring at?" was the best he could manage.

Her brows knitted together. She appeared to be wrestling with some ambiguous concept, trying to haul it out of the shadows of her mind and into enough light to allow her to wrap words around it.

"You don't know how unique you are, do you?" she said.

He wasn't sure if she was about to compliment him, or slam him. It didn't matter, both would embarrass him deeply. She was being as serious with him as she had ever been and it was making him squirm.

"People trust you, Jack," she continued. "I can think of just one person who wouldn't follow you without thinking twice about it."

"And who's that, Phil?" He tried to sound flip. Sarcastic. It came out angry.

"You."

Jack felt like a plastic grocery sack whose handles snapped off, leaving all his insecurities spilled out across the floor for Phil to see. He couldn't speak. Her cold analysis made him as angry as he'd ever been with her. Gritting his teeth to cage a nasty reply, he sat waiting for Phil to say something, anything, to release him from her torture.

"You can stay here and hide in my closet if you like," she said with finality, "but I'm going." She got up and went downstairs, leaving him to stay or follow, whichever he chose.

Jack's eyes shot to Phil's closet. The tiny grotto was crammed full of clothes. The floor was a jumble of still more clothes, shoes, and long forgotten toys. A corner of his mouth lifted in a sardonic half-smile.

"I wouldn't fit anyway," he told himself.

Shrugging the blanket off his shoulders, he joined her by the front door where she was pulling on her winter coat. Digging into the entryway closet, she drew out a hunter's jacket and tossed it into his arms. The coat was two sizes too big for him and smelled of stale beer and cigars. One of her mother's many ex-boyfriends must have left it when he left her.

Jack knew he looked ridiculous. Still, it would keep him from freezing. He jammed his hands into the pockets, tucking one side of the coat tight under the other by crossing his arms. He kept his mouth shut.

As they walked back to his house, he imagined the confrontation with his sister going in multiple directions. The worst scenario, which he swore he wouldn't allow to happen, was the one in which his friends championed him while he sat by hangdog and silent. It was one thing needing their moral support. It was quite another to let them fight his battles for him.

When they reached his house, they darted upstairs and into his room before his parents could ask about his borrowed coat and why he ran off without his own. Peter and Collin arrived soon after and Phil started to fill them in on her plan, but Jack cut her off.

"Collin, you told me this afternoon that I needed to talk to Grace and Kelly about what's been going on. Phil? Peter? You both told me the same thing, and you were right. Grace and Kelly are downstairs and I'd appreciate it if you would hang out with me while I talk to them."

Jack's stomach felt queasy. He was grateful his friends were there — humbled by the fact that, when he needed them, they dropped whatever they were doing and came to his aid. Despite those feelings, he hoped he made it clear that he was to do the talking. Or, at least to start it off. He couldn't stop Phil from putting in her two cents if she felt the need.

Peter posed an even bigger problem. He struggled in school, but Jack knew that was because Peter's personality leaned toward physical activity and direct exploration. He wasn't designed for the passive bookworm approach. Though a poor match for the way classes were taught, Peter had an agile mind and a savage mouth.

If Kelly and his sister resisted his attempt to talk reason and turned nasty, Peter would become just as ugly. He would turn a difficult discussion into a verbal mugging. Somehow, Jack had to prevent Peter from feeling he had to defend him. To do that, he had to keep his own cool and wasn't at all sure he could.

CHAPTER 10

Dreading what needed to happen, Jack led the way down to the basement. With plodding steps, he descended the stairs and sat on the carpeted floor facing the couch. Phil, Peter, and Collin trooped behind him, grim faced and determined. They took up places flanking Jack.

After their group project exploded in their faces, Grace and Kelly retreated into ignoring each other. Kelly was balled up at one end of the couch, arms hugging her knees, and glowering at the wall. Grace was curled up just as tightly, one hand pressed against her chest, the other holding a paperback copy of Macbeth in a death grip so tight the spine was splitting.

Jack decided the best thing to do was to wait for the girls to notice him. Slowly, they lifted their heads out of their shared isolation and stared at him with confused and expectant expressions.

Grace sneered. "Well?"

He had their attention. If he didn't get things started now somebody else would. It took all his effort to make his voice sound confident. "Grace? Kelly? I've got a problem."

"We've got problems of our own," Grace said testily. "We don't need to add yours to them."

"You do when you're the problem," Peter snarked.

Jack watched as his sister's jaw muscles begin to quiver. Her face flushed pink then roared into a deep maroon. Jack had a fleeting image of a cartoon version of his sister with steam squealing out of her ears.

Collin saw the same tantrum signs as Jack and scrambled to smooth things over. "What Peter means…"

"Guys! Shut up and let Jack deal with this in his own way," Phil snapped.

Jack squeezed his eyes shut. Ignoring everything his sister said, he started over. "Kelly? I know that you are worried about what's going on in your country. Maybe it makes you feel better, maybe safer, to hang around me and my friends. The thing is, I am finding it annoying, being in your shadow all the time."

"Well that's just tough," Grace exploded. "This is my house just as much as it is yours."

"I know that," Jack fired back.

Swallowing hard, he inhaled through his nose and let it seep out of his mouth. Taking another deep breath, he used brute force to exert his will to stay calm over his anger's call to erupt.

"But you never had to always be in the same place as me before," he said as he let the air escape his lungs. "And the two of you never argued with each other so much before, either. Whatever is causing this problem, it isn't just affecting me. So, it's your problem, too."

Grace's eyes opened wide; her mouth pursed in anger. "Don't you tell me what my problems are, you little…"

Kelly laid a soft hand on her arm. "He's right."

Grace turned on her. "No! He's not! He can't tell us what to do. Where me and my friends get to go in my own house. He's being a jerk."

"He's being honest," Kelly insisted. "That's more than we have been with him."

To Jack she said, "We have been invading your space. On purpose. I've been so scared and worried I couldn't see what we were…what I was doing to you…"

She flashed a feeble smile at Grace. "…or to us. Something needs to change. It's time we told them everything."

Collin, always quick to pick up on subtleties, said more than asked, "So this isn't about Al Qaeda."

"Oh yes," Kelly said, "it has everything to do with Al Qaeda. Just more to do with one member in particular."

"Start from the beginning," Jack said, curiosity obliterating his temper, "and don't leave anything out."

Kelly looked to Grace for support.

"You can trust Jack, Kel. I don't know what he and his friends can do, if they can do anything at all. But I do know you can trust them."

Jack raised his shoulders and pushed his neck to the side, trying to stretch away the awkward feelings Grace's words stirred up inside him. The foundation their relationship was built upon shifted underneath him. No longer "big sister" and "little brother," separate and independent from each other, they were family in a way they had never been before — a family working together to solve a serious problem. For once, they were on the same team.

Relief washed over him when Grace returned to her old and familiar snottiness. "Jack? If you tell anyone, or screw things up for Kelly and her family in any way, I'll make your life a misery."

"Sure," said Peter with a sneer. "Because, you know, the past month has been so wonderful for Jack. Who'd want to mess that up?"

Grace stared Peter down with a boiling glare.

This was a side of his sister Jack had never seen before, but he recognized it for what it was, the same fire that fueled his own stubborn determination. He shoved those thoughts out of his mind with the aid of another neck-stretch. This was neither the time nor the place to try to get his brain wrapped around the new quirks he was discovering in his sister. Grace meant what she said, and it sobered Jack. The enormity of what Kelly was about to tell them must be huge.

"You have our word. Anything you tell us stays with us," he said.

Phil, Peter, and Collin added their vows of silence to Jack's.

"Okay," Kelly drawled in a hesitant voice.

Jack could see she wasn't convinced this was the right thing to do. He guessed that she was going to share her story with them because she didn't know what else to do. She was desperate.

"I am afraid of a man named Qasim Batesh," Kelly began. "He was an Al Qaeda terrorist who was making his way up their ranks."

"Was?" asked Collin.

Kelly's forehead creased as she considered her answer. "I suppose he still is," she said. "It's just, that he was captured several years ago and has spent those years in a prison on the outskirts of my city."

Phil's intuition helped her guess the rest of the situation. "As the situation at home gets worse, the probability that he will escape or be released increases."

"And it was your dad's testimony that got him locked up," Collin said frankly, not giving Kelly a chance to respond to Phil.

Jack came to Kelly's defense. "Guys! Let her tell it."

"It's okay, Jack," Kelly said, forcing a smile onto her somber face. "They are both right. Their understanding makes this easier."

Her feeble smile faded as she returned to her story. "Dad's testimony was supposed to be anonymous, but while in prison, Batesh learned the truth. He swore himself to vengeance.

"We had already moved to this country by then, but word got to us that I was to be the instrument of his revenge. Being the youngest, and my family's only daughter, Batesh swore to make me his terrorist bride and then, after enough torture and humiliation leaves me broken and brain-washed, I am to be used as a suicide bomber."

They all sat dumbfounded as the horror of the plan sunk in. Jack felt like an idiot. In that instant, he forgave Kelly, and Grace too, for any inconvenience they were causing him. It seemed so petty a thing to have been upset over compared to the burden the two girls were struggling under.

"Oh, come on!" Peter said forcefully, ending Jack's self-berating. "That's way over on the far side of the world. And this Batesh guy is still in prison. And even if he does get out, he still has to make it over here to get to you. That's not such an easy thing to do these days."

"He already has a plan on how to get into the United States," Kelly said in a voice just above a whisper.

"What!" Grace shouted.

Kelly stared at her hands while picking polish off her manicured nails. "Before they were captured, Batesh and his followers had a plan to enter this country to commit attacks," she said.

"But that's what he got locked up for, right?" Peter asked, his tone revealing how much he wanted it to be the truth. "The authorities will be ready for him if he escapes and tries to go through with it."

"No, they won't," Kelly said as tears began welling in her eyes. "No one outside of Batesh's terrorist cell knows the details of his plan."

Kelly tunneled deeper into the couch, causing its fake leather to make a farting sound. Any other time, this would have driven the boys into laughter. Not one of them so much as cracked a smile.

Kelly's voice was feeble and sounded apologetic. "No one, that is, except Mom."

"She has got to tell someone!" Phil exploded.

Jack took a long, hard look at Phil. If she was shaken by what she had heard, that was reason enough for all of them to be worried.

"She won't," Kelly said, her tears falling in earnest now.

Jack knew there still had to be more to hear. "Kelly?" he pressed as gentle as he could. He felt as if he were coaxing a terrible secret out of a frightened child. "Why won't she tell?"

"Chess," Collin answered for her.

Grace sneered with a sarcastic wrinkling of her nose. "Chess?"

"A version of it, yeah," Collin said. He turned to Kelly. "Your mom is afraid that, if she tells everything she knows up front, the government would have no reason to help her in the future. She'd have nothing to bargain with. No moves left to make."

Kelly nodded shamefully.

"That's ridiculous," Peter scoffed. Whether for his own benefit or for Kelly's, he was still trying to downplay the severity of their predicament.

"Is it?" Phil asked. "Kelly's mom lost her husband to these people. I can understand her doing anything to not lose her children, too."

Peter was about to make a comeback, but shut his mouth. His shoulders sagged. Jack knew Peter was done. They all were. No argument could ever be strong enough to stand against a mother's love for her children.

The adage, "Hope for the best. Plan for the worst," was one of Jack's favorite catch phrases. It served him well in the past, but this went far beyond anything he expected to face in his freshman year of high school. He had no clue where to begin planning for the worst. He couldn't even imagine what the worst could be.

Panic began creeping over him. Fighting against it, he tried to reassure himself. *The best thing that can happen is nothing. Batesh remains in jail and we're good,* he said inside his mind.

His pessimism reasserted itself and he started to list all the things that could go wrong. *Batesh escapes. He makes it to America. He goes after Kelly and her family. They all die. We all die trying to prevent it. What can I do against something like that?*

He felt like he was falling into a hole that had no bottom. As he wrestled with his growing feelings of inadequacy, his friends began spitting out random suggestions, making him feel more desperate with every word.

Phil said they needed to go to the police. Kelly forbade them to defy her mother's wishes.

So much for the most sensible plan, Jack thought.

Peter insisted they were all making a big deal out of nothing.

Maybe he's right. But what if he isn't? What then?

Collin alone kept quiet. His eyes darted left and right as he analyzed the situation as if reading it from the pages of a book. He wouldn't speak up until he had something substantial to say.

And our own personal genius can't think of a single thing that'd help.

Jack's insides felt on fire. His skin prickled. Breathing was becoming difficult. Panic was setting in.

"Stop it!" Jack barked aloud.

He was talking to himself, but everyone jerked their heads around, assuming he was yelling at them. With every eye upon him, he felt pressured to come up with something brilliant, but had nothing.

"Stop throwing stuff at the wall just to see what sticks," he said. "Let's calm down and think things through. We need a plan that is workable. One that makes sense. Kelly isn't in any immediate danger, so we have time."

They all settled down to work on the puzzle, but Jack struggled to focus. He kept thinking of how he'd dreamed of being involved in stopping an evil plot like this. Now that one was thrown into his lap, he questioned if he was the right man for the job. He thought he was going to be sick.

Phil gave him a tap on the knee with her foot. When he looked at her, she tilted her head in Peter's direction. Shifting his eyes where she indicated, he saw a wiggling Peter chewing on his lower lip and picking at carpet threads.

Waiting. No plan. Uncertainty. These things were Peter's kryptonite. The longer he was exposed to them, the more reckless and volatile he would become.

Jack realized he had to take charge of the situation. If he didn't, who would? The problem was that he didn't know what to do. They couldn't keep sitting there agonizing under the crushing weight of an unsolvable problem, but what options were there?

His mind burst open. "We are going about this all wrong," he said aloud. "We are trying to solve the problem of social and political deterioration that's going on halfway around the world, and we can't. It's too big."

Kelly whimpered.

"No! Listen," he insisted. "We don't need to solve that problem. Our problem is much simpler. What we need to do is keep you safe, not prevent whatever is going to happen over there from happening. We can't stop it and besides, it's ... it's ..."

"Above our pay grade," Collin said in his matter-of-fact-way.

Jack beamed. "Exactly! Our job is to deal with whatever shakes loose here at home. That, we can do!"

Everyone was focused on him, hanging on every word. Kelly's tears slowed to a trickle. Phil, Peter, and Collin were bright and eager to get into action. Grace was beaming with pride. Jack tried to ignore that because it put him off balance.

"At the moment, we don't have enough information to work with," he continued.

Kelly sniffled.

"That's a good thing," he said. "After all, time is on our side. Things aren't horrible yet."

Jack's assessment of the situation was a partial lie. Not having enough information was never a good thing. It does, however, give a spy the perfect place to start. Gathering intelligence.

"That's right," Peter said enthusiastically. "Remember, this Batesh fella is still locked up."

"And," Phil said, "after being in jail for so long, maybe some indispensable part of his plan to get into this country was destroyed. You did say that plan was made years ago."

"It hasn't," Kelly croaked. She sounded as hopeless as Jack felt.

"You don't know that," Collin said.

Jack's gut tightened. Collin didn't go in for sugar coating things. He was always blunt and always went straight to the heart of the problem. Jack had no idea what Collin's next words would be and, given that both Kelly and Grace were terrified, didn't know how they'd react.

Collin went on explaining, "Your fear is telling you it's true, but that is a very different thing than knowing it's true."

"What he said," quipped Phil, as if surprised by Collin's insightfulness. Jack knew she wasn't. Her reaction was part of the pretend game they were all going to have to play in order to give Kelly some sense of security. For the time being, Kelly would be told positives. He and his friends would deal with the negatives.

"That's right," Jack agreed. "We need to know more. Now, ever since I found out you were worried about what was going on in your home country, I've been studying news reports from that area. I'll keep that going. Peter?"

Peter's face lit up. "Yeah, Jack?"

"Since you're on the swim team, you've got more friends than the rest of us. Well, except maybe for Phil. Start asking around. Find out if anything strange or out of the ordinary has been seen."

"Sure thing, Jack," he said.

"And see if you can get close to Jenny Wade," Jack added. Giving out tasks loosened his thoughts and ideas began flowing out of him. "She's on the swim team too, and everyone knows her brothers are thugs. Maybe she overheard them talking about something going on that's a bit sketchy."

"She'll think I'm hitting on her," Peter objected.

"She's pretty," Phil countered with a grin. "If it works out between you two, that'd be okay, wouldn't it?"

Jack bit his tongue. Phil's attempt to lighten the mood was a good thing, but it scraped against his role of handing out tasks.

"Collin," he said gravely, "Blain MacGregor is in the chess club."

"That's right," Collin said.

"Join it."

"Why?"

"Because his dad happens to be the Deputy Chief of Police."

Collin scratched his head. "Sign-ups ended months ago."

"Who's their best player?" Jack asked.

"William Mugambi," Grace blurted out.

Jack turned to her; his jaw dropped open.

"He's in our class," she said sheepishly. "A senior."

She smiled at him. She wasn't acting like someone who was trying not to be left out of the action. She was trying to help.

Jack faltered. He preferred it when his sister was part of the scenery in his life, not an active participant.

Stunned and blinking, he returned to giving instructions to Collin. "Challenge this William Mugambi to a game. Then rip him apart. When he demands a rematch, which he will, rip him apart again. Tear him to shreds every time you play him. In less than two weeks, you'll be on the team."

Grace was incredulous. "He can do that?"

Jack answered in total confidence. "He can do that." A proud smile slid across Collin's face.

"Phil?"

"Saving the best assignment for last, Jack?" Phil asked, grinning widely.

"Not exactly," Jack said cautiously. Just as she had done with Peter, Jack declined his head in Kelly's direction.

Phil's countenance fell. "Really?" she groaned.

"You are the best qualified," Jack said.

Phil bristled. "Why? Because I'm a girl?"

Jack rocked his head from side to side, eyebrow raised, the corners of his mouth turned down, exaggerating a contemplative look. "That too," he said.

A hint of a smile fluttered onto Phil's face. Jack was relieved to see that Phil understood he was complimenting her fighting skill, not making a dig. He hoped that would be enough to cover what he had to say next.

"Grace? Kelly? Phil is going to be hanging out with you guys for a while. It may raise some questions. Tell people she's one of my friends and that you felt sorry for her."

He heard Phil's breath hiss out her nostrils as if she were an angry bull. He wished he hadn't because it pushed him beyond his ability to resist taking the tease further. "You know. A charity case."

"When this is all over, Jack Straw, you are going to pay for that," Phil growled.

"I'm sure," Jack said.

She shot him a nasty smile.

Returning to Kelly, he explained, "Seriously. Out of all of us, Phil makes the best bodyguard. And when she can't be there, I'll be tagging along with Grace. She and I will make up excuses for it as we go. The rest of the time, stay close to your brothers and your mother, or hang out here with us. The point is, you will be kept safe for as long as you need to be."

Kelly erupted in tears of relief. She blubbered unintelligible words of thanks. Jack didn't understand why she had to carry on like that but, since she did seem to need to, he locked his teeth together and let her get on with it.

He was relieved when Grace bustled Kelly upstairs to clean her up. Then Grace and Phil walked her home. While they were gone, Peter and Collin said their goodbyes to Jack and took off for their homes as well.

When Grace and Phil returned, Jack met them at the door. He could tell Grace was peeved.

"Jack, you need to talk to Phil," she said, ignoring the fact Phil was standing right beside her. "I told her she didn't need to walk me home. Kelly is the one in danger, not me. It took her well out of her way to come back here after dropping Kelly off. It's cold out. She should have just gone home."

"I'll talk to her," Jack said. He had no intention of doing so, but if it made Grace happy to think he would, that was reason enough for him to lie.

"See that you do," Grace said. "Now, I'm going to bed. Tonight wore me out. Good night, Jack."

She reached out with a hesitant hand and, leading him by his shoulder, pulled him into a hug. Feeling awkward, he fingertip-patted her back.

Releasing him as quick as she grasped him, Grace trotted upstairs to her room.

"Weird," Jack muttered.

"If you say so," Phil said.

Jack was puzzled by Phil's response. "Well, I do."

"She's your sister, Jack." Her lips tightened with exasperation. "You can be so dense sometimes."

"You don't have any brothers or sisters," Jack pointed out, "so take my word for it. She's being weird."

Phil shrugged.

Changing the subject, Jack said, "Thanks, by the way."

"For what?"

"I knew I didn't need to ask. That you'd look out for Grace anyway."

He shook his head in dismay. "She doesn't even realize that, as long as Kelly is in danger, she is, too."

Phil cupped his cheek in her hand. "You know, Jack, you can be so sweet sometimes."

Her hand was still cold from the November night air. Despite the chill of her fingers, he felt his face burn with blush.

"No, I'm not," he pouted, trying to sound macho. "I just don't want to have a bunch of explaining to do to Mom and Dad."

"I don't believe you," she said. Caressing his cheek as she slid her hand off his face and slipped it into a glove, she continued, "But Jack?"

"Yeah, Phil?"

"You're still going to pay big time for calling me a charity case."

CHAPTER 11

Jack leaned back in his beanbag and intertwined his fingers behind his head. Phil was next to him, taking her turn at the video game, while Peter and Collin did schoolwork.

"This is awesome," he announced. "Grace and Kelly haven't been bugging me lately. I get to watch Phil get slaughtered in this game. You guys are hanging out, my stitches have dissolved, my hair's growing back, tomorrow's Friday, then it's the weekend and no school!"

"Okay for you," grumbled Peter as he scribbled on his paper. "I've still got to finish this math worksheet. Was supposed to take thirty minutes. I'm coming up on an hour."

"Bet you get all the answers right, though," encouraged Collin from behind his book.

"That's not the point. Tomorrow's test is going to be timed! I can't work fast and do well. I just can't!"

"Then don't," Collin said. "Fast isn't always better."

On the screen, Phil's player exploded. "Man!" she groaned, tossing the controller to Jack.

She spun around to better face them. "Collin's right, Peter. Decide which means more to you, answering more questions but getting fewer right, or getting through fewer problems but getting far more right."

"How do I know which'll get me the better grade?"

"I asked which means more to *you*," Phil said. "If you have to choose between one and the other, and neither is going to win that grade, then what does it matter to anyone but you?"

They all sat in silence, feeling a little stunned. Collin was usually the insightful one.

"We hanging at the park this weekend?" Phil asked, breaking the spell. "Supposed to be the same nasty weather we've been having, but I'm game if everyone else is."

"No," Jack said. "Too bad, too. I was looking forward to getting out of the house."

"Done," Peter announced, throwing his pencil across the room so that it clacked against the far wall. Jack wasn't sure if that meant he'd finished the sheet or was giving up.

"You said Grace and Kelly aren't still crowding you?" Peter asked as he packed his schoolwork away.

"No, they're keeping their distance," Jack said.

"How do you think they are getting along with each other?" Phil wanted to know. "They seem to be doing better to me."

"They are," Jack agreed. "Earlier, I walked by Grace's room and heard the two of them cracking up over something."

"And what about that other thing?" Phil asked.

Jack was confused. "What other thing?"

Phil rolled her eyes in disgust as she retrieved the game controller.

Peter laughed, "Phil doesn't think we know about you being all bent out of shape over Kelly hitting on you."

"Well I didn't know," Collin said putting down his book. "I mean, aside from that one time that Jack told us about when we were at the park. What was going on?"

"When Kelly was freaking out," Jack explained, "she was kind of flirting with me. Not seriously or anything, just...I can't explain it. She was being goofy. Or maybe I am. In the end, I think she was nervous and scared and wanted to keep close to me."

"That's plain creepy," Collin said.

Jack nodded in agreement. "I don't think she was hitting on me. She was just being a little *too* friendly."

"Still creepy," Phil said as her avatar picked up its pace.

Jack shrugged. Kelly's extra attention made him uncomfortable but, at the time, it made him feel special, too. Now that he knew her fascination with him was a ploy to keep him close to her, he felt foolish for reading too much into it.

That betrayal — manipulation — whatever he called it, left him confused over how he felt about Kelly now. Every once in a while she'd still tease him, but she'd always done that and, now knowing for sure she was playing, it didn't bother him. Being used hurt and was much harder to forgive than her keeping secrets and invading his space.

"That's all in the past," he said, trying to convince himself as much as his friends. "All we have to do now is keep our eyes and ears open until this blows over."

The next few days proved Kelly was in a much brighter place. Jack grew accustomed to Kelly hanging around more and he was even getting along better with Grace.

A week later, however, as Jack walked with Phil, Kelly, and Grace to school, Kelly asked him, "Have you seen this?"

"Seen what?" Jack asked.

Kelly handed Jack her phone. It was open to a news website and the headline read, "Massive Weapons Bust In Chicago."

"Yeah," Jack said. "I read about it last night. Why?"

"What if it's Batesh, building an arsenal?"

"The article says the weapons belonged to the Mexican cartels. There's nothing linking it to the Middle-East."

"You don't know how these people work," Kelly grumped, taking her phone back from him.

"Maybe not, but I still don't think there's anything in it to worry about."

Jack slowed his pace and fell back to walk beside Phil. "You catch that?"

"Yeah. It's not the first time she's made something out of nothing."

"What do you mean?"

"Remember over the weekend there was a story about protests in Texas over the building of a mosque near a school?"

"Yeah?"

"Kelly told me it was Batesh, setting up a base for his campaign of terrorism here in the US."

"That's ridiculous," Jack said.

"You know that and I know that, but Kelly's convinced it's true."

The truth was as clear to the both of them as was the fact Kelly's initial sense of security had worn off and she was becoming paranoid. As he walked, his thoughts turned to the Thanksgiving holiday that was fast approaching. His hopes for having an enjoyable break were now ruined.

That weekend, he took advantage of Grace and Kelly secluding themselves upstairs to study for exams. Calling his friends together, he needed to discuss this negative turn Kelly had taken because, he noticed, it wasn't just bringing him down. His friends' moods were becoming splattered with Kelly's gloom as well.

Pairing his phone to the game room's speaker system and firing up one of his playlists to drown out their voices he dove straight in.

"Kelly's losing it," he said bluntly.

"No kidding!" agreed Phil. "She's driving me nuts."

"Short trip," Peter joked.

Phil jabbed her elbow into Peter's arm.

Collin tried to look on the bright side. "At least she and Grace are still talking to each other. And to us. That's more than they were doing. Things could be worse."

Peter rubbed his arm and, ignoring Collin's observations, asked, "So, what do we do now? Give up?"

"No," Jack said. "We keep at it. Sooner or later, she'll figure out how unrealistic she's being. Until then, we need to convince her that we are on top of things."

His friends nodded in agreement.

Jack wanted to move on. If they kept complaining about Kelly, he knew he wouldn't be able to stop himself from joining in. He had to keep himself, and them, focused on things to do. He was their leader and that meant his job was to take them somewhere productive, not to let them go on whining.

"So. What have we learned?" he asked them all.

"You already know I managed to get special permission to join the chess club," Collin said. "Played a few games with Blain. He's not a bad player. We're meeting at his place tomorrow night for a game. Unfortunately, he doesn't know anything and he says his dad never brings work home."

"Stick with it," Jack encouraged. "His dad wouldn't hide something as big as a joint federal-local investigation from his family."

"Right, Jack."

"Peter?"

"Everyone knows there's lots of newcomers. No one has specifics, though. Middle Eastern? Mexican? Asian? Martian? Nobody cares too much about it, and no one's paying that much attention. As far as they're concerned, it's all the same — just more strangers hanging around the mall. No big deal. Sorry, Jack."

"That's okay. It was worth a try."

Peter puffed up with a cocky sway. "Yeah it was! Jenny hasn't told me to get lost. At least not yet."

Phil grinned at him. "Told ya!"

"She almost did though," Peter went on, growing serious again. "When I asked about her brothers. She doesn't get along with them at all and, most of the time, pretends they don't exist. They're up to something dirty, I just haven't been able to find out what. Jenny doesn't know and goes well out of her way not to know."

Jack was disappointed, but did his best not to show it. "You've done great. Keep doing what you're doing. Something may come up."

"Sure thing, Jack."

"All right, Phil. You're up. And I hope you can shed some light on why Kelly is more frightened now than she was before we got involved."

"I can, Jack. Kelly's still keeping secrets."

"You mean there's more?" Peter exclaimed. "Because things weren't bad enough?"

"That's not what I meant," Phil said hastily. "I mean, she has access to information we don't."

The squeak of the floorboards overhead silenced them. Once the footsteps passed out of the kitchen Jack said impatiently, "Come on, Phil. Spill it."

"Not surprisingly, the Middle-Eastern refugees have formed a very close-knit group. They are cautious, scared, and don't trust anyone outside their own community. They especially don't trust governments, police — officials of any kind."

"That makes sense," interrupted Collin. "But what does that have to do with Kelly being more scared than ever?"

Phil explained. "They talk to each other using direct messaging on social media apps. Just before Kelly started her recent nutso stuff, she got a direct message. From what little I could see before Kelly caught me looking over her shoulder, it spooked her bad. She was as pale as a moonbeam. I thought she was going to pass out."

"So, you were looking over her shoulder," said Peter. "What were you able to read before she busted you?"

"Nothing."

Peter scowled. "Nothing? You mean you were staring right at her screen but couldn't make out a word?"

Phil's jaws flexed at the criticism. "I don't read Arabic," she said between clenched teeth.

Jack stretched his brain for some way to find out what Kelly had been reading. He could just ask her, but felt that would feed into her paranoia. Besides, he didn't know how she'd react to the news that Phil was reading her emails and messages over her shoulder.

He writhed, growling, "We need to see whatever it was!"

"I agree," Phil said soothingly, "but how?"

Collin walked over to the couch and, after pulling out his phone, sank into its cushions. Within seconds he asked Phil, "This the app?" while tilting his phone toward her.

"No. It had an image of an envelope in a lightning bolt."

"I know the one," Collin said, his fingers flying again. "I'll have to download it to my phone. Give me a sec."

Jack moved to sit next to Collin as he waited.

"All right," Collin said, "the app's loaded. Phil, do you know Kelly's username?"

"Kelly-twenty-oh-seven," Phill said. "I think that's her birth year."

Collin scoffed before asking, "What about password?"

"No clue. She's pretty good at hiding that."

"Is it long, or short?"

"Short, I think."

"Anyone know her birth month?"

"May," Jack said, "but I've no clue about the date."

"We'll try them all," Collin said. "Hope this app doesn't have a lock-out policy."

Collin's thumbs jigged over his phone's keyboard. It took longer than Jack expected and his earlier hope for success thinned.

"That's not it," Collin said.

Jack swore softly.

"Hey, Collin," Peter said. "Try capital J, lowercase n, fifteen, colon thirteen."

"What's that?" Phil asked.

"Remember when Kelly told us about her dad? About how he died for them. She quoted the Bible, the Gospel of John, verse fifteen, line thirteen."

Phil's eyes widened as her eyebrows lifted up her forehead.

Peter's face reddened. "What! My folks have been dragging me to Mass every Sunday since I was born. Something was bound to stick."

"Well I didn't think of it," Collin said, his face pale in the phone's glow, "and I've had to sit next to you for almost as long."

"It doesn't matter," Jack said. "Did it work?"

Collin hunched over his phone. "Yeah! I'm in!"

Jack's stomach heaved with conspiratorial triumph.

"Now, let's see," Collin went on. "Direct Messages…"

A list of usernames appeared on the screen.

"About two weeks ago," he mumbled as he started scrolling down. "Gotta be this one!"

He double tapped the screen and a message written in beautiful Arabic letters filled the screen.

"Okay, you found it," Phil said, enthusiasm making her voice warble. "Now what?"

"Now I save off a copy to my phone. Then log Kelly off. And we're done."

"Done?" Jack demanded.

"For now, yeah."

"How do you plan on reading that message?" Peter asked.

"I know of a few translator programs. I'll just have to try them one at a time and hope for the best. Worse comes to worst, I'll download an Arabic keyboard and retype the message manually into a translator app."

"How long will that take?" Peter asked.

"Could be tomorrow. Could be next week. Won't know until I get started."

"Until then," Jack grumbled, "we're stuck with nothing."

"All we can do is cope, I guess," Phil said in surrender to the problem.

"Good job all of you," Jack told them as they bundled up to face the cold on their way home. "Collin will figure out this message issue then, well, we'll see."

CHAPTER 12

Once alone, Jack turned down his music and sat on the floor, notebook in his lap, and his algebra book open beside him. Just as he started to get the hang of the quadratic equation, his phone rumbled. Grace was texting him from her room.

"Pathetic," he sighed at her laziness as he read, *You alone?*

Yes, he replied.

Seconds later, she was descending the stairs. Her face was drawn, as if she hadn't had a good night's sleep in quite some time.

"Can we talk?" she said.

"Sure, just give me a sec."

Grace eased herself down onto the couch.

"You and Kelly have another falling out?" he asked after solving a grueling polynomial.

"No," Grace said.

Her brow furrowed in thought. Jack could tell she was looking for the right words to describe what was bothering her. He rolled off his seat to sit cross-legged on the floor, facing her. He picked up one of the many pillows scattered across the floor, bunched it up, and hugged it to his chest. Outside, sleet splattered the single row of windows near the ceiling of the basement. It sounded like the hiss of static from an AM radio station putting out a lousy signal.

"Jack," Grace said, "Kelly's becoming unglued."

"Yeah. I've noticed."

He gave that answer its due moment then said, "I haven't seen her much this weekend and Phil says she hasn't seen her either. We were wondering what was going on."

Grace pulled her legs up under her and wrapped a blanket around her shoulders like a shawl. "She says she wants to spend more time with her family. They are as scared as she is over how things are unfolding back home.

"Besides, whenever she or her brothers leave the house, Kelly says her mom gets weird and accuses them of not taking Batesh seriously, of disrespecting the sacrifice their father made, and demands to know why they feel they need to go out at all. That sort of thing."

Jack hugged his pillow tighter. He had no personal experience with the kind of fear Kelly and her family must be feeling, but that didn't mean he couldn't sympathize with it. It had to sit somewhere between awful and hellish.

Still, he'd spent all of his spare time calculating how best to provide security coverage for Kelly without being too obvious or too intrusive. Part of him felt angry that all his scheming turned into a waste of time since Kelly wasn't around to benefit from it. Another side of him felt ashamed for being so self-centered and petty. That goulash of conflicting emotion made him irritable, not more charitable, magnifying his self-recriminations for being a heartless jerk.

Monday morning began with disappointment. Jack was hoping the overnight sleet would be enough to shut down school for a snow day. It didn't happen and he found himself galumphing beside Grace to Kelly's house through a damp and slushy late autumn freeze.

Gray clouds blocked out the sun. On the roads, the goop was gray and gross. He tried to think of how to describe the sloshing sound of tires plodding through the muck. The best he could come up with was "depressing." He always liked the soft squeaky sound a new snowfall made beneath his boots. This snow squished.

Stamping in his boots as Grace went to ring Kelly's bell, he sulked on the sidewalk. His clammy-feeling feet couldn't be wet. His boots were sturdy and in good repair. Still, his feet felt like lumps of clay and his socks were bunching up under his toes. After taking three times as long as he thought she should have, Grace rejoined him. Kelly wasn't with her.

"Is she coming?" he asked grumpily.

"No," Grace said.

Jack's silence demanded to know why.

Grace shrugged. "She said she isn't feeling up to it. She's staying home."

Angry and disappointed, Jack turned to clomp the rest of the way to school when a blue van, more rust than paint, tore past splattering his coat and snow pants with filth.

Kelly's decision to play hooky; his balled-up socks; the rotten mix of rain and sleet that started falling anew; now this. They all combined to force his attitude into a nosedive. By the time he arrived at school he was in a monstrous mood.

Spotting Phil in a secluded corner beside a stairwell pulling her boots off and replacing them with cross-trainers, he made his way over to her. Hurling his backpack into the crease where the wall met the floor he began tugging at his own boots. A frustration fueled yank sent the boot he was wrestling with flying off his foot. Frozen by fury, he watched as the boot skidded out into the hallway, his sock still inside. Jack swore loudly.

"Language!" Phil said, looking around for any teacher who might have overheard his foul exclamation.

He said something equally nasty about his language before stomping away with uneven steps, one foot booted, the other bare. The ice-cold floor-tiles stung his toes as he walked over them. Retrieving his boot, he returned to Phil and hurled the offending footwear at the wall to join his backpack.

"You're cheery this morning," Phil said.

"Kelly decided to stay home," he said as he began to struggle with his other boot.

"So?" asked Phil.

Jack stopped sparring with his boot and glared at her. "So what?"

The corners of Phil's mouth twitched. "Exactly!"

Jack glowered at her, which made her grin widen.

"So Kelly's with her family. Big deal!" she said. "She's safe. Batesh is still locked up. If she decides to skip school, that's on her. What does it matter?"

It mattered to Jack. When he promised to keep Kelly safe, he made it a personal vow. He had sworn to protect her, and if anything happened to her, it would be his fault.

Jack blinked, staring at Phil, his own thoughts making him realize he was angry at Kelly for not letting him play hero.

He felt silly. So silly, he had to laugh at himself. "You're right. So what? Let's get to class."

The skies stayed dreary for the remainder of the week. On Thursday, the weather took a turn for the worse, blanketing everything with so much snow that Sensei canceled class that evening. As soon as he got the word, Jack grabbed his cell-phone and began calling his friends.

"Hey Collin," Jack greeted him over the phone. "Guess you heard class is canceled tonight?"

"Yeah," Collin's voice said through the phone. "I was looking forward to going, too."

"So was I. Look. I'm calling everyone. Why don't you come over here and hang out?"

"Sure. Be there in a bit."

When Collin barged into Jack's basement Peter, his voice full of hope, was asking, "Is it still coming down? Do you think we'll have school tomorrow?"

"Probably," Collin said, pulling off his coat. "This storm isn't supposed to last and the snow-plows are all set to run once it starts to lighten up."

Peter's shoulders dropped.

"What difference does a little snow make? Apparently, if you don't feel like going to school you can just not go," snarled Jack.

"Don't pay any attention to him," Phil said. "He's crabby because Kelly asked for our protection then hasn't been around for us to protect."

"Well, she hasn't," Jack snapped.

"Quit being such a control freak, Jack," Phil shot back. "The goal is to keep her safe. Is she safe, Jack? Is she?"

Jack's jaw tightened. "Yes," he admitted.

"Then let's move on. I assume you had something on your mind when you asked us over?"

"I did," Jack said.

Arguing with Phil was a risky move when she was right. Jack knew her well enough to know that she never went looking for a fight. He also knew she never backed down from one, either, and was grateful she gave him an opportunity to retreat.

"Who has anything new to report?" Jack asked.

Peter was the first to offer information. "All I've got are new twists on old news."

"What does that even mean?" asked Phil.

"Well, like before, everyone agrees there has been an increase in the number of strangers in town. No one seems to care all that much."

"What's the new bit?" asked Collin.

"Nothing, when you listen to the stories individually. But taken together, some interesting patterns crop up. For example, that gas station on Venture Avenue? Loads of kids are saying the new-comers hang out in the parking lot the later it gets, even though it's freaking cold. They've set up a couple of burn-barrels. So far, the cops haven't shut them down. The mall comes up a lot, too. Especially that end by the food court."

"Is that it?" Jack asked.

"Pretty much. Crowds have been seen every morning in that empty lot a block away from school. Supposedly, those people are looking for work. More headscarves and a few face coverings are being seen. A van has come up a few times. There's even been a fight or two between the new kids and those of us who've lived here forever. Nothing's ever come of it, though. Just stupid being stupid."

"What's the deal with the van?" Jack asked, his interest piqued as he remembered the van that sloshed slop out of the gutter and onto him.

"Not much to tell. It's just some blue van. Rumor is there's a new carpet cleaning business in town."

"What's going on with Jenny?" Phil asked.

"Her brothers are up to something. She let that slip. I can't ask her much directly. That's the fast track to an argument. But she did say they were being more scummy than usual."

"That's not what I meant," Phil said. Her eyes narrowed into mischievous slits.

Peter shot her a quizzical look.

Phil smiled. "I saw her last weekend at the CostLess. She and a brown-haired girl I don't know…"

Collin interrupted. "Her cousin Allison. She lives on a farm about two hours away."

"How is it you always know this stuff?" she asked.

Collin shrugged the question off.

"Well, it doesn't matter," said Phil shaking her head. "What does matter is that they were looking at different flavors of lip gloss and giggling…a lot."

"What does that have to do with anything?" Peter asked.

"If you don't know, I suspect you'll find out soon," said Phil wearing a devilish smile.

"Moving on!" Jack snapped. "Collin?"

"Something's up, but I don't know what. I went over to Blain's a few days ago to play chess. While I was there, I got the opportunity make a quick rummage in his dad's desk. I found a business card for Homeland Security, but otherwise, nothing. Blain is not lying. His dad does *not* bring work home."

"Keep at it," Jack encouraged. "That may change."

"It doesn't have to," Collin said, a hint of impatience in his voice.

"Sorry," Jack said, realizing he'd stepped in too quick. "Go on."

"Since he doesn't bring his work home, that means, if there is an increase in his workload for whatever reason, he has to stay late at the station to deal with it. According to Blain, his dad has been working loads of extra hours lately."

Jack waited long enough to be sure Collin was done. Satisfied, he said, "Interesting. See if Blain knows why his dad's been putting in the overtime, or if any federal agencies have taken over local investigations, or if his dad ever gets weird calls in the middle of the night from Washington."

Collin's lips pursed and his eyebrows sagged, giving Jack a sarcastic look.

"I know, it sounds stupid," Jack said, "but stuff like that happens often enough in the movies. We know it's nonsense, but Blain doesn't know you know that. He might enjoy the opportunity to set you straight about how things get done. It might get him talking and something useful could slip out. You never know, so it's worth a shot."

"Makes sense," Collin agreed. "I'll run with it and let you know."

"Great," said Jack. "How's translating that message coming?"

"Slower than I expected, but I got enough of it translated to tell you it isn't anything good."

"How so?"

"It's full of cryptic threats. Things like, 'We know who you are,' and, 'We know where you live.' That sort of stuff. Nothing specific and I can't tell if it's legit or just some troll thinking they are being funny."

"Kelly thinks it legit," Phil said. "At least now we know why she's been so jumpy lately."

"But there's still nothing we can do about it," Jack said.

"At least now we know," Peter said.

Jack's lips puckered and he grunted. It didn't matter to him why Kelly was so frazzled. What mattered was that he was helpless to do anything about it.

Eager to move on, he finger-combed his red bangs away from his eyes and said, "I can tell you Phil's got nothing. Kelly has been holed up in her house so there's no news there.

"As for me, details from Kelly's home town is pretty thin. I did manage to stumble across a soldier home on leave who was on the Internet doing a bunch of bragging on LiveFaces. He was talking so much smack it was embarrassing to watch. He hinted at some big secret surrounding that area. He even suggested he could be called back off leave because he was so vital to some counter-intelligence initiative. Ridiculous!"

Collin cringed. Out of all of them, Collin had the least use for social media, aside from keeping in touch with his friends.

"You know what those sites are like," Collin scolded. "The whole thing could have been a hoax to get followers. Bet the guy isn't even a soldier!"

"Probably. But something about what he was saying rang true. He even started trying to back track, like he said more than he should have. Not long after, he ended his broadcast. I tried to replay the post, but it's was taken down fast. Why would they do that if it was fake news?"

"Maybe they did it because it *was* fake news," Collin said.

"Maybe. I'm trying to find another source to confirm what he said."

"Jack," asked Peter, his voice leaden with concern, "if he was bragging about being part of some counter-intelligence op, doesn't that mean there's something that needs countering? Isn't that what we were afraid of?"

CHAPTER 13

Jack spent the next several days searching for anything he could find about the potential attack. He slept little and gave his schoolwork just enough attention to keep from making Fs on his assignments. Frustrated, he realized he would have been better off sleeping or pouring more effort into his studies. Nothing he found confirmed the soldier's boast. Still, enough speculation was flying around to keep him at it.

His eyes shot to the corner of his computer and checked the time. Three in the morning. In less than six hours he would be taking a biology exam, an exam he was in no way prepared for.

He knew he should get some sleep, but it wasn't going to happen. All the websites he was scouring led him to believe that tonight the prison near Kelly's home-city of Wahat Jamila would either remain secure or all prisoners were going to be liberated carte blanche.

At seven he was still manic, surfing for news. Kelly's town was too small for the major outlets to cover it in depth so he had to flash from page to page, creating an uncomfortable strobe effect on his screen. Each new webpage made him blink and each blink felt gritty. Rubbing his sore, yellow eyes offered no relief, making the red veins that spider-webbed across them fatter and darker.

The last tidbit of information he ran across indicated that NATO forces had begun to withdraw from the prison's region, but not fast enough, and aggressive steps to speed up the process were emerging. Violence was starting to erupt. That was three hours ago. Now, his mom was yelling at him from downstairs to, "Get a move on!" He couldn't put off leaving for school a second longer.

Jamming his unstudied biology into his backpack, he shoved earbuds into his head, switching from surfing on his laptop to surfing on his phone. He breezed past his scowling mother, ignoring the toast she was trying to press on him and forgetting to grab his lunch. The trudge to school was made on autopilot.

"Any word?" Peter asked after Jack walked straight into him.

Jack yanked his earbuds out. "None."

Collin pulled up alongside them. "Me neither."

"Do you think Kelly knows what's happening?" Peter asked.

Collin looked at Peter, amazement twisting his face. "Of course she knows."

Phil trotted up to join them and didn't waste time on causal greetings. "I just had a chat with Grace. Kelly is skipping school again."

"Nothing we can do about that," Jack said. "At least she is at home with her family around her. She'll be all right."

Phil scowled in concern. "I wouldn't be so sure about that. Grace said she saw go-bags stacked in the living room. It's only a matter of time until they bolt."

Jack swore. Light, easy to carry travel bags? Packed with essentials only? Stacked so that they could be grabbed on the run?

Phil had it nailed. With fear increasing in Kelly's family, they would soon vanish.

"Nothing we can do," he said again, voicing the frustration they were all sharing.

Dejected, they merged in with the crowd of students entering the building to escape the snowy cold. All too soon they had more immediate problems to deal with. With the exception of Collin, whose biology exam would be given later in the day and would be twice as hard, none of them were prepared for their test. Rather than replacing concern for Kelly, Jack's impending academic doom added to it, making his already stormy mood darker.

"Did you double check your answers, Jack?" his teacher asked as he lay his exam face down on her desk.

Jack lied, saying he had.

She picked up his packet forcing him to stand there as she looked it over. She studied the first page, scanned the second, and scarcely glanced at the third and fourth.

She fixed eyes as bleary as his own onto him. "And you're sure you don't want to use the remaining class time to review your work?"

Jack didn't lie this time. "Honestly, Mrs. Ray, I don't think I can do any better."

As his teacher glared at him, he was fully aware that twenty-five sets of eyes drilled into the back of his skull. It made him itch. Pressing his luck, he asked Mrs. Ray if he could listen to music on his phone for the remainder of the period.

"Keep the volume low," Mrs. Ray said in a tired sigh as she slid his paper back on top of the one other test handed in thus far.

Not a good sign, Jack thought.

He walked back to his desk feeling very ashamed over what he knew was going to be an abysmal score. Taking his seat, he muttered angrily, "I don't have time for feeling sorry for myself," and returned to his manic scanning for news out of the Middle East.

"Thousands of out of work Greeks have crowded the streets in demonstration against…"

No.

"British members of parliament are demanding the Prime Minister give explanations for…"

No.

"Police in Paris have begun a city-wide manhunt for a man who is believed to be the most prolific assassin for hire in the world. Reports suggest this man and an accomplice, rumored to be a boy as young as fourteen years of age. Both escaped as police were closing in on their location. Anyone having any information is being asked to…"

Interesting! But no.

"American lawmakers are calling for a full investigation into…"

No.

"Are you tired of your ordinary mattress? Then you should try our…"

No.

"We have just received an update from our Afghanistan correspondent. Hours ago, American advisors were airlifted out of the town of Wahat Jamila. At this time coalition forces, supported by United States artillery units, are pulling back in a strategic withdrawal. Hundreds of residents are fleeing with the retreating forces leaving homes, shops, and government offices deserted. The prison on the outskirts of the city, a main object of contention between the Taliban and NATO, has become a focal point for hostilities. Even with the U. S. and NATO objecting to the indiscriminate release of prisoners, it is expected the Taliban will have full control of the prison before nightfall."

"No!" Jack shouted aloud.

"Mr. Straw!" Mrs. Ray snapped. "People are still taking their exam!"

"Sorry," Jack said. "I just thought of what I should have put for number 17."

The room buzzed for a moment before his classmates returned to their work. Phil and Peter kept their attention on him. Swallowing hard against the queasiness in his gut, Jack gave them the 'thumbs down' hand signal.

As soon as the bell rang Peter and Phil crowded around Jack's desk demanding details. He insisted they wait until Collin joined them so he wouldn't have to go over it twice. The truth was, he needed time for his own mind to absorb what he'd heard.

They packed up their things and moved out into the hallway where Collin caught up with them. Jack thought about spinning the bad news to make it sound less explosive. He opted against that, and told them what he'd heard, as he'd heard it.

As he feared, the news spooled them up with anxious tension. Even Collin, who was always cool as the weather outside, started to shift on the balls of his feet and comb his fingers through his hair.

"Calm down!" Jack said too forcibly.

Several students standing nearby careened their necks at the sound. Jack scowled and slunk away.

His friends followed, staring at him in wide-eyed desperation. They wanted — needed — to take action. Anything would be better than watching their mission, as they had come to call it, go sideways. They felt helpless and overwhelmed.

Their expectant expressions dug into Jack like daggers. His friends stood looking to him for a plan and he had none to give them. His jaws clenched and his breath grew thin.

"Listen," he hissed, speaking little louder than a whisper. "Yes, Kelly's home town was taken over. And yes, the prison has fallen into Taliban hands. But that doesn't mean anything to us.

"We're talking about someplace way over on the far side of the world, remember? Even if this Batesh guy was still alive to be freed, he has to get here. That's close to impossible these days. For all we know he might not even have been in that prison anymore. They move those guys around, random and often."

"Kelly and her family would know," Collin said.

"Not necessarily," Jack argued. "A lot of what happens over there takes place in the dead of night and in secret. The truth is, when it comes to Batesh, where he is and what he's doing, we don't know anything."

"So, what do you think we should do?" asked Phil.

"Nothing. Because there's nothing we can do," Jack said.

His friends stared at him blinking and waiting for more. Doing nothing, he realized, was the wrong plan.

He started over. "What I mean is, we don't do anything differently. Remember, our main objective was, and still is, to keep Kelly safe, not to worry about what's happening on the far side of the globe.

"We keep our eyes and ears open. We keep tabs on Kelly as best we can. Unless something happens that gives us a new issue to attack, we stay on our toes, keep quiet, and keep watch."

"That might be a bit tricky," Peter said.

"Why's that?" Jack snapped.

"Well, today is the last day of school before the Thanksgiving break. Collin's family and mine are going out of town. Our parents decided to take joint vacations this year instead of the traditional Thanksgiving dinner we usually do."

Collin confirmed Peter's words with a nod.

"I don't see how that causes much of a problem," Jack said in an attempt to keep everyone calm. "This thing in Kelly's home town? It just happened. It isn't like Batesh is going to pop up in the lunch-room in the next five minutes. It'll take months, at least, before he can get a plan like that rolling, if he can do it at all. I have doubts that he can."

The vice-like pressure crushing down on Jack's chest eased when he heard them grumble in semi-agreement.

"The best thing we can do right now," Jack went on less urgently, "is to get through today. We can meet over at my place after school and talk about this in more detail."

Above them the bell rang, letting them know they had five minutes to get to their next class. When the bell tolled again, they'd be marked tardy if they weren't sitting at their desks for their next class. Jack couldn't have cared less about being tardy, but it gave him an excuse to shut down their pointless fretting.

Collin and Peter headed down the hall toward their next classes. Phil and Jack were supposed to go have Math together. Phil started off in that direction but Jack didn't move.

"What's up?" she asked.

"I'm gonna bail on Math. Tell Mrs. Beasley I'm in the toilet and that, when I'm out, I'm headed for the nurse's office."

"Where are you really going?"

"To find Grace. She can get word to Kelly, just in case she hasn't heard, though I'm sure she has. Grace can also find out what Kelly and her family plan on doing. If Kelly isn't willing to work with us, we'll just have to do what we have to do in spite of her, for her own good. And we are going to use Grace as our mole."

"What a sweet little brother you are," Phil simpered as she crinkled her nose playfully.

"I know," Jack said through a laugh. "Ain't I a prince!"

The high school campus consisted of two buildings. One held classrooms while the other was dedicated for use as gymnasium, lunchroom, and auditorium. For generations the prevailing rumor was that the school was designed by an architect with a gambling habit.

Aeriel photographs showed that the two buildings looked like a pair of dice. One corner of the Gym Building was rotated so that it pointed toward the flat side of its mate. Throw in the not-so-coincidental placement of rooftop air-conditioning units, four on the first, set at each corner, and three on the second running diagonally, corner to corner, and the image was complete.

Inside, the school was segregated by grade. Jack and the other freshmen were located on the east half of the first-floor. Sophomores took up the west. In keeping with the outside theme of rotated dice, someone had the brilliant idea to rotate the second-floor by ninety degrees so that the juniors occupied the north half leaving the south to the seniors.

The upperclassmen were much envied. The school colors were royal blue and gold. The juniors' area was painted in tasteful shades of blue accented with gold and the seniors got the reverse; soft gold, accented with blue.

Freshmen had to suffer through their year surrounded by walls painted with primary colors. To Jack, it felt like kindergarten all over again. Those colors ensured he and his classmates were teased for being the babies of the school.

Sophomores had it worse still. Their color scheme consisted of bright, neon colors. Electric lime, pink, and blue screamed off the walls triggering migraines. Even those not prone to headache left school each afternoon massaging their temples and rubbing their overtaxed eyes.

As soon as he was free from the nauseating decor of the first-floor and entered senior-country, Jack's breathing became deeper and smoother. The more adult surroundings brought out a more mature and measured version of himself.

The situation with Batesh still weighed on him, but it didn't eat at him like it had while staring at walls that looked as though they had been colored in by sugar-crazed toddlers armed with crayons and highlighters.

His tranquility was short-lived. Two thick boys materialized in front of Jack. Both were wearing letterman jackets sporting football patches and awards.

They grimaced down at Jack. One grunted, "You're Straw, aren't you?"

His heart gave a massive thump, landing it in his throat. "I'm Jack, yeah."

More glares.

"Look," Jack said as he tried to move past them, "I've got someplace important to be."

"Hold it a minute," the other football player said moving to block his path. "We heard what you did for Ackerman's little brother. Pretty cool!"

Jack's jaw dropped. Harassment from the football team abated after he was released from the hospital, but he was too distracted with Kelly's problems to notice. "Er, thanks, but it was something anyone who was there would have done. It just happened to be me."

The two jostled each other. "Told you!" one said to the other. "Paul said the Straw kid was okay."

"Thanks," Jack said again not knowing what else to say, "but, like I said, I've someplace I have to be and…"

The two looked at him on the verge of laughing. "And?"

"…and I don't have a hall pass."

Unable to contain themselves, the two boys erupted in laughter.

"No problem, dude," one said, digging his meaty fist into his jacket pocket. "We've got a whole stack."

He pulled his hand out of his pocket holding a thick pad of the precious pink slips. Tearing one off, he handed it to Jack.

"Here ya go. But, don't fill it out, 'cause that's forgery and you'll get in loads of trouble. Just carry it folded so teachers can see the slip but not that it's blank."

"See you 'round, Straw," the other boy said before the pair sauntered off.

Jack watched them go whispering to himself, "The inmates are running the asylum."

Rousing himself, he returned to his search for Grace.

Seniors enjoyed schedules very different from lower grade levels. Underclassmen had courses one after the other. Every moment was mapped out from first bell to dismissal. Seniors had gaps in their schedules. They were expected to attend study hall or tutoring sessions in those open periods. Jack, along with everyone else at his school, was well aware that Study Hall was more a social event than an academic endeavor.

Jack made his way to that rambunctious room. Grace, he knew, spent every free period she had there. He suspected his sister's grades would benefit more if she signed up for tutoring. Their parents felt the same way, judging by how often they griped at her for wasting time in Study Hall.

The room's appeal was apparent to Jack the moment he opened the door. Popular music was playing out of a small boom-box. A few students were dancing. The rest either milled around drinking sodas or sat on the floor, on tables, or on counter tops. Chairs in this room seemed to serve more as foot stools than seats. Located in the farthest corner of the room sat a single teacher pretending to fulfill the duties of chaperone.

Despite the laid-back atmosphere, Jack was aware of how out of place he was. As soon as he entered, every eye turned on him, curious and suspicious. The expressions on the faces of the girls shifted into sweet condescension. To them he was a stumbling cute puppy. He might as well have been wearing a baby-blue bow attached to an oversized collar.

Their voices cooed, "Aww," making Jack turn pink.

The boys' faces slipped in the opposite direction. He was being scowled at and sized up by the older, bigger dogs protective of their territory and feeling the need to assert their dominance. Jack wanted to find Grace, say what he came to say, and get out of there fast.

He waded into the crowd, surprised that no one confronted him about being there. The chaperone might be oblivious, his face hidden behind today's newspaper, but the students couldn't take their eyes off him. Even the dancers stopped their churning and stared.

A rough hand clamped down on his elbow. "What are you doing here?"

Jack spun around and jerked his arm free. His knees bent and his spine curled in preparation for a fight.

Grace made an audible gasp and took a quick hop back, putting distance between the two of them.

They were not close siblings, but the thought of getting into a physical fight with Grace never once entered Jack's mind. The last time he hit her he was three and she took his toy car, refusing to give it back. Seeing shock and fear in her startled, wide eyes, knowing he was the cause, made him feel like a cockroach.

"Sorry," he mumbled as he switched to a more relaxed posture. "I didn't know who grabbed me."

She ignored his apology but kept her distance. "What do you want?"

"I need to talk to you."

Her eyes darted around the room. They were the center of attention and Jack could tell that for once, Grace didn't like it.

"Now?" she hissed.

His face twisted with impatience.

"No," he answered back. "I came up here to tell you I wanted to talk to you next week. Of course now!"

Turning, she led the way to the door. "Out in the hall."

Once the door was shut tight behind them, she rounded on him. "I thought we had an agreement. You stay away from me at school and I keep away from you."

"I don't remember ever agreeing to anything like that," Jack fired back.

Grace was frustrated with him and Jack could see her eyes narrowing. Speaking through clenched teeth she said, "You can't just come up here and bug me."

"This is the one time it's ever happened!" Jack assumed that would make it obvious how serious what he had to say was.

"One too many," Grace said as she wagged her finger in his face.

"Will you shut up and listen," he said much louder than he intended.

A teacher burst into the hall from a nearby classroom. "What is going on out here?" she asked the hallway as a whole. Her gaze landed on the two of them. "Miss Straw! Explain yourself," she demanded.

"This is my brother, Mrs. Daws. A minor family crisis," Grace said hastily.

"Well, wrap it up quickly. And quietly!" As though it were an afterthought Mrs. Daws glared at Jack like a bit of trash blown into her yard. "And you get back to where you belong."

"So, what is it that's so important?" Grace asked after Mrs. Daws returned to her classroom, leaving her door ajar and scowling through the crack.

Jack related what he had heard on the radio. When done, he figured Grace would understand why he felt she had to talk to Kelly.

All he got from her was an unimpressed, "So?"

"So," he snapped in exasperation, "what is Kelly doing? Has she said anything about having any kind of a plan? How will her family take the news? So, everything!"

"Keep your voice down," Grace whispered harshly. She shot a quick look at Mrs. Daws's door.

"I don't have any idea what Kelly is doing," she went on once satisfied Mrs. Daws was not going to re-emerge and give them detentions, "aside from trashing her senior year. I don't think there's any way she'll have good enough grades to graduate."

How thick could his sister be? "I think she has a lot more to worry about than grades, Gracie."

"Well, that's none of your business, is it."

"You two made it my business when you asked for my help. It's a bit late for changing your mind now that we are involved and things are getting ugly. Besides, you are supposed to be Kelly's friend. Doesn't that make it your business, too?"

"I am her friend!"

Grace's voice was the one that had risen this time. Mrs. Daws shot out of her room like a rocket. "That is enough! Both of you get to where you are supposed to be. If the holiday break didn't start today, I'd put both of you in detention. Now move!"

"After school I'll talk to Kelly," Grace said in tones Jack alone could hear. "I'll tell you what I find out at home. Now beat it."

Jack glanced over at Mrs. Daws. She was standing in the hall, arms akimbo, and her face was flushed an angry crimson. He had no choice but to bite his tongue and retreat.

CHAPTER 14

True to her word, Grace talked to Kelly after school. Sticking to generalities, Grace told Jack that Kelly and her family already knew about the prison break. They were troubled by it, but had not made any decisions about what to do.

"Kelly did say that they would have to go into hiding at some point, but swears she doesn't have a clue when that will be," Grace ended her report.

Jack's mouth tightened into a grim line. Grace's news left him with nothing to look forward to except more waiting and more watching. It also meant the level of uncertainty increased tenfold. At any given moment, Kelly might just not be around anymore. He tried to prepare himself for that — for when she'd no longer be his mission — but he found he was having a hard time letting go.

Hissing his breath out between clenched teeth, he was thankful Peter and Collin were going out of town. It would give them a break from the unpredictable actions Kelly's family might take. Also, they would get a well-deserved vacation from the futility their constant, but fruitless, scavenging for information left them all feeling. He and Phil, having to make do with no school and just hanging out, were more than capable of holding the line while they were gone. In his mind he imagined both Phil and himself taking turns babysitting an uncooperative Kelly. He dreaded what lay ahead.

As it turned out, keeping tabs on Kelly was easier than he expected. She spent most of the holiday at his house. Thanksgiving was not something she and her family celebrated. For them Thanksgiving was nothing more than a week off from school or work.

According to Kelly, being at home turned unbearable. Her mom was impossible to live with. She was short tempered, nagging and, when the strain became too great, verbally lashed out without provocation.

Kelly added that her brothers were little better. They weren't as volatile as her mother but they had withdrawn into themselves. Their faces were always sour and they stayed locked in their room for hours on end. When they did talk to her, after she engaged them first, she was rewarded with one-word responses or grunts.

One day into the break, Kelly couldn't take anymore and retreated to the Straw's game room, filling it with tension and boredom. The next day had all the signs of being as dreadful as the first. Phil suggested they play a board game.

Initially, no one was interested in the game but agreed to play because anything was better than sitting around staring at each other. As play progressed the mood lightened. By the end of the game they were laughing and teasing each other as if none of them ever heard of a man named Qasim Batesh.

The hideous spell cast by worry was broken. The following day, they all went to the movies. Later in the week, they visited the bowling alley where Grace proved herself to be a pretty darned good bowler. She and Jack turned it into a sibling rivalry with Kelly and Phil taking neither side but needling both equally.

The day before Thanksgiving, a light snow began to fall. The accumulation was too thin for Kelly's suggestion of building a snowman but good enough for Phil's idea of a snowball fight. Combat began with Phil and Grace on one team and Kelly and Jack on the other. Those alliances soon fell apart and it turned into girls against boy. Jack got pummeled. Later, over hot chocolate, he wanted to pretend he was offended by the treachery, but couldn't stop grinning.

Thanksgiving Day arrived and his house was filled with the beautiful smells of the cooking feast. Places were set at the table for his family as well as for Kelly and Phil. When Jack's parents learned Phil's mother was going out of town with her current boyfriend, they insisted she come and eat dinner with them.

It was one of the best holidays Jack could remember. The house was filled with laughter, silliness, and love. He and Grace didn't fight. Arguing over the last dinner roll didn't count since neither of them actually wanted it, they just wanted to playfully pester one another.

After dinner, they tried to keep awake and play another board game, but full bellies had them feeling drowsy and sluggish. It wasn't a school night but everyone was in bed by ten. Even Jack slept well into the morning. When he did tumble out of bed, he picked up where he'd left off, enjoying the girls' company. He even sat through a Sunday afternoon 'chick-flick' during which Phil only needed to snap at him once to, "Grow up!"

"Hey, Jack!" Peter yelled from the far end of the school hallway Monday morning, the first day back at school. "How was your break?"

He came strolling up grinning from ear to ear. Collin was with him and, despite his trademark deadpan demeanor, Jack knew him well enough to spot his lighter stride. He took it as proof that both of his friends had a great time.

Before he could tell them that his Thanksgiving was fantastic as well, Kelly and Grace walked past on their way upstairs to senior country. Kelly tussled Jack's hair in passing. "Hi, cutie-pie."

Jack's face flushed red. "Uh…hi?"

To everyone's surprise Grace giggled at her brother's embarrassment and joined in the game. "Hello, boys," she cooed to Collin and Peter, giving them a seductive wink.

Both girls erupted in laughter and continued on their way, leaving Jack and his friends staring after them.

"What just happened?" Peter asked.

"Thanksgiving at Jack's must have gone well," Collin said.

"It did," said Phil, walking toward them. She had a definite bounce in her step, too, and was smiling from ear to ear. "Why? What's going on?"

The boys laughed.

"What? What'd I miss?"

"I'll tell you on the way to class," Jack said.

"Wow!" said Phil after she had heard the story. "Things certainly have changed for the three of you."

"The three of us?"

"Well, yeah. I mean Kelly looks to have a better outlook on life. She and Grace are back to being besties. And you and Grace are finally acting like you are related."

"What do you mean, 'acting like we are related'?" Jack asked trailing behind Phil into their classroom. "We are related. She's my sister."

Phil hoisted her backpack onto a desktop and began rummaging for a pencil. Jack noticed she had an amused smile on her face. He stood there waiting.

"Oh, for heaven's sake, Jack! You and Grace used to act like each-other didn't exist. If nothing else, this crisis, if it even deserves to be called that, has brought you two closer together."

Jack dropped his backpack onto the floor and slid into his desk. "I've no clue what you are talking about," he said as he began digging for his own supplies, letting his grin tell her he was aware of the change, too.

He and Grace would never be best friends, but maybe brothers and sisters didn't always have to be. He puzzled over the conundrum of a relationship that was emotionally deeper than friendship while at the same time functioned on a more superficial level.

Papers rattling in front of his nose pulled him out of his thoughts and back into the classroom. "Dude!" the boy in front of him said. "Quit daydreaming and pass these back."

Jack took one of the handouts and twisted in his chair to pass the stack along. Turning back around he glanced at Phil. Her eyes may have been scanning the handout, but she was smirking and shaking her head.

"You are such a goof," she whispered.

"Oh, yeah," he drawled.

With that, his deeper contemplations were forgotten. All that mattered was that everyone's attitude was better for having time off. The improvement in their general mood worked like a cool rainfall on parched crops. Peter and Collin were included in the fun Jack, Phil, Grace and Kelly enjoyed over the Thanksgiving break. Kelly seemed to be able to put her fears of Batesh, if not out of mind, at least into perspective.

Thanksgiving being over meant the Christmas Holidays were on their way. As far as Jack was concerned, another break from school couldn't arrive quick enough. The pace of his classes increased as teachers scrambled to cover all the material they needed to get through before mid-term, intent on starting the New Year back on schedule.

With two weeks left before the break, they were all at the mall on a Saturday afternoon. The boys and Phil had been in the basement cramming for their exams when Grace and Kelly invited them to go shopping. Anything being better than studying, they agreed in earnest. Collin, alone, was disappointed.

The stores were crowded with holiday shoppers. Cheery Christmas carols were being piped through every speaker in every store as customers jostled and elbowed their way around each other. Clothes on discount tables were piled in wadded heaps. They reminded Jack of his bedroom floor and he asked himself why he had agreed to this.

Worse still, Grace and Kelly were looking at dresses for the Junior/Senior Winter Formal. A similar dance, less formal and lower budget, for the freshmen and sophomores was planned for the day after. None of them knew if Phil intended to go, but she did want to look at dresses. Jack tried to remember if he had ever seen Phil in a dress and all he could come up with was a Halloween nurse's costume covered in fake blood, holding a plastic meat cleaver.

"This is more boring than studying," groaned Peter.

"Way more," said Collin.

"Why don't you go check out the suits?" Phil suggested as she held a slender red dress against herself. The gown was covered in sparkling glitter and reminded Jack of a craft project he'd made in kindergarten. His lip lifted in a sneer.

Peter stuck his tongue out and made barfing noises.

Collin yawned.

"Shoo," Phil shouted.

"The bookstore is two stores down. We could go there," Collin suggested.

"Or the arcade," Peter countered.

Both boys looked to Jack for the deciding vote. He felt guilty for pulling Collin away from studying, but not that guilty.

"Arcade!" he said without hesitation.

Collin moaned, but Jack knew his friend's disappointment was temporary. Collin liked video games just as much as the rest of them and he was wicked good at them. Once he started playing Jack knew he'd cheer up.

The boys picked their way through the press of shoppers, none of whom seemed to be paying too much attention to where they were going. More than once the three had to stop to keep from being walked into. Jack cringed when he heard Peter snap obscenities at someone to watch where they were going.

Outside the store, things were just as bad. The Muzak was louder which meant the crowd's noise was louder, too. Everyone was trying to talk over everyone else. In the end, the building rumbled with a unified gurgling of noise.

Jack darted to his left and led them through a door labeled "Employees Only." Rounding a corner in the empty corridors, he ran down an off-limits flight of stairs, his friends dashing along close behind. Bypassing the mob outside was well worth risking a stern talking to by mall security.

Cautiously, he pushed open the matching employees-only door on the first-floor. He didn't want to hit anyone on the other side of it or do anything else that would draw attention to himself and his friends. They slipped back into the throng of shoppers as if they had been a part of it all along.

The arcade, like everywhere else, was three times as crowded as usual. Kids of all ages had been dumped there so that their parents could get on with their present buying uninterrupted. Jack, Collin, and Peter separated, making their way to their favorite games where they joined the huddle of watchers and waited for an opening for them to take their turns.

As he waited, Jack noticed two mall security officers were stationed inside the arcade. All the rest of the year, one security guard kept an eye on the kids as part of his roaming duties. He cased the rest of the room. Whatever the mall directors' reasons for tightening security at the arcade, Jack decided there was nothing to fear. No immediate danger lurked behind the games. The terrorists he was so worried about weren't going to leap out from behind the plastic Christmas Trees that were strewn up and down the mall and start a killing spree. He laughed at the idea and turned his attention to the game being played in front of him.

The boy playing was small, about ten years old. His game finished fast. No sooner were the words, "Game Over," beginning to flash on the screen, an older and chunky boy budged his way in shouting, "My turn! My turn!" The smaller boy stumbled away from the machine, grabbing the frame to keep from falling to the ground.

"Hey!" Jack shouted. "Stop being a jerk!"

In an instant one of the mall-cops was beside the machine. "You boys settle down or I'll throw you outta here! Got that?"

The chubby boy grunted something unintelligible and jammed his tokens into the slots. As the guard began to walk away his radio, which was tethered to his right shoulder, squawked. Jack could not make out what was said but the expression on the man's face was clear enough. Somewhere, trouble had broken out. As if confirming his suspicions, the two guards both trotted out of the arcade.

He turned away from the game to find Collin standing next to him.

"I saw it," Collin said.

"Let's grab Peter and go make sure the girls are okay," Jack ordered.

He pushed himself up on his tiptoes and spotted Peter playing his usual game. "You go wait out front. See which way they go. Peter and I'll be there in a sec."

"The guards took off towards the store we left the girls in," Collin told them as soon as they sprang out of the arcade.

"Of course it was," Jack moaned. "Let's move!"

They tried to follow at a run but the crowd was too thick. Bobbing and weaving, they made their way back slower than Jack wanted.

As they neared the first-floor entrance to the store, Jack heard Phil shouting at him from above. Jack stopped dodging in and out of the crowd and looked up. Kelly looked to be in a daze while Grace was pale and terrified. His eyes locked onto Phil's. She cupped her hands around her mouth and shouted, "We'll meet you at the car!"

When Jack, Peter, and Collin reached the car it was already running, ready to race out of the parking lot. Jack didn't waste time asking questions. He, Peter, and Collin tumbled into the back seat. Grace rammed the car into reverse and started to back out of the space they were in. Kelly stared out the passenger side window nibbling on her thumbnail. Phil was crammed onto the same seat as Kelly, half her rump on the middle console.

The traffic in the parking lot was thick. Cars were traveling in whatever direction their drivers felt like going, ignoring all signs, arrows, and general rules of the road. It wasn't until they merged onto the highway and the traffic began to thin out as they put distance between themselves and the mall that Jack risked distracting Grace with questions.

"What happened back there?" he asked.

Kelly still seemed to be in shock. He could see her hands shaking. Grace was thin lipped and the red flush of anger replaced her bleached look of fear. Phil was the only one in the front who seemed at ease. "A couple of guys said something to Kelly. Whatever they said, it scared her to death," Phil said.

"What did they say?" Collin demanded to know.

Kelly swallowed hard. Her voice was a barely audible whisper. "They said, 'We know who you are. He's coming.'"

Peter blurted, "Batesh! Has to be."

Jack noticed how Kelly flinched at the sound of her tormentor's name.

"Unlikely," Collin said thoughtfully. "I can't see how he could have made it here in such a short amount of time."

"Maybe," Peter admitted, "but he could be using operatives who are already here."

"What happened next, Phil?" Jack asked to put an end to Peter's doomsaying.

Before Phil could respond, Grace broke in. "Phil happened."

"What the heck is that supposed to mean?" Peter asked.

Grace went on as if Peter hadn't interrupted. "Phil was in the fitting room. She must have heard me yelling at the men pestering Kelly because she ran at them like she was insane."

"Trust us," Collin said, "she is insane when she's mad."

Phil smirked but said nothing. Grace returned to her story.

"She came up behind one of the men and before anyone knew what was happening, she kicked his knees out from under him. As he fell down, the other man took a swing at her. Phil ducked under his fist and when she came back up, she punched the guy straight in the nose."

Cheers for Phil flowed out of the back seat.

"It didn't end there," Grace said, grinning from ear to ear as she was getting into the tale. "Phil starts screaming at them. I mean, like screaming yelling. And do you know what she's yelling?"

The boys begged her to tell.

"She was yelling stuff like, 'No, I won't go into the dressing room with you!'; 'No, I don't want to see your thingie!'; 'Get away from me, you perv!'; 'Where's my daddy?'

"By the time she was done the two men were surrounded by outraged parents. Everyone was so focused on them nobody saw us slip away. It was pure genius."

Phil spoke up at this point. "It was impulsive and stupid."

Jack could see Phil's face in the rearview mirror. Her eyes were narrow slits and her nostrils flared. He'd seen that look on her face several times before in the dojo. It was the one she made when she was disappointed with herself.

"What'd'a mean?" asked Peter. "It sounds to me like you were awesome! Man! I wish I could've been there to see it."

"We should have stuck around and waited for the cops to show up," Phil said.

Everyone in the car could tell she was furious with herself and kept quiet.

"We could have gotten all this out into the open. We could have pulled the real authorities into the game. But because I had to go all crazy-woman, we missed the opportunity."

Kelly laid her hand on Phil's knee. "I'm glad you didn't. I would have had no choice but to deny the men had said anything to me. You would have been in a lot of trouble."

"Why on earth would you lie like that?" Phil asked.

Jack watched as Phil's anger with herself was blown away by her frustration with Kelly, her family, and the absurdity of the situation they were in.

"Why won't you get the help you need?" she snapped.

Kelly's face flushed as she slumped lower into the car seat. "Mom said we can't. She has much more experience with this kind of thing than I do. I have to trust her."

Phil's body tensed. Jack knew that her mouth may have stopped, but this was far from the end of the matter as far as she was concerned. Her anger threatened like an impending storm. No one spoke the rest of the way to Kelly's house. Wordlessly, they got out to escort her to the door. After opening the front door, she turned to thank them.

"I appreciate all that you've done for me. Especially you, Phil. You were amazing today."

She flashed a weak smile at Phil before continuing. "I need to go in and explain to Mama what happened. I don't know how she's going to react."

Phil pushed Kelly aside and barged into the house. "Let's find out."

Phil

BriNLee

CHAPTER 15

A torrent of Arabic words erupted from inside the house. Kelly trotted in after Phil and answered in kind. Jack, followed by Collin and Peter, went in as well. Grace, left with no other choice, came in last and shut the door behind her.

Phil was ignoring the woman yelling at them and planted herself in an armchair. "Tell her,"she commanded Kelly.

"I will. But now, you have to go," Kelly pleaded.

Phil kept her eyes locked onto Kelly. "Tell her, or I will."

"Tell what?" Kelly's mother asked with some difficulty, speaking with a thick accent.

Kelly began speaking in Arabic. Though no one understood a word that was spoken, they knew Kelly was telling her mom what happened at the mall. Her mother's face paled and she crumpled into the seat next to Phil's.

"What I don't understand," Phil said after Kelly had finished, "is why you won't let anyone help you."

Kelly began to translate but her mother waved her into silence. She understood. "Kalila tells me what you do for her. You are very kind."

Kelly's mother stopped speaking. Her head was shaking from side to side as her face and mouth worked in silent agitation. Without warning she slammed her palms down on the arms of the chair. A stream of Arabic flowed out of her.

"Mom says her English isn't good enough to give you the answers you deserve," Kelly translated for them. When she was done speaking, she looked back at her mother who continued in her native tongue. Kelly interpreted.

"Not everything is as clean as it seems. My husband gave information to the Americans about Al Qaeda activities in our village. Because of that, we had to leave. However, my husband did not escape.

"Without him, without what he knew, we were of little use to the Americans after we arrived in this country."

"We know all this," Phil blurted out. Kelly translated that, too. Her mother smiled at Phil as she said something.

Kelly hesitated, then translated, "She said you are young and impatient...and a little rude."

Phil stiffened in her seat. She didn't like being called a child. She liked being told to be patient even less. Biting her tongue, she hunkered down into the chair, scowled, and waited. Kelly's mother was speaking again.

"There are many things you do not know. Things nobody knows."

Kelly's eyes widened as her mother began speaking, the words falling fast from her mouth. Rather than translating, she was asking her mother questions. They began to argue. When they were finished, Kelly looked crestfallen. Whatever her mother said sucked all hope out of her.

Her mother gestured toward Phil, indicating for Kelly to pass on what was said.

"Soon after your government was through with us, American operatives across the Middle East began to be discovered. Many were killed. Mom was brought back in and questioned. They thought she was responsible for leaking their names, seeking revenge for the husband who didn't escape."

They all stared at Kelly's mother in drop-jawed surprise. In a rush Kelly said, "Mom swears it isn't true. She swears on Father's soul."

Kelly reached out and held her mother's hand. She said something in Arabic then said the same thing to all of them in English. "I believe her."

Jack looked at Kelly's mother. He studied the face, prematurely wrinkled by a harsh life. Her eyes, though sunken and weary, were gentle and kind.

"I believe her, too," he said.

That was good enough for the rest of them and they all nodded.

"What do you plan on doing next?" Jack asked.

"Nothing," Kelly's mom said in her heavy accent. Switching back to Arabic she explained to Kelly.

"This situation is very delicate. Move too soon and we will draw unwanted attention to ourselves. We will either give the enemy time to adjust or your government time to come after us. If we move too late..." Kelly stopped translating. They already knew what that meant.

There was nothing left to discuss. Kelly's mom asked if Kelly could stay at Jack and Grace's for the rest of the weekend because she, along with Kelly's brothers, had much to prepare and wanted Kelly kept safe and out of the way. It was decided.

Grace went with Kelly to pack a few things. Kelly's mother gazed into the carpet, her mind thousands of miles away, lost in a foreign country. Jack, Phil, Collin, and Peter sat in silence, squirming in their seats, thinking the squeaking springs were as loud as thunderclaps, and waited for Grace and Kelly to come back.

Not soon enough for Jack, they were back at his house. Grace and Kelly disappeared into Grace's room. Jack and his friends likewise retreated to the basement where Jack shared his plan for moving forward. Jack thought it sounded a lot like what they were already doing.

The reminder of the weekend, he stayed close to his sister and Kelly, kept company by his friends as much as they were able. The girls seldom emerged from Grace's room. When Sunday night rolled in, Jack lay awake until three in the morning. Sneaking downstairs, he filled a quart sized Ziplock bag with a splash of milk, a tiny bit of vinegar to sour it, some water, a slice of bread to thicken the mixture, and that night's leftovers to add something recognizable to the mix. Luckily, it was a casserole that contained lots of mixed vegetables.

Returning to his room he squished the lot together until the slop reached the desired consistency. In the morning, he dressed for school as he always did. Passing the first-floor guest bathroom, he darted in and stashed the Ziplock beneath the sink. Taking up his normal spot at the kitchen table, he played with his cereal instead of eating it. Having stayed up so late, he didn't need to fake looking worn out.

"I have to use the bathroom," he said with just enough stress in his voice to perk his mother's ears.

Leaving the bathroom door ajar, he retrieved the hidden bag and positioned himself over the toilet. He groaned, made a loud retching sound, counted, "one-one-thousand, two-one-thousand, three-one-thousand," then made a second fake heave even louder than the first. Holding the Ziplock waist high, he dumped the contents into the toilet, producing a delightfully believable splash.

Needing to move fast, he zipped the bag shut and rammed it down the front of his trousers. Dropping to his knees in front of the toilet bowl, he waited for his mom, timing a miserable groan to coincide with her arrival.

He protested the first time she suggested he stay home.

She followed with, "I think it'd be a good idea, honey," and he pretended to cave.

Peter and Collin both wanted to skip school too, but Jack wouldn't allow it. Collin had perfect attendance, which was an important component to the advanced program he was enrolled in. Jack wasn't going to allow his friend to tarnish that record if he didn't have to.

As for Peter, he could ill afford to miss classes. Peter worked harder than the rest of them for grades that didn't reflect that effort. Jack refused to make Peter's life more difficult.

Grace had no choice but to go to school. Although Kelly took full responsibility for Grace's earlier failure to turn in an acceptable project, she was placed on a very strict form of probation. Absences, excused or not, would be academic suicide.

Kelly's year, on the other hand, was over. It didn't matter if she showed up at school or not, she wasn't going to graduate. Kelly left with

Grace as usual, but was intercepted by Phil at the end of the block. Phil snuck her in Jack's back door less than five minutes after his mom left for work. They spent the remainder of the day playing video games, pretending to study, and over all, being bored out of their skulls. As soon as Grace returned home, Kelly disappeared into her room.

"Wow!" Phil groaned as she rubbed her face with the palms of her hands.

"I know," Jack agreed, rotating his fingers deep into his temples. "I can't remember the last time I was so bored. Still, I can't blame Kelly for that."

Phils eyebrows rose. "So, what? You saying it's my fault?"

He looked at her through narrow eyes and with one corner of his mouth raising in a smirk said, "Well, yeah. I kinda am."

"Look here, Straw. It's your house. It's not my fault you don't know how to entertain your guests."

They both laughed. The odd thing was, Jack couldn't think of anything he and Phil would have done differently if it were only the two of them. All he knew was that they would have had loads more fun.

"Why don't you stick in a movie?" Phil suggested. "Something Kelly would hate."

Jack laughed and plugged in an action flick with lots of fights and things blowing up. Phil flopped onto the couch and Jack sank into his beanbag on the floor, their boredom headaches beginning to subside. Just as things started blowing up on screen, Peter and Collin came trooping in through the outside door.

"Anything exciting happen around here?" Peter asked, peeling off his snow gear.

"Not one blessed thing," Phil moaned, "and that's a fact."

Her voice sounded as flat and worn-out as Jack had ever heard it.

Just before lunch, he noticed that her eyes were swollen and her shoulders sagged. She tried to put on a good act, but Jack knew her too well not to realize she was suffering from cabin fever.

Phil spent as little time at her own house as possible. She and her mother didn't get along and the string of boyfriends her mother kept bringing home, a new one showing up every couple of months, didn't help. As a result, Phil kept herself on the go. Today, being stuck in the same place all day with the same people, even if it was with her best friend, was tough on her.

"What went on at school?" Jack asked. He hoped hearing news from the outside world would cheer Phil up.

"The usual," Collin said. "Had to deal with dumb teachers and even dumber students."

They laughed. Despite his quip, Jack knew Collin held most of his teachers in high regard, especially his math and science teachers. Others, he shared with them, made him question how they managed to feed themselves.

A malicious grin spread over Peter's face. "Well, there was one unusual thing."

Phil's eyes popped. "Which was?"

Peter's grin broadened. "You and Jack weren't there."

Collin choked down a laugh.

"What? We're out sick. At least that was the story. Didn't everyone buy it?" Phil asked, her curiosity piqued.

"That's just it. They did buy it. Best friends, *supposedly*? Both come down sick at the same time?" Peter was now smiling so wide his teeth were showing.

Jack's face scrunched in confusion. "I don't get it. What do you mean, 'supposedly' best friends?"

Peter and Collin erupted in laughter.

Phil shook her head and chuckled. "Poor, clueless Jack."

She grimaced at Peter and jutted her hip to the side while crossing her arms. "Who do I get to kill for starting that lovely little rumor?"

"Rumor?" Jack asked.

"He's catching up," Collin giggled.

Peter said, "I heard it from Jenny. I was pretty mad at the time. I mean, even if you two were…"

Phil's eyes flashed and Peter rushed to add, "Not that I think you are…were…whatever! But, hey, it's none of my business.

"Anyway, Jenny thought I'd go looking for trouble so she wouldn't say who she heard it from."

"That's okay. I'll deal with it when we go back," Phil said.

"You mean people are saying Phil and I got each other sick by making out?" Jack blurted.

"And he's arrived at last," Phil said, patting him on the top of his head as if he were a dog who'd just learned how to sit on command.

"Let's finish the movie," she suggested light-heartedly.

"Can't," Collin said. "I've got to get home for dinner."

"Me, too," said Peter. "But after, I'll come back and let you know what you both missed in class. You know that hag, Mrs. Fishburn, had to go and give us an essay that's due before we break for Christmas."

"Figures," groaned Jack. "Bet she gives us another one that'll be due the day we get back, too."

As promised, they all met back in Jack's basement after supper to work on homework. By nine, pitch black enveloped the outside and they wrapped up what they were working on so they each could get home and ready for school in the morning. Phil, Peter, and Collin were pulling on their coats and hats when Jack's phone rang. Not recognizing the number he answered in a gruff tone, expecting it to be a telemarketer.

"Is it Jack? Grace's brother?"

The voice sounded stressed.

"Yes," Jack drawled cautiously. "Who is this?"

"I am Kalila's mother. She gave me your number. For emergencies. Is she there with you?"

"She's upstairs with Grace. Why? Is something wrong?"

Phil, Peter, and Collin froze. They huddled around Jack trying to catch some of the conversation. Jack switched on the phone's speaker.

Words began spilling out of the phone in a mad rush.

"I call Kalila earlier. No answer. I call again. Same. No answer.

"It is time. We leave tonight. She was supposed to meet us. She knows where. But she hasn't come."

"I'll go up and check on her," Jack said.

With Kelly and Grace safe, planted upstairs in Grace's room, he had nothing to worry about. He was, however, angry that they hadn't come down and told him of this plan as soon as they found out about it.

"When did you last talk to her?" Jack asked.

"Two hours ago! She should have been here by now!"

Jack's face burst with surprise. "Two hours?"

This news shattered Jack's confidence in Kelly's safety. A few minutes delay he could understand. And, he knew, those few minutes would seem unbearable to a worried mother. But two hours? Something had to be wrong.

"Yes," Kelly's mother confirmed. "Two hours! Since, I've been calling and calling. I call your sister, too. No answer."

"My sons are already gone. They went ahead to make sure we would be safe when we arrive. We had no reason to suspect the danger would be here. Not so soon!"

"It'll be all right," Jack said, not at all believing that. "I'll find her and bring her to you."

"Oh, yes. Please. Please find her."

As soon as Jack hung up he was bombarded with questions.

"You heard everything I did," he snapped. "Stay here and I'll go upstairs and see what I can find out."

He wanted to run up the stairs but forced himself to remain calm. Passing through the living room he saw his parents on the couch watching TV. His dad had his feet up on the coffee table, a pillow under his heels, as his mom dozed under an afghan with her head resting on his thigh.

That simple expression of the love that existed between them was a scene he had grown up seeing every night, but for some reason, tonight it struck him how happy his parents were together. As he climbed the stairs to the second-floor he was filled with a deep appreciation for just how good his life was. That sense of warmth and peace wrestled against his fear for Kelly…and for Grace.

Jack knocked on his sister's bedroom door. No response. Fear won.

Cautiously, he cracked the door. "Grace? Are you and Kelly in here?"

No answer.

He pushed the door wide and went in. The room was small and dark and empty.

He dashed back down the stairs. "Dad? Do you know where Grace and Kelly went?"

"Yeah. Kelly's family is out of town dealing with some kind of family emergency. She's staying here for the next couple of nights. They went back to Kelly's to get a few things she'll need. Why?"

Jack was no longer there. He was hurtling back to the basement.

"Why would they do something so stupid?" Collin asked after Jack had filled them in.

"I don't know," Jack hissed.

He paced back and forth, pulling at the hair on the top of his head. Concentration was impossible. Worry for Grace drove him out of his mind, leaving him unable to come up with any kind of plan. He felt sick.

Phil, Peter, and Collin were huddled in the room waiting for him to give orders, but he had none to give. Their silence made things worse.

As he paced, he started drowning in resentment. All his life, he dreamed of this kind of adventure, but this was too soon! He wasn't ready. He didn't want to be in charge. Not for this. But what other choice did he have?

Sucking in a noisy breath, he pulled out his phone and dialed Grace.

No answer.

He tried again.

Nothing.

He tried Kelly.

It went straight to voice mail.

He stared at his phone, his thumbs hovering over 9-1-1. Closing his eyes, he swallowed hard and made the call.

"911. What's your emergency?"

"My sister and her best friend are missing. I think they've been kidnapped by terrorists."

"Say that again, please."

"My sister's friend was targeted by terrorists. Now she and my sister are both are missing!"

"Is this some kind of joke? We have your number recorded. Making fraudulent emergency calls is a crime."

"I'm not making this up!"

"Listen carefully, kid. I am reporting your number to the police. They will find you and when they do, you are going to be in serious trouble."

Jack hung up. Dejected, he stuffed his phone into his pocket. "We have to go looking for them on our own."

That was all the push they needed. They broke apart and finished tugging on winter jackets and snow boots. Exiting the basement door, which led straight outside, they disappeared into the darkness.

"So, how do we do this?" asked Peter, his words forming a hazy mist in front of his lips.

"We'll start at Kelly's. If they aren't there, I have no idea where else to look," Jack said.

He led them to Kelly's by the route he knew she and his sister would take. As he walked he struggled to come up with a plan should they not be there. All he could think to do was to wait it out and see if they showed up.

As far as plans go, Jack knew that one sucked. The alternative, however, was to wander the streets with no plan other than the lame hope their paths would cross.

The slow departure of the sun made the temperature plummet. Snow was starting to fall again. The wind was brutal. Night was coming on. That plan sucked even worse.

CHAPTER 16

As they walked, Jack's heart felt as if it were being ground into the sludge beneath his boots. He fumed, thinking the girls went shopping or something equally stupid. Desperately trying to convince himself that he would find his sister safe at Kelly's house or back home, he imagined roaring and screaming at them for being so reckless. After, he would deliver Kelly to her mother and get her, Batesh, and this whole nightmare out of his life.

Deep in the pit of his stomach he knew that wasn't going to be how this was going to end. Everything he'd learned from studying spy-lore told him things were starting to go sideways and were only going to get worse from here on out. One thing he prided himself on was his ability to imagine possible scenarios that could stream out of single events — the ability to see the big picture. In this case, he couldn't envision an outcome that turned out well for any of them.

His gloomy premonitions made him cautious.

Instead of marching straight up and banging on Kelly's door, Jack motioned his friends to stop half a block away. In hushed whispers, he directed them to hide in the shadows. They settled in behind a pickup truck, cold and damp, as the night's temperature plummeted to below freezing.

The exposed parts of his face began to sting as the sloppy drizzle that had been falling started to freeze on him. His friends huddled close around him, shivering but not once complaining.

Their faces were hard and determined. Whatever was about to happen, he knew they would see it through with him, wherever it led. Jack didn't know if that was a good thing or not.

He was torn between feeling responsible for their safety and fear for his sister. The urge to ditch them for their own good and to go on alone was growing inside him like a weed. If he did, he knew he wouldn't be able to achieve anything beyond getting himself killed.

Batesh and his men would do their worst then disappear. They'd murder the rest of Kelly's family then go on to cause even greater mayhem on a much larger scale.

Batesh had to be stopped. Jack knew he couldn't do it alone, but felt he had no one to turn to. No outside help was coming. His 9-1-1 call proved that. His parents wouldn't believe him either. By the time he convinced them, if ever he could, it would be too late. He needed his friends' help, but a dismal voice in his head kept nagging, *You are going to get them all killed.*

He swore under his breath.

"What's wrong?" Phil whispered.

She was crouched down next to him.

"I don't like where this is headed," he said. He shuddered more out of fright than cold.

"I don't either," she agreed, "but we've hit the point of no return."

The point of no return. It was a phrase they came up with years ago, and he was well aware of what it meant. They'd hit that critical point where the ultimate decision had to be made. Bad stuff was starting to happen. Currents of destruction were in motion. At this point, every single time, in every single movie, book, and biography, the heroes faced two choices. They could either turn back, saving themselves, and allow whatever was going to happen, happen, or they could try to stop it, accepting the very real likelihood that they and the people they cared about would die in the attempt.

Many nights, after binging action movies, they laid awake and talked about it, wondering if that's how things went in real life. Living it for himself, he knew the point of no return was real and he'd reached it.

Am I willing to die trying to stop Batesh? he asked himself.

He wasn't sure.

A second thought smashed into him like being hit with a baseball bat. *Am I willing to die trying to save Grace?*

There was no hesitation. *YES!*

With that thought, the point of no return passed. He'd made his mind up as to which way he was going, and there'd be no turning back. Things were going to turn out terrible for them all, but things were going to turn out terrible no matter what he did. Of that, he was certain. The difference was in being able to say he at least tried.

The fact was, Grace was missing. As far-fetched as it sounded, he knew she and Kelly were kidnapped by the terrorists. He had no evidence for that. He wanted to be wrong, but every inch of him trembled with conviction. He knew he was right and he knew he had to try and save them.

Ramming his self-doubt down his gullet, he turned his attention to Kelly's house. It was a single-story home built on a small plot of land. To the left of the house was a vacant corner lot. The cross street just beyond the lot was typically busy with passing cars but, due to the late hour and crap weather, it was deserted. On the other side, as well as to the rear, the house was penned in by strip malls. All the shops were closed and black. At Kelly's, all the lights were on.

Jack thought that the house's isolation would be good for them in that they could poke around outside without having to worry about being seen. The down side was that the lack of neighbors meant that all hell could break loose and no one would ever know. A rust-bucket car, never before seen by Jack, parked at the curb, was the worst aspect of his reconnaissance.

"What do you guys see?" he asked the others, hoping they picked up on something he missed.

"Nothing," Collin said. "But it looks like somebody's in there."

Jack rolled so that his back rested against a tire. They were miserable. Hands and feet were growing numb with cold. Their noses were becoming runny. Involuntary sniffling broke the silence. Every so often,

Jack heard someone's jacket rattle as its owner gave a violent shiver. They couldn't sit forever doing nothing.

"Jack," Peter began.

Jack cut him off. "Shut up. Just…shut up. Nobody say anything. Give me a chance to think."

He leaned down and looked at the house from beneath the truck. He focused on the light glowing out the window at the side of the house facing the stores. Sitting upright, he berated himself. "Come on! Come on! Think!"

He leaned over again to stare at the house. Nothing had changed.

Sitting back up he said, "I need to know what's going on inside the house!"

"I'm going with you," Phil said in tones that forbade argument.

"Fine," Jack spat. He wanted to be moving, not talking. "You and I will sneak over to that side window.

"Peter? You and Collin keep an eye out. If anyone else shows up, you start yelling like crazy then get out of here. Once you start screaming they'll know where you are and will come for you. Go straight to the police. Make them believe you. Whatever it takes."

"What'll you two do?" Collin asked.

"What?" Jack hadn't thought about an exit plan for Phil and himself.

"If others show up?" Peter demanded. "What are you and Phil going to do?"

"Run like mad," Phil said.

"Yeah," Jack agreed. "We'll meet you at the police station."

Phil looked at him, skepticism burning in her eyes so hot it forced him to avert his own. He would never run away — not if Grace was in danger — and Phil knew it.

Collin startled them by springing up and hoisting his hips onto the edge of the truck. He stretched his arm inside the bed, rummaged with a racket that to Jack sounded like a battlefield, then dropped back down beside them. He was holding a roll of duct tape and began wiping the snow and ice away. Pulling a small piece off the roll, they cringed at the loud, sticky, ripping noise it made.

Satisfied that the weather hadn't ruined the tape, he said, "I've an idea I want to try, in case they leave."

"There's no time for trying stuff," Jack snarled. He was too terrified about what might be happening to his sister to be patient with any of them.

Collin looked crestfallen, but Jack didn't care. "Just keep watch like I told you. Come on, Phil."

Without waiting to see if she was ready or not, Jack tucked his feet underneath him and darted out from behind the truck. Running through the snowy yards, halfway between the houses and the street where the shadows were the deepest, he dashed hunched over towards Kelly's house.

Fearing that he ran too far without ducking for cover, he dove behind a low retaining wall circling a barren and ice-covered tree. Seconds later Phil plowed into the ice and snow beside him.

"We need to get across that street," Jack said, his words forming puffs of steam in the freezing night air.

"I know," she said.

Lifting herself as if she were doing a push-up, she scanned the area.

With slow, deliberate strength she lowered herself back down. "We'll have to make it all the way to the side of the house. There's no other cover between here and there."

"I saw that," Jack agreed. "Do you think it'd be better to go at the same time or one by one?"

Phil pushed up again. "I'm not sure," she whispered. "I don't think it makes much…What is he doing!"

Jack lifted himself up to see what set Phil off.

In the dim light from the streetlamp, he saw Peter, crawling on his hands and knees across the street, keeping the battered car between himself and the house.

Jack watched in bewildered horror as Peter scrabbled underneath the car. For a few seconds he fiddled with something then crawled out. On his hands and knees, he scrambled back to their side of the intersection. Once in the shadows, on the opposite side of the street from where he and Phil were watching, Peter's silhouette popped to its feet and tore back to where they left him and Collin to keep lookout.

Jack and Phil dropped back to the ground.

"What was that all about?" Jack asked.

Phil shrugged. "Guess they decided to try Collin's idea."

Jack sighed. "Foolish!"

"Probably," Phil agreed. "But at this point, I think foolish is all we have to work with."

Jack ground his teeth knowing Phil was right. If they are going to survive this, they'd have to rely on foolhardy and desperate action. Jack shuddered, and it had nothing to do with the cold. Every choice from here on out would have life-or-death consequences. He shoved Peter's actions out of his mind. Whatever Peter and Collin were up to, it didn't matter anymore. Their caper was done and over. They'd gotten away with it. Jack had to focus on his next reckless move.

"We'll cross together," he decided. "That way neither one of us is left alone."

"Sounds good," said Phil. "On three?"

Jack counted down. They both sprang up and bolted across the street. They made no attempt to disguise their destination and pelted straight for the side of Kelly's house where the window shone its light into the darkness. The sound of their heavy snow boots galumphing through the muck on the roads echoed into the night. The thunderous racket terrified Jack.

Reaching the house, they dropped flat on the ground, making themselves as small as they could. The window they planned to look through was still lit. Beneath the window stood an air-conditioning compressor. In order to see inside, they would have to climb on top of it.

He motioned Phil to stay where she was. Lying flat on his belly he crawled to the other side of the compressor, making room for her. Fear made his senses hyper-acute. The snow and muck grinding underneath him crunched like a kitchen disposal. Even his breathing seemed to roar like a tornado.

By the time he took up his position on the far side of the compressor, his heart was pounding in his chest and despite the frigid nighttime air, he was drenched in nervous sweat.

Struggling to catch his breath he waved to Phil letting her know it was now her turn. She duck-walked to the compressor since she didn't need to pass under the window. Once in position, Jack could see her shoulders rising and falling as she panted. Stress was taking its toll on her just as it was him.

Jack started to climb onto the air-conditioning unit. He moved slow, struggling to keep silent. The thick coat and heavy boots he wore made stealth difficult. Inch by inch, he made his way up until, after what seemed an eternity, he was on all fours with his head just under the windowsill.

As if the sound of his neck moving would be loud enough to alert the terrorists to their presence, Jack lifted his head slowly, like a turtle eeking itself out of its shell. He kept rising up until his eyes broke the plane of the windowsill.

The brightness inside stung his eyes and he had to blink several times to clear his vision. Thanks to hours devoted to improving his memory, a moment was all he needed to sear the scene into his brain. He ducked his head back down much quicker than he had poked it up. Easing himself off the compressor, he squatted in the shadows next to Phil.

Closing his eyes, he mentally studied the picture he had captured in his mind. He could see it as if he were still looking through the window. Opening his eyes he leaned into Phil, too terrified to do more than whisper half sentences into her ear.

"Two men. That side of the window," he hissed, pointing to the side of the compressor he had just been on. "Grace and Kelly are tied to chairs between them. Grace has a gag in her mouth. Kelly doesn't.

"One guy in front of this window, his back to it. The last one over there," he pointed over Phil's shoulder, "by the front door.

"Didn't see any guns, but one of the men guarding Grace and Kelly has a long knife."

"Doesn't mean they don't have guns," Phil said. "Guns are loud and draw attention fast. Besides, knives ..."

She stopped talking. Jack knew what she was about to say. Guns meant death. Blades implied a painful death. These people were all about creating fear.

"Kelly's family?" Phil whispered, prodding Jack forward.

"No. They're waiting at some meeting place, remember? I think these guys are hanging around to see if they show up."

"So, what do we do now?" Phil asked as quiet as possible.

Jack slumped against the house. He had no plan. It felt as if his brain had crashed into a brick wall.

"You go get the others," he whispered.

Making his plan up at the same time he was explaining it, he continued, "Bring them back to the front of the house. Collect as many rocks and bricks as you can carry. I'll sneak around back. Once you are out front, start trashing the house. Break as many windows as you can. While you're doing that I'll run in and free the girls."

"Jack! There's no way that'll work! You won't have time to cut them loose, even with a distraction. You're going to get yourself killed."

"It's all I can come up with," he snarled louder than he intended. Pulling his head down, he looked around to make sure no one had heard and was coming around the corner of the house to attack them.

Phil pleaded with him in a hiss. "For the moment, Grace is okay. Let's go back and hook up with Collin and Peter. Together we will come up with something that isn't suicide."

"I'm not leaving Grace!"

"There's nothing we can do for her now. We need to work together."

Kelly screamed. Even muffled by the sealed windows it shattered the stillness of the night.

In a single swift movement, Jack leapt to his feet and pounced back on top of the compressor. All thoughts of stealth abandoned, he stood staring into the house.

One of the two men guarding the girls was struggling with Kelly, trying to stretch thick silver tape across her mouth. The guard who had been by the front door was drawn in closer to the center of the room where the struggle was taking place while the man by the window laughed. The final man was saying something to Kelly while sneering hideously.

With dramatic flourish, he pressed the evil looking knife he was holding against Grace's throat.

Jack launched himself off the compressor, diving head first through the window. He collided against the man standing just inside. Shards of glass sliced through his coat and into his back as he and the man slammed to the floor in a tangle of flailing arms and legs.

Taking the man by surprise gave Jack the advantage. He scrambled to his feet before the terrorist could recover and drove his heavy snow boot into the man's mouth. With a wet crunch, teeth broke free and mingled with the glass on the floor.

Turning in a quick circle, Jack saw that the closest enemy was the one who was trying to gag Kelly. Jack hunkered down and closed in. The man swung a wild haymaker aimed at his head. Bobbing beneath the fist, Jack bounced back up and slammed his knee between the man's legs as hard as he could. Groaning painfully, the man dropped to the floor like a lead ball.

Jack spun around and went after the man holding the knife on his sister. Before he could take a single step in her direction, violent hands clawed at his hair and he was jerked away. The goon who was guarding the front door now had ahold of him.

Phil exploded through what remained of the window. As she hurtled toward the floor she wrapped her arms around the waist of the man Jack had kicked in the teeth, who was staggering back to his feet, his hand clasping his ruined mouth. They fell to the ground tangled together. Phil snatched a broken shard of glass off the floor and began slicing savagely at his face.

Her arrival distracted the man holding Jack, giving him the opportunity to slam the heel of his boot down onto the top of the man's foot. The bones cracked loudly, but the terrorist managed to keep his fingers tangled in Jack's hair.

Jack clamped the man's hand against his scalp to keep it from being ripped off his head. Spinning under his captor's arm, he twisted it so hard the hand was forced to relax its grip. Jack shoved the man away, losing several locks of hair in the process.

Phil scrambled off of the man on the floor and darted into the gap between Jack and his assailant, landing a spinning back kick on the man's jaw.

The large bay window at the front of the house shattered inwards. A hail of glass along with an iron porch chair flew into the house. Behind that destruction came Peter and Collin.

The man Phil had kicked was dragging himself to his feet. Collin snatched up a table lamp and smashed it down on the back of his skull. Eyes rolling up in their sockets, he dropped to the floor, unconscious.

The man whose face was now devoid of teeth and was crisscrossed with slash marks was in Peter's powerful grip. With a running rush, Peter slammed the man into a wall nose first.

The fight was over in seconds, but it took too long. Finally free to go after the man with the knife, Jack discovered he was already gone. Grace was slumped in her chair, her neck pumping blood over the front of her body.

He ran to her. She was gasping for air, but growing weaker. Throwing himself to his knees beside her, he wrapped his arms around her as she breathed her last breaths. He never felt so useless. He knew she was dead, but couldn't let go of her.

Phil ran to the kitchen and, grabbing a paring knife, cut Kelly free. Kelly crumpled to the floor sobbing and wailing. The sounds of her crying mixed with the groans of the men littering the floor. Jack suffered in silence.

Outside, tires locked as a large blue van slid to a halt outside Kelly's now destroyed house.

"Jaaack!" Collin bellowed.

Phil grabbed Kelly and forced her out the back door. It took both Peter and Collin to pry Jack away from his sister.

Men were now pouring into the house. Bullets fired in haste whizzed past their heads. They had to run. Jack looked over his shoulder one last time at Grace before plunging into the darkness, running for his life.

CHAPTER 17

Jack stumbled into a shambling walk. Phil was at his side goading him to pick up the pace. She begged, pleaded, even swore at him to get him moving, but he ignored her. All he could hear was Grace's final rattling exhale, carrying the last of her life away from her body.

Phil grabbed his sleeve and began dragging him along. He swung violently away from her, fist raised. It took every ounce of self-control he had in him to squelch the impulse to smash whoever was yanking him forward.

His fist fell limp by his side. This was Phil. His best friend. He'd never hurt Phil.

Jack's feet ground to a halt. He thought he'd never hurt Grace, but he got her killed.

"Jack! What are you doing?" Phil shouted. "You can't stop. We have to keep moving!"

She grabbed him hard by the shoulder and pulled at him. Deep in his core, far beyond conscious thought, he felt unquestioning trust in Phil and allowed himself to be dragged along.

Peter was in the lead and brought them gasping to a stop in a neglected playground behind an abandoned church. Jack straggled in last with Phil still clinging to him, pulling him along. A poisonous tasting lump in his throat blocked all air from reaching his lungs. His eyes were so clouded with tears the ground swam beneath his feet. Spasms flexed through his chin and his lower lip quivered as he fought against a total meltdown. The rest were all so out of breath they couldn't speak. Even if they weren't gasping for air, none of them had any words to express their horror or to comfort Jack.

Shuffling to a crooked picnic table, Jack threw himself down onto its top. Making no protest, he let Phil ease his coat off of him. Glass embedded in his back caught and twisted. It should have hurt but didn't, and any pain he did feel he didn't care about.

She tossed the coat to Collin. "Pick the glass out of that," she commanded. "Peter. Head back. Keep out of sight and keep watch."

With nimble fingers, she pulled the larger shards out of Jack's back. Jack was numb to it. He felt his t-shirt being lifted up and off. The cold made his skin cringe and pimple with goose bumps but his mind didn't register anything.

"Kelly," Phil said as she pulled out her small pocketknife and flicked the blade open, "I need some help over here."

Kelly was sitting curled in a ball at the bottom of a dented slide. Her legs were pulled up tight against her body and her eyes were buried in her knees. She didn't move.

"Kelly!" Phil snapped. "Jack needs you!"

Kelly lifted her head and dug the heels of her hands into her eyes, squashing the tears out of them. Moving in a defeated stupor she stood and joined Phil at the picnic table.

Phil handed her phone to Kelly. "Shine the light on his back. We have to get as much glass out of him as we can before we have to start moving again."

Kelly mechanically followed orders.

Jack felt the pinching of Phil's fingers and the scratching of her blade as small grains of glass were being picked out of his skin. It hurt. It didn't hurt. He didn't care which. His mind was oblivious to it all.

As his body temperature began to plummet, the tears that were seconds ago pouring over his cheeks turned to slush and froze in his eyelashes. He blinked hard to break them out.

"Why?" he rasped.

"Why what, Jack?" Phil said in a peculiar mothering voice he'd never heard from her before as she continued to pull glass out of his skin. Jack, in a vague, distant way, thought it ill-suited her.

"Why, Kelly? Why did you and Grace leave the house?"

Kelly whimpered, "My scrapbook was hidden in my room. In a hole in my closet's wall. When my family left they didn't know to look for it. My friends. My dad. My life. It's all in that book. I couldn't leave it behind."

"A book." Jack shook his head in disbelief. "My sister died for a book."

Kelly blanched at his words. "Jack! I...We..."

Jack's voice was colder than the surrounding night. Incapable of feeling sympathy, he was at his most dangerous. "Don't. Just...don't," he warned her.

"Best leave it," Phil said to Kelly, her voice little more than a whisper.

Finishing her work on Jack's back she slipped his shirt back over him, guiding his arms through the sleeves as if she were dressing a child. "Collin? How's that coat coming? He's starting to freeze."

"I'm done," Collin said handing the coat to Phil. "I got most of it out, but there'll still be some in there."

Peter's slapping footfalls interrupted them as he came running up. "They're coming. They're moving slow, which means they don't know where we are, but they'll be here in less than five minutes."

"What do we do?" Collin asked.

Jack stood and took his coat from Phil. In a voice as emotionless as Death's he said, "The park is two blocks over. We play Hide and Seek."

Making no effort to keep out of sight, Jack led them to the park. Sprinting past the snow-covered playground equipment, they darted into the tree line. Hunkering down behind the largest trunks, Jack gave his orders.

"Phil, you and Collin take Kelly to our spot. If any of Batesh's men show up, Peter and I'll lead the clowns the opposite direction. Then, we'll ditch them and link up with you there."

Without saying a word, Phil, Collin, and Kelly left. Looking over his shoulder, Jack watched Kelly stumble over snow buried branches and fall to her knees. Phil helped her up and, taking her hand, guided her through the underbrush. Once out of sight, Jack turned back around and burrowed into the snow next to Peter. He watched and waited and stewed in his misery.

After Peter fidgeted for the fourth time, he hissed at him to keep still. He knew Peter's nerves were being tested. Anticipation of the enemy's arrival was twisting inside Peter like a knife. Jack was having a hard time being sympathetic.

He was so filled with hatred there wasn't enough room inside himself for any other feelings to crowd in. When he thought of Grace, and she was all he could think about, flames of rage fanned into blistering white heat. Even the agonizing sorrow he first felt over her murder was burned away by his hatred for the men who killed her.

Five men jogged into the playground area. It was Peter's turn to elbow him into silence as a low, guttural growl slipped past his lips. Jack bit the inside of his lip so hard it bled. It took all the self-control he could pull together to keep from flying out of the woods and attack them.

Just as Jack knew they would, the men spotted their footprints in the snow.

It didn't matter. He and his friends knew every stump and rabbit trail the woods concealed. The pitch-black night, the ice, the snow — none of it made any difference. This was their forest. They had played in it since they were first-graders. As far as Jack was concerned, they owned it and no one could ever get the upper hand on them as long as they were in it.

He expected the men to rush straight in after them. He wanted them to. Despite what he told Phil and the others, he had a very different plan in mind. After leading their pursuers away from Kelly, before he and Peter rejoined them, he intended to take them out. All the way out, if he could.

Two men began to follow their tracks when a third called them back. They argued. The one who ordered them to stop the chase puffed up and jabbed his finger at the pair, clearly not taking kindly to his orders being questioned.

Jack felt the sting of impatience. His entire body craved revenge.

"What are they waiting for?" he snarled.

The man who was giving the orders took out his phone and made a call. Though Jack could hear everything being said, he couldn't understand a word of it. He regretted sending Kelly away. She could have translated for him.

Making her leave with Phil was the right choice, but his ability to tell the difference between what was right and what served his lust for revenge was blurred. He wanted everyone associated with Batesh dead. With each passing moment, he became more and more determined to see that happen no matter what the cost.

Jack watched as the phone was stuffed into a coat pocket. The man said something. The two who wanted to follow them into the woods shouted their objections. The other two, who until now had remained silent, entered into the argument. From their body language he could tell they were siding with the one in charge.

Shouting for silence, the leader of the group threw his hands into the air. He turned his back on them all and stormed away. His two allies hesitated for a moment, then turned and followed him. The remaining two stood still and watched them go.

"Come on," Jack whispered to Peter. "Those two will be coming in here any second now."

"Where will we lead them?" Peter whispered back.

"Into the canyon. We'll climb out on that tree that's growing out of the wall. Remember? The one you were hiding behind last time we played Hide and Seek. There are plenty of big rocks on that side of the rim. Once we're out, we'll start stoning them."

Peter shot Jack a mistrustful glance. "I thought the plan was to ditch them and hook up with the others."

"Can't risk them picking up our tracks in this snow and following us," Jack lied. That couldn't happen once he and Peter were out of the canyon.

The two men turned back to face the tree line.

"Time for us to go," Jack whispered.

Using all the stealth they had learned from years of playing their games, he and Peter crawled into the forest. Once they reached a point he felt certain they wouldn't be seen Jack motioned to Peter that it was safe to get up. Remaining just as silent, they crept to the nearest trail.

"Ready?" he whispered.

In the cloudy, moonless black Jack heard more than saw Peter nod his head.

"Let's go!" shouted Jack. He took off running down the trail making as much noise as he could.

"Right behind you," yelled Peter.

Behind them, Jack heard the two men crashing into the woods. If he and Peter were making a ton of racket, those two sounded like artillery fire. A sudden thud echoed through the wood, followed by angry yells. Jack grinned out with burning hatred, knowing at least one of them tripped and fell flat on his face.

Despite the darkness, the trail stood out like an incandescent silver thread. Their boots sloshed through the heavy wet snow. Surefooted, knowing exactly where he was headed, Jack led the way into the heart of the park. The spot he chose to lead the men to was the point farthest away from any houses or roads.

"The path splits up ahead," Jack hollered for their pursuers' benefit. "Stick to the right!"

"Got it!" Peter shouted back.

Jack was grateful for Peter's trust. Peter knew just as well as he did that the two paths rejoined further on. The one to the left was wider and easier to follow. The right one was winding and narrow, riddled with roots and half buried rocks. The farther down it you went, the worse it got. Even with that knowledge, Peter didn't question his decision to go right.

As the path began to deteriorate, Jack slowed to a walk, then stopped.

"Don't move," he whispered.

He was straining his eyes, boring into the darkness. "There! Just ahead. It's that tree that blew down across the trail in last month's ice storm. We'll use it to hide our tracks and cut over to the easier trail."

Peter snickered. "We'll be at the canyon long before they are."

"Yeah. If they fall for it, we'll have plenty of time to make obvious tracks down into the canyon and to climb out. Once out, start gathering rocks. Biggest you can find. Get as many as you can but keep an ear out for them. When they are right under us, let 'em have it."

By the time the men shuffled down to the floor of the canyon, he and Peter had amassed quite an arsenal.

"Now!" screamed Jack.

Heavy stones, requiring both hands to lift, were hurled down on top of the two unsuspecting men. The initial volley knocked them to the ground. Before they could get up, another salvo rained down, followed by another and another.

Hatred escaped Jack's mouth in earsplitting screams. After he and Peter ran out of stones, he stood at the lip of the gorge glaring down at his handiwork. Below him the two men were bleeding and groaning, trying to crawl away. Their suffering filled him with a bitter satisfaction he wasn't altogether sure he enjoyed.

"Let's get out of here," he said.

They raced toward the creek bed where the others were waiting for them. As they ran, Jack struggled to understand why he wasn't filled with more of a sense of satisfaction. What he did should have made him feel like he'd gained some small bit of payback for Grace's murder, but it didn't.

Instead he felt scummy and gross. And it did nothing to ease his pain. He couldn't help thinking hatred and vengeance weren't what Grace would have wanted for him. As that notion settled into him, he became furious with himself.

CHAPTER 18

When Jack and Peter's boots hit the gravel of the creek bed, Phil charged into Jack's face. Even in the dark he could see that hers was drained and pale.

"What was all that shouting?" she demanded to know.

Peter told the story.

Collin listened, his face cold and solid as a tombstone.

Phil was horrified.

She shoved Jack. "What were you thinking?"

Jack's temper blew. "I was thinking I didn't want them to follow us when we take Kelly to her mother. I was thinking that unless we dealt with them, her whole family would be caught. I was thinking we have been on the defensive for months and that it's high time we started building some kind of offense."

"Really, Jack?" Phil moved to stand nose to nose with him. "Really! Or were you looking for something else?"

Jack's fist flew back.

Phil didn't move.

This wasn't going to be some playful swipe at her. Not even Phil could dodge or block a blow from such close range. She was going to stand there and let him hit her if that's what he wanted to do.

Jack snarled and spun away.

Skulking to one of their milk crates, he dropped down onto it. "Whatever!"

Phil turned her back on him. "This has gone far enough," she said to the rest of them. "We've been lucky so far. Both what Jack and Peter did just now, and the fight at Kelly's place? We came out on top because we took them by surprise. Next time, they'll be ready for us."

"What do you suggest we do?" Peter asked.

"We call the police," Phil said with finality. "I'm sorry, Kelly, but we have to. This whole thing has gotten way out of control."

Kelly whimpered, but nodded in agreement and said nothing.

"I don't think calling the police is such a good idea," Collin said.

Phil bristled. "Oh, really! And why is that?"

"Because if we call them, if they even listen, all they can do is come collect us."

"So?"

"Well…" Collin drawled.

Collin was being cautious. Despite his anger and pain, Jack was listening to every word. Collin, he knew, was more worried about Phil being pig-headed than he was about facing her temper. Whatever his reasons, they had to make complete sense otherwise Phil would argue her way around them.

"Still stalling," Phil snapped.

"Look," Collin said, "if I were Batesh, I'd be using some kind of a scanner to listen in on what the police were up to. If a bunch of cars get dispatched to pick us up, they'd know about it."

Phil sneered. "What are they going to do against the police?"

"Set up an ambush," Collin said with a shrug, "or make sure they get to us first. I don't know what they'd try, but I know they'd try something."

"And how do you know that?"

"Two reasons. First, they are determined to get Kelly. Look at what they've done so far. None of this has been an attack against the country. It's not rooted in some political or religious idealism. It's personal. It's Batesh's need for revenge. Nothing else."

Jack saw Phil deflate. Collin was right and she knew it. "What's the second reason," she asked in a defeated tone, not needing to hear any more.

"Like I said, Batesh has abandoned his cause to destroy America and turned that fanaticism toward destroying Kelly and her family. That's the only possible explanation for the risks he's taking just to capture her."

Collin paused like a professor waiting for his students to fill in the gaps. Everyone was looking at him, waiting for him to finish the thought for them.

"Isn't it obvious?" he asked.

"Not to us," Peter said more in support of Collin as opposed to being frustrated with him. "Help us out, buddy."

Collin looked at each of them then said, "Qasim Batesh is insane."

Everyone was silent. Jack breathed loud deep breaths and thought about everything Batesh had done. Slowly, his brain twisted into comparing himself to the terrorist. Ambushing Batesh's men was a crazy thing to do. A stupid thing. So why did he do it? Collin said the need for revenge drove the terrorist mad. It was a madness Jack could relate to. Having something in common with such a despicable man made him want to throw up.

He raised his eyes toward the cloudy skies. Never had he felt so ashamed. Peter, Collin, Phil and Kelly were standing in the dark not saying a word. He couldn't afford to let his judgment slip into chaos. They were all depending on him. He wished that weren't the case, but it was.

Even Phil, who was more than capable of taking the lead in a crisis, wouldn't be able pull them together and keep them going for the long haul. That had always been his job. Now, when they most needed him to take charge, he couldn't flake out and expect someone else to do it.

"We can't stay here forever," he said grimly. "Kelly's mother is waiting for her. They have to get out of town as soon as possible. Once they're safe, then we can decide how we are going to deal with this mess. I, for one, am on board with Phil's plan. We see that Kelly makes it to her family then we go straight to the police."

Agreements were murmured.

"Phil, have Kelly tell you where she is to meet her mother. Then you lead us there. The rest of us don't need to know where it is. If we run into trouble, we'll drop back and deal with it. If we get taken, we won't know anything to tell.

"But Phil? That means it's all on you. No matter what else happens, your mission is to deliver Kelly safe and sound. If that means you ditch us, then you ditch us. Got it?"

Phil gave grim nod. "We'll leave in five minutes. Jack, I need to talk to you."

He led her far enough away so that the others couldn't overhear. Before she could say anything Jack started talking. "Phil, this is the only plan I've got, so don't argue about it.

"I wasn't going to. It's a good plan. I'd have never thought of doing it that way."

"Oh! So that's not what you wanted to tell me. That my plan is crap? Because honestly, I kinda think it is. I just don't have a better one."

Phil chuckled. "I'll take your crap plan over someone else's brilliant idea any day."

Jack was thankful for the pitch-black night. Phil couldn't see him turn pink.

"What I wanted to say," Phil went on, "is that I'm sorry for yelling at you. I was just worried. Like, freaking out, worried."

"You had every right to yell at me. I was out for revenge. I was being stupid and, like you said, Peter and I got super lucky, so you keep on yelling at me.

"From here on out, I'm going to focus on getting us out of this mess alive. And I meant what I said. We're going to deliver Kelly to her mom because that's what I promised Grace. But after that? I intend to leave getting justice for Grace in the hands of the real authorities. Not us. Not me."

They stood there in the dark, neither one knowing what else to say. Jack broke the tension. "We better get moving."

Jack assigned the order they'd move out in. Phil would go first, taking point. He gave her a fifteen second head start then sent Kelly, flanked by Peter and Collin, after them. Counting off fifteen Mississippies in his head, he followed his friends out of the woods, bringing up the rear.

They trudged through town, staggering themselves on either side of the road, trying to make themselves look inconspicuous. Jack thought they stood out like a neon sign.

The freezing night air bit and burned his exposed skin. Admiration for Phil's cunning as she led them on a meandering route provided some inner sense of warmth. She often doubled back or made quick dashes between houses and down alleyways making it impossible for them to be followed without their noticing it.

All her precautions, however, did little to ease his tension. Every nerve was on edge. As he walked, his eyes darted left, right, even to the roof tops and up telephone poles. At random intervals, he pivoted and stared back down the street behind him. All he could see were street-lamps making polka dots of light in the muck on the roads. Through it all, he felt the vile nausea of Grace's murder.

There was no sense of relief that the enemy was not there. Anticipation of an attack was cutting so deep that he almost wished the terrorists would come for them, just to get it over with. If they did attack, his mind could shift onto them and off of Grace.

Ahead of him, Collin was messing with his phone as he walked. Jack wished he could distract himself as easily. That thought didn't quite fit, though. In fact, it set Jack's teeth on edge. Collin never allowed himself to become distracted when faced with a problem that demanded complete focus. Collin was the most single-minded person Jack knew. Trudging through the winter slop, he wondered what Collin was up to.

Phil turned their procession into a narrow alley between a tire store and a pharmacy and stopped. Both businesses were closed. Weak light, trickling in from their shared parking lot, bathed the alleyway in a dirty yellow glow, making Phil's shadow a tall, thin distortion on the brick wall. Like a horror film special effect, her misshapen shadow-arm motioned them to join her.

One-by-one they slipped into the alley and huddled around each other as much for warmth as for secrecy. Kelly pointed to a small gas station and convenience store across the road.

"That's it," she said. "The people who own it are refugees in this country, too. They help others who need to disappear. Mom is in there."

Jack studied the building. The light inside the store, dingy and yellow, was as weak as the light leaking light into the alley where they stood. No customers milled around inside, nor were any out at the pumps. He guessed the man at the register was somewhere in his late sixties. Looking between the cigarette ads and drink special decals plastered to the window, Jack watched him sitting hunched over the counter turning the pages of a newspaper.

"Peter? Collin? Either of you got any money?" Jack asked.

"I've got a ten," Collin answered.

"That should be enough. I want you to go check the place out. If you think it's safe, buy a couple of sodas. Hang around inside like you are trying to get warm. We'll come join you. If anything looks fishy, buy a bag of chips and leave, walking away from us."

"Hey! That's good thinking, Jack," Peter said.

Jack ignored him. He was too numb inside for something as simple as praise to boost his mood.

"Get going. Out the back and come from around the far side of the tire shop."

"Gotcha," Collin said. They took off at a trot.

Peering out of the ally, Jack waited for them to come into view.

"Kelly? Is there any kind of signal you are supposed to give to let your mom know you are here?"

"Just sending a text," she answered timidly.

While they were recovering at the abandoned playground, Jack felt Kelly was keeping her distance from him. Even now, she pressed herself against the wall of the pharmacy with Phil between them. Maybe she was afraid he would blame her for Grace's death. Perhaps she didn't know how to approach him because nothing she could say would make things any better. He didn't care. All he wanted was her out of his life.

Across the road, Collin and Peter entered the store. They split up with Peter heading toward the toilets and Collin going to the large coolers at the back wall. Collin said something to the clerk.

Jack watched as the cashier turned his attention to Collin. With perfect timing, Peter darted into the storeroom. Collin browsed around the store for a bit then moved to the soda machine. He said something else to the clerk and undercover of that distraction, Peter popped back out of the storeroom.

Even with so much going on, Jack's thoughts clung to Grace. He was thankful Kelly was leaving him alone. Grace had depended on him to keep both her and Kelly safe. He'd failed spectacularly, but not completely.

Grace was dead but Kelly was still alive. No matter what, he owed it to Grace to keep her that way until he reunited her with her mother. After that, he was done. With a cold bitter jolt, he realized how bad he wanted her gone.

Back in the shop, he could just make out bits and pieces of his friends. Collin's head bobbed over a row of shelves. Peter made a U-turn around an end cap.

They were being thorough in determining if the store was safe to enter or not. Jack knew he'd have their verdict soon. The next time he saw them in full view, they were at the counter.

Jack held his phone out to Kelly. "They bought sodas. Send the text."

After she handed his phone back, Jack stepped bold and confident — complete opposites to what he was feeling — into the parking lot. He went as far as the street, looking in all directions for trouble. "Move," he commanded over his shoulder. "Now! Walk quickly, but don't run."

Bells tied to the front door clanged as it closed behind them. They were still ringing when the big silver refrigerator door at the rear of the store burst open. Kelly's mother raced down the far isle and pulled Kelly into her arms. Two men Jack didn't know were coming up behind her.

Instinctively, Jack shifted into a fight-ready posture. "Who are they?" he asked. Behind him Phil, Collin, and Peter bristled at his grim and dangerous tone.

"Friends," Kelly's mother said, confused by his hostility. "They are friends. Here to help."

She looked at them, taking in the overwrought nerves and haggard expressions. Her eyes widened when she realized what the rusty stains on their clothes were.

She turned to Kelly. Jack didn't need a translator to know she was demanding an explanation.

As Kelly told their story, her mother's hand flew up and covered her mouth to keep from shrieking. Tears flowed from her wrinkled eyes. Kelly's tears were streaming down her face.

When Kelly could no longer get words past her sobs, her mother pulled Kelly to her bosom, rocking her while cooing reassuring words. She let Kelly go and threw her arms around Jack. He stiffened and didn't hug her back.

Releasing him she said, "I am so, so sorry. I know. Those words are meaningless, but I have no others to give, except this: everyone will know what you have done. What it cost you. You will be known as a true hero."

"I'd rather I wasn't," Jack said.

Kelly's mother was stunned by the coldness in his voice.

He didn't know why he said it. Habit, more than anything else. Ever since he began toying with the idea of being a spy, he avoided so much as having his picture taken. He did all he could to not be noticed, not to stand out. Secrecy had become a way of life for him.

He tried to explain. "After this is over, I'm going to want to disappear. I can't do that if I have a reputation following me around."

Wizened eyes looked deep into his own. Too knowing. Too understanding. Jack could tell she knew what lay ahead in his life. Her uncanny insight unsettled him but not near so much as did her words.

"You are thinking like so many others I have known," she said, sadness dripping off her words. "Secretive people. Dangerous people."

Staring straight into his eyes, ensuring there could be no misunderstanding she hissed, "Government people."

She gripped his arms and implored, "I beg you, choose a different path, if you still can."

"If I can?"

"Yes. If you can. Things may have already gone too far for you to stop what you, me, Batesh, yes even Grace by her death, have set in motion."

Jack flinched at the mention of Grace. Since Kelly's mother already knew his ambition he saw no point in denying it. "It's what I want."

Kelly's mother shook her head in disappointment. "Nobody wants that life. Necessity, loss, and pain forces it upon those who live it."

"That's your opinion. And I do want it. I've been working for a long time to make it happen," Jack objected.

"A child playing a game!" she hissed at him, fanning his words away with her hand.

Jack had heard enough. He stepped away from her. Behind him, she made a mournful sigh.

The store owner said something in Arabic.

"Kalila. We must go," her mother said, sounding exhausted.

Kelly thanked Peter and Collin with tears still running down her cheeks. Phil was wrapped into a tight hug which she struggled to reciprocate. Before Jack knew what was happening, Kelly had gathered his hands into hers.

Kissing his cut and bruised knuckles, her tears splashed onto the backs of his hands. She pressed her cheek against them. She pressed her lips onto his forehead. Without uttering a single word, she wiped her tears out of her eyes and joined her mother. Nothing needed to be said. Kelly and her mom, along with the two men, scurried out the back of the building and into the night.

A car rumbled into life.

They were gone.

"Leave," the old clerk demanded. "Leave now."

CHAPTER 19

"Glad that's over," Peter said once they were back in the alley across the street.

They huddled around Jack who was staring at the filthy gray slush under his feet. His heart beat slow and hard. Each thud felt like a punch.

Out of the corner of his eye he caught sight of Phil casting a furtive glance at him as if Peter's naive words would slice him open like a sword strike.

"It isn't over," she said in a whisper, as if stealth still mattered. "Not by a long shot. There's Batesh's men to deal with. And the cops. Even when we're done there, the fallout from this is going to drag on for months. Years."

"Forever," Jack whispered.

Like Peter, he was hoping that once they were rid of Kelly, he'd feel better. Relieved, if nothing else.

He was grieving for Grace, he understood that. But hadn't the mission been accomplished? Wasn't Kelly delivered alive and safe to her mother? She wasn't his problem anymore. Despite his pain, shouldn't he feel somewhat relieved? Shouldn't he have some sense of accomplishment?

Nothing.

He felt nothing.

In fact, he felt less than nothing because, now that Kelly was off his hands, he was left with no sense of purpose. Lacking that, an emptiness inside him yawned open like a demon's maw, threatening to swallow him whole. All the pain and misery he felt over Grace's murder flooded in to fill that emptiness.

Grace! How am I ever going to explain what happened to Mom and Dad?

The thought had occurred to him earlier, but he'd refused to dwell on it. He found it much easier to focus on his mission of delivering Kelly to her mom. Now that mission was over, he had nothing left to distract him from facing the horrific duty of telling his parents that his sister, their daughter, was dead ... and it was his fault.

Phil's words drug the truth out into the open. This was far from over and he had nowhere to hide from what lay ahead.

Far from over.

He couldn't get that mantra out of his head.

Thoughts of his mom and dad crowded in on him and weighed him down as he sank to the bottom of despair. What would he say to them? What could he say? How could any good intentions he started out with justify what he allowed to happen? How could Mom and Dad not hate him?

"You're crazy," he heard Peter snark back at Phil.

Jack turned his attention onto his friends. Anything was better than wallowing in despair's suffering.

"No, she isn't," Collin muttered.

Collin's voice sounded distant; half connected to what was going on around him. Pressed against the wall of the tire store he was doing his best to shield himself from the arctic wind just like the rest of them but, inside his mind, he was somewhere else.

Jack felt keenly aware, now more than ever, that Collin was on their periphery, not far enough away to be separated from them, but distant enough to not belong. Like he was on the journey to Kelly's drop off point, he stood fiddling with his phone.

Seeing Collin so focused on his phone pestered Jack like an itch along the inside of his spine. An itch he couldn't even begin to reach.

Why can't he ever just be one of us? an annoyed voice inside his head asked.

Jack inhaled blew out steam and frustration. He had to keep frosty. He had to keep his mind clear. One thing he knew for certain — Collin never did anything without good reason.

"Why do you keep messing with that thing?" he asked.

"I'm trying to find Peter's phone," Collin said.

"Come again?"

Peter's eyes bloomed with excitement. "That's right! We were so busy running for our lives that Collin and I never had a chance to tell you. Remember when you and Phil were stalking up to Kelly's house? I'm guessing you saw me slide underneath the goons' car? Well, I taped my phone inside the front bumper."

"That was the plan you had when we were hiding behind that truck?" Phil asked Collin.

"Yeah," he answered without taking his eyes off his phone. "I'm using the Find-My-Phone app to track their movements. Trouble is, the signal is spotty. Must have something to do with the phone being inside the bumper. I just didn't know where else to tell Peter to tape it so it wouldn't fall off."

"That was some pretty good thinking," Jack said. "It's a shame it isn't working."

"Oh, it's working. Just not all the time. I get a signal, then it goes away. That's why I need to keep…Wait! I've got something!"

They crowded around him.

A map filled the tiny screen. In the top corner was a small red dot. Collin pinched his fingers together then, spread his thumb and forefinger across the screen. The dot shrank as the map grew larger.

"So, the phone is here," Collin said pointing at the blip. And we are here."

He pointed to a part of the city farthest away from the dot.

"So how do we get from here to there fast?" Jack asked.

"Jack!" Phil gasped. "I thought the plan was that we were going to the police after we got Kelly reunited with her mother."

"It was."

Phil glowered at him.

"I mean, it is. But look!" He pointed to the screen. "Peter's phone is on Iroquois Street. Five blocks over is Pueblo. The police station is on Pueblo. It's on the way!

"We can go, make sure the terrorists are wherever the phone is, then go to the cops. That way we can tell them where the jerks are!"

Phil, face full of mistrust, stared at him. He glared back with eyes full of black hatred. Seeing that blip on the screen opened floodgates of rage, the one emotion he was capable of feeling aside from crippling pain and sadness. Preferring anger to suffering, he let his hatred pour out of him, threatening to drown anyone or anything that stood in its path.

"Collin?" Phil said without taking her eyes off Jack.

Tension in Collin's voice made it squeak. "Yeah?"

"Do you have a fix on that phone or not?"

"I do. It isn't moving. Maybe that was part of the problem. It's been at the same spot for the last few minutes."

"Fine," she spat. "Jack? We'll go check it out. It makes sense. But that's all. You got that? No snooping around. No assaults."

"That's the plan, Phil," Jack said. "We go, see what we see, then head straight to the police station."

She continued to stare at him skeptically. She had every right to be skeptical, but he was telling her the truth. All he had in mind was to discover if the terrorists were with the car or if they ditched it somewhere knowing he and the others could identify it.

Peter broke the standoff. "We better get going. It's a long way across town and we still need to keep out of sight."

"What difference does that make now?" Jack asked, breaking his eyes away from Phil's. "Kelly's out of reach. Without her, Batesh's men have no use for us. Once they see she's gone, that'll be the end of their interest in us."

"I doubt they'd be that nice about it," Peter said, "but it wasn't them I was thinking of. It's everyone else. Jack, look at us. We're filthy. And you..."

"What about me?" Jack asked defensively.

Peter looked at him, his eyes cold as the grave. "Aside from all the dirt? It looks like someone slammed a brick on a ketchup packet right in front of you. You're covered in blood."

Jack stiffened. "That blood is Grace's," he muttered.

"I know, Jack. I know. I wasn't trying to poke fun or anything. It's just…I mean…well, I don't know what I mean. I don't know how to talk about it, but I wasn't trying to…"

Peter stopped talking. He swore. "Look. All I meant was that if we are going across town, as messed up as we are, we need to be careful. Do you want to get there without drawing attention? Or do you want to get stopped along the way and never make it? That's all I was trying to say."

Jack looked at Peter. Then Phil. Then Collin, who was dragging the heel of one hand over his eyes. They each had pale faces and clueless expressions. Slowly, the truth dawned on him. They were suffering with him. They were in pain because he was in pain and, just like him, they had no clue what to say or to do.

Aside from Phil, this was the first time death had touched any of their lives, and she was just as far out of her depth as the rest of them. She was a newborn when her dad died. All she had were her mother's memories and a few photographs.

Jack spoke softly. "You guys don't know what to say because nothing can be said. Grace was murdered. Her death was senseless and it can't be undone. All we can do is keep moving and learn how to cope as we go."

Phil sidled up next to him. "Do you want us to take you home? Maybe after you tell your parents…"

Jack flinched away. "No! Not until this is over."

Tears dribbled out of his eyes. "Let's find that stupid car then tell the police everything that's happened. After that, I'll tell Mom and Dad. They shouldn't have to go through trying to figure out how to deal with Batesh. I want to finish this for them and for Grace."

She turned away from him and he was glad she did. He didn't want her or anyone else to see him blubbering.

"So that's that, then," she said to the group while he pulled himself together. "We'd best get started. We've a long way to go and we're pressed for time. Collin, lead the way. Take the shortest path you can that avoids the busier streets. And keep an eye on that app. If you lose the signal or if the car goes on the move, you tell us."

They hustled out of the alley's protection. A cold blast of winter wind slapped them across their faces. Collin kept the pace brisk but not at a run. Moving too fast would make them just as conspicuous as taking the bus, if any were still running in this blizzard. Faces set hard against both their pain and the elements they marched doggedly on until finding themselves hunkered down, exhausted and panting, behind a row of dumpsters outside the seediest motel in town

Callin

BriNLee

CHAPTER 20

The motel was a long, thin, two-story building painted the ugliest pale-yellow Jack ever saw. The doors may have once been blue, maybe green, but were now so battered and faded they pock-marked the yellow walls like mold on cheese. At intervals, rusty metal trestles ran from the ground up to the second-floor walkway and from there up to the roof.

Dead center of the hideous motel was a breezeway. It cut straight through to the other side of the building. Access to the second-floor, an iron staircase with concrete steps, lay half way through the breezeway opposite ancient, out-of-order, vending machines.

"There's the car," Collin blurted out in excitement, pointing to the rust bucket sedan used to transport Grace to her death.

"Quiet!" hissed Phil. "We see it."

"Yeah," whispered Peter. "But we can't see much else from here."

Jack agreed. "Stay here," he ordered.

Crawling on all fours he scrabbled down to the far end of the row of dumpsters. Three quarters of the way down, his gloved left hand slipped off the curb and broke through the layer of ice covering the gutter. With a loud plop, his hand landed in a puddle of rancid leakage from the dumpsters and sank past his wrist. The disgusting liquid trickled over his glove's cuff, flooding it.

Steam rose out of the hole he'd made in the thin ice carrying with it a stink so foul Jack gagged. Clamping his teeth tight to keep from vomiting, he removed his glove and poured the goop out.

A sharp staccato voice cut through the icy night.

Jack froze. He didn't understand a single word of Arabic but in this case, he didn't need to. The man's tone made his words clear enough. "What was that?"

Looking back at his friends he saw that they were anxious, waiting for his orders. At his signal they would stay put or bolt.

Another voice, calmer, said something and trailed his words with a chuckle.

Jack raised his hand, palm facing his friends, and clenched his fingers into a tight fist — the hand signal for, "Stay!"

After wriggling his hand back inside his wet and smelly glove, Jack continued his crawl. Lying flat at the end of the row, he pushed his head out past the last dumpster.

From this vantage point he could see the two men. One was standing on the sidewalk beneath the second-floor walkway hiding from the wind behind a corner of the breezeway. The other had his back to Jack and was returning from the narrow parking lot, having been drawn out by Jack's ruckus. The first thug lit a cigarette with the embers of the one he was smoking and handed it over to the other when he rejoined him.

Scanning the first-floor walkway, then the second-floor, Jack couldn't see anyone else. Several windows had lights shining behind thick polyester curtains. The lit rectangles were scattered to the left and right of the building. However, Jack paid particular attention to the fact that the three rooms to the right of the lookouts and the corresponding rooms on the second-floor all had lights on.

Jack turned his eyes to the parking lot. Motel management was pinching pennies by not keeping the lot free of snow. Battered cars and shabby mini-vans were parked according to the drivers' best guess of where the lines might be. Not a single vehicle was less than ten years old.

The worn-out rust-bucket that had been bugged with Collin's makeshift tracker was parked in front of the three lower-level rooms being guarded. An industrial work-van was parked beside it.

The van looked familiar.

Jack closed his eyes and concentrated on the van's image. He felt angry, but it wasn't the pervasive hatred he felt over his sister's murder. The van itself made him angry but he didn't know why.

His eyes shot open in recollection. That van was the same one that had splashed muck and sludge on him before school when he and Grace went to pick up Kelly.

If only he had known who owned that van!

At the time he had written the incident off as nothing more than having a crappy day. Now it took on a whole new meaning. He felt as if being splattered that day was a deliberate act of taunting; like they were being stalked the whole time without their knowing it.

Fuming, he crawled back to where his friends were waiting for him.

"Six rooms," he said in hushed tones as he squatted down in the filthy snow next to them. "Three up. Three down. Two men are standing guard near the stairs. You can't see them because of that blue van. Anyone recognize it?"

Peter leaned over and peered throughout the crack between the first and second dumpster.

"Yeah," he said sitting back again. "Now that you mention it, that matches the description of the van I was telling you about. The one seen cruising around belonging to some carpet cleaners."

"I remember," Jack growled still mentally kicking himself, wondering if somehow he could have prevented Grace's death.

Phil got to her feet. Pushing up onto tiptoe she looked over the top of the dumpster. She dropped back down.

"What?" Jack asked, forced out of his self-recrimination. "What did you see?"

"Shadows. Moving behind the curtains."

"In which room?" Collin asked.

Phil swallowed hard. "All of them."

As her words dropped from her lips, they heard doors opening and voices filling the night air. Jack scrambled back to the end of the row, listening for any change in the voices telling him he moved too fast, made too much noise.

"Crap! Crap! Crap!" he heard Phil hiss. She was right behind him, back on her feet and peering over the dumpster.

Squatting down next to him, she whispered, "There are so many of them. At least six coming out of every room! All with guns. Jack, we have got to get out of here!"

Jack poked his head past the dumpster's edge and pulled it back immediately. He closed his eyes and pictured in his brain what he had seen.

Armed men were seeping out of the motel rooms and making their way to the van, the junker Collin was tracking, and other battered cars in the lot. They were all dressed in bits-and-pieces of military garb, but were not wearing uniforms. Most were armed. Many were laughing with one-another. They were so bold, not even trying to hide the fact they were scumbags. It made Jack furious as his imagination told him they were mocking Grace's death.

Just like Phil, Jack knew they had to get out of there, which suited him fine. Being so close to these men made him sick. They were disgusting and he wanted to get to the cops. That would be his revenge.

Jabbing his head out, he took one last look before leading his friends to the police station just a few blocks away.

A tall, lean man came out of one of the second story rooms. He paused in the doorway, looking up and down the block. He was being cautious. Flanked on either side by two bodyguards, he walked to the railing and scanned the area a second time.

Jack couldn't make out any details. The light pouring out from the room behind transformed him into a silhouette. Something familiar about the man nagged at Jack like a swollen mosquito bite.

The men beside this stranger were rigid. Their movements were far more deliberate and precise than Jack thought natural. They respected this guy. He had to be the one in charge.

Jack watched as the man reached inside his military style coat. With a slow and casual movement he placed a cigarette between his lips. The bodyguard to his right made a brisk movement and, flicking a lighter, lit the cigarette.

In that flash of flame, as the man inclined his head to dip the cigarette's tip into it, Jack caught sight of a twisted nose and scruffy ponytail. He knew this man from Internet pictures. Qasim Batesh was here!

Jack hurled himself back behind the dumpster. He was breathing in gasps. Steam was puffing out of his mouth.

"Jack?" Phil asked. "What is it? What did you see?"

"Batesh. He's here."

"What? So fast? Impossible!"

She swore, thought for a moment then asked, "Are you sure, Jack? I mean, there hasn't been enough time for him to…"

"He's here," Jack snarled.

"Then we need to get out of here."

Jack didn't move. His fingers dug into the snow and mud. He balled the muck inside his fists. Closing his mouth, his jaw flexed as he grit his teeth.

Outwardly, Jack became as frozen as everything else around them. Inside, a volcano was building toward a scorching eruption.

"Jack," Phil pleaded.

He made no answer.

Phil swore.

The men at the motel began shouting. They heard.

Jack sprang to his feet to run but, locking eyes with Batesh, became paralyzed like a bird staring into the eyes of a serpent.

Phil was on her feet beside him, screaming at him to move.

Still yelling, Batesh's men began closing in on the dumpsters.

"What are you two doing," Collin shouted in stunned confusion. "They're coming this way!"

"Batesh," Phil yelled, there being no more reason for stealth. "He's here."

Jack's stupor was shattered by fear for his friends' lives. "Run," he shouted. "Run!"

Like hounds on a hunt, voices were rising behind them as the mob of terrorists converged on the dumpsters. Jack and the others dove into the shelter of a collapsing gas station next to the motel. His name echoing in the frozen night stalled their flight.

"Jack? It must be you, Jack Straw! Yes, I know who you are. Your sister and your friend Kalila betrayed you. I know all about you. And your friends — Collin Jensen, Peter Rochelle, and, forgive me, Peelomeela Nightingale?

Filled with impulsive bravado, Phil shouted, "Philomela, you moron."

Batesh laughed. "Of course. Forgive me. And Kalila. You are there, too? Yes?"

A breath of relief rushed from Jack's lungs. Batesh didn't know Kelly escaped him.

Batesh started in again. "Ah, well. It does not matter. I will see you soon enough, Kalila. And you, Jack. I am most anxious to meet you."

"What does he mean by that?" Peter asked.

Jack's stomach lurched. "It means we've stood here too long."

They stared at him.

"Batesh is distracting us," Jack explained in a rush. "They're coming for us! We've got to run! You three take off. Hide someplace. I'll lead them away."

"No!" Phil shouted. "We stay together."

"You heard. Batesh wants me the most. Besides," he looked Phil straight in the eyes, "the worst they can do to me is kill me."

Phil flushed stoplight red. The brutal truth of his fear for her should she be captured was as disgusting as it was clear. Her lips quivered as she tried to object but no sound slipped past them. Jack felt a pang of stabbing sadness for her. This was the first time he'd ever seen her let being a girl matter — yet another reason for wanting to kill Batesh with his own hands.

"You two. Protect Phil no matter what. She is not to be taken. Got it?"

"Never," Peter swore.

Collin didn't say anything but gave Phil one of his rare smiles. She would be safe with them.

Voices erupted nearby. Batesh's men were almost upon them.

"Go," Jack ordered. "Now!"

Jack watched his three friends run through the burned-out building and over the crumbling brick wall at the back of the property. He knew before he ordered them away there was no time to lead Batesh's forces anywhere. Straightening his body, he turned to face the oncoming battle, a smile playing across his face. Moments ago he was out of his mind with rage and fear. He'd allowed his feelings to overpower his common sense. As a result, he and his friends were put into unnecessary peril.

The enemy was closing in.

He heard them slinking up to where he stood waiting. Like a toddler cuddling in the security of a favorite blanket, a sense of calm settled over him. Cool reason had returned.

Earlier, attacking Batesh and his men would have meant pointlessly throwing his life away. Now, some good would come from his death, but Jack had no intention of dying. Not yet. He still had a mission to accomplish. Batesh was going down.

He couldn't run. The risk of Batesh's men splitting up and chasing both him and his friends was too great. By staying put they would be forced to deal with him and him alone, giving Collin, Peter, and Phil a few more precious seconds to get away. If necessary, he would force them into a fight if that was what it took to keep them from chasing his friends. He knew he had no chance of winning such a fight, but it would buy his friends time.

He could hear the men outside the burnt shell of a building, surrounding it. When they burst in, the looks of surprise on their faces made Jack grin. The last thing they expected was to find him waiting, patient and calm.

Jack counted four of them. As he prepared to take them on, a hubbub of chatter broke out between them. One man stepped forward and Jack recognized him as the one in charge back at the park.

"What is this?" he growled at Jack.

"What is what?" Jack answered innocently.

The man scowled. "Don't play games. Where are your friends? Where is Kalila?"

"Oh! Them," Jack drawled with all the childish sarcasm he could muster. "They said you guys were nothing but a bunch of nasty cheaters and they don't want to play with you anymore. They went home."

With a face looking like a red grape, the man started shouting orders. Four of the men separated themselves from the others and took a step toward the back exit of the building.

Jack positioned himself to block them. "If Batesh wants me he can have me. You are not going after my friends."

"Silence that dog," the man screamed, "but don't kill him yet. Then, go after his friends!"

One of the four stepped forward and swung his fist at Jack's head believing he was facing an untrained child.

He was mistaken.

Dropping into a low squat, Jack lashed out with his foot, aiming for the man's kneecap. Hitting its mark with incredible force, the knee snapped backwards with a gruesome crunch. The man crumpled to the ground, writhing in agony.

The others were on him in an instant. Jack whirled like a tornado, striking out with hands and feet. He fought like he'd never fought before and the carnage he was causing was devastating, but it wasn't near enough. Outnumbered and outclassed, one boy against several well-trained men, he was soon subdued.

Lying where he had fallen, the men who surrounded him began taking turns kicking him. All he could do was ball up and try his best to make sure they made contact with his arms and legs and not more vital parts of his body. The outcome, however, was inevitable. He missed a savage boot aimed at his head.

Starting at the far edges of his eye-sight, blackness tunneled in, blocking out everything around him. In the end, nothing was left but the black.

CHAPTER 21

Jack woke kicking and screaming. A throbbing pain was pounding in his head. What felt like electric shocks blasted through his shoulders.

His arms were wrapped around a horizontal metal pole that was threaded between his elbows and behind his back. The pole itself was held in place by hooks at either end attached to chains running up to the ceiling. His wrists were bound across his chest, preventing his elbows from raising much beyond his shoulders. Dangling three feet above the smooth concrete floor, his bare feet flailed wildly, kicking at the air.

The room he was in smelled of caustic chemicals. They made his eyes water just as much as the pain. Hearing voices off to his side, Jack jerked his head around, making the chains supporting him rattle like they were in the hands of a ghost.

He had to blink several times to clear his vision. Cobwebs still cluttered his foggy brain. His watery eyes refused to focus.

Batesh looked over at him, smirked cruelly, then returned to the whispered conversation he was having with his men. Seeing him, memory of the past several hours flooded Jack's mind. Forcing himself to settle down, the searing pain in his head subsided to a dull ache.

By pressing his hands into his chest he was able lift his body a little and thereby reduce the pain in his shoulders from tortuous to mere agony. It wasn't a lift he could hold indefinitely, but by alternating his lifts with hanging, he could control when he was in discomfort and when he could have relief, at least for the moment. Eventually, his strength would give out and hanging would be all that was left to him.

Looking around him, Jack saw that he was in a large warehouse with rugs, carpets, and drapes hanging from similar poles as his throughout the room. On the floor were piles of scrap fabrics and trash. A single brown door leading to offices was at the far end.

Across the room, the group of men dispersed.

"And now I turn my attention to you," Batesh said as he pushed a squeaking and clanging aluminum staircase in front of Jack.

"I don't have anything you want," Jack said hoping for the best.

"You have Kalila. If that were not the case, you and your troublesome friends would have been dead days ago. Much easier to kill a man than to try and control him."

Jack clenched his jaw. Batesh didn't yet know Kelly had fled with her family. That ignorance was all that was keeping him alive. If he wanted to stay that way, he had to keep Batesh from learning the truth.

Climbing the stairs, Batesh grabbed Jack by the face, turning it from side to side as he inspected him with eyes narrowed in curiosity. "Oh, you may look like a boy," Batesh continued calmly, "but you and your friends wage war like adults."

Batesh's iron grip transferred to Jack's neck. He wasn't squeezing the windpipe. His massive hand was cutting off blood flow through the carotid arteries, starving Jack's brain of oxygenated blood.

"Let's see if you die like a man or a boy," Batesh pondered more to himself than to Jack.

Pinpricks of light began to dance in front of Jack's eyes. His legs were kicking wild and spastic as everything began to go black again. Despite sucking in air with rasping pants he felt starved for a breath. It took less than seven seconds for him to pass out.

Ice struck Jack in the face as a bucket of freezing water was thrown over him. He gasped and his feet jigged in the air.

Batesh descended the stairs and drug the rickety apparatus away. Returning, he stood on the floor where Jack could see him clearly, arms folded across his chest, studying him.

"Very good," he said as if complimenting Jack. "No tears. No begging for your worthless life. Impressive, from one so young."

Jack glared at him.

Not in the least concerned, Batesh continued talking as if they were friends. "You see, Jack, you can learn a lot from how a person faces death."

"And what did you learn from me?" snarled Jack.

"All I needed to. For example, it will be a waste of my time to offer you your release in exchange for Kalila. Not fearing death, you'd rather die. Just so, threats to kill you if you don't tell me what I want to know will prove fruitless as well."

"It's a struggle," Jack quipped. "You can't bribe me, can't threaten me, and can't kill me. You could, of course, give up trying to get your hands on Kelly."

Batesh lunged forward and, with a viscous blow, struck his fist into Jack's gut.

"I will never stop! Not until I have her here! With me! I will show her pig of a father of hers what it means to betray me!"

"He's dead," Jack wheezed. "You won't be showing him anything."

Batesh stepped back, using his sleeve to wipe spittle from his lips.

"As for killing you?" he went on as if Jack hadn't spoke, "You must know I am going to kill you, Jack. I was always going to kill you. And your friends,"

Batesh paused and made the same arm motion an umpire would when calling a runner safe. "Dead. All dead. Just a matter of time.

"The struggle, as you put it, isn't what to do with you. My dilemma is how am I going to get the information I need before I do it.

"There is only one way. Torture. Not the most effective method. No doubt I will have to wade through hours of tedious lies before you give me the truth. But, it is all I have left to use. Now, as much as I'd like to begin this very moment, I have another engagement for which I'm late. But at least you now have something to look forward to until I return, yes?"

Jack's brows furrowed. *Where is he going? What else is this madman planning?*

Batesh crossed the room and began rooting around in a tool chest. As if reading his mind, Batesh laughed, "Oh, yes. I have more, what is it you Americans like to say, 'Fish to fry' than taking my revenge."

He lay a number of tools on a small table which he drug, banging and bouncing across the floor, to rest in front of Jack.

He picked up a hammer. "For the joints."

Returning the hammer to the table he lifted a small saw. "For between the joints."

He next picked up a clothes-iron. "To cauterize the wounds. Can't have you bleeding to death. We will begin just as soon as I return."

Trying to appear brave Jack asked as cordially as he could, "You didn't say what the electric drill was for."

Batesh sneered at him. "For the fun of it, of course."

Jack felt sick. He wanted to burst out in tears but refused to give Batesh the satisfaction.

"I will leave a few of my men to keep you company, Jack. Feel free to, what is the phrase you kids use? Ah yes! To hang out, until I return."

Batesh strode to the brown door laughing maniacally. Opening it, he called for someone inside the office. A man joined Batesh in the doorway. Jack recognized him immediately. His leg was bandaged with sports wraps over the outside of his pant leg. To help him walk, he was using a mop handle. This was the man he'd kicked in the kneecap before he was captured.

The two men began shouting at each other. Batesh reached into his jacket and produced a pistol. He waved it in Jack's general direction then pressed it against the man's forehead. Both Jack and the man got Batesh's point. If anything happened to Jack while Batesh was away, the man's life would be forfeit. That fact was information Jack determined to use to his advantage.

Seconds later, Jack heard car doors opening and slamming outside. Engines roared into life and tires crunched in the slush. Batesh was gone … for now.

Jack's mind blazed with everything he tried to learn about military tactics for Escape and Evasion, or E-and-E. He knew that opportunities to escape presented themselves in two ways. The first was the result of meticulous planning. That took weeks, even months to prepare and Jack knew he didn't have that kind of time.

That left the second method of escape, watching for any opportunity to get free, no matter how slim, then taking daring, foolhardy risks to exploit it. That was his best option, he decided, because if he was still a prisoner when Batesh returned, he would be one dead kid soon after.

The worst that could happen is that I'll die before Batesh gets his chance to torture me.

Jack called to the man at the far end of the warehouse, using his most taunting and juvenile voice, hoping to force an opportunity to present itself by engaging with this man who hated him, "What's your name? Or should I just call you gimpy?"

"Don't speak to me, dog."

"It's Jack. Not dog. But hey, it's all good. I get it, you being mad about a little kid like me taking you out."

Jack watched the man's face twitch as his anger was building.

"Look," Jack said, trying to keep up the pressure, "I am sorry about your leg and all. You know how it is, kill or be killed, right? So…no hard feelings?"

The man clomped over, his mop handle tapping out his hurried steps. He stopped in front of Jack.

"I sure do hope," Jack teased, "that leg of yours isn't going to keep you from going out and playing with your friends later. I mean, they did have to leave you behind this time. Right?"

Jack shook his head pityingly. "It'd be a real shame if you had to miss out on all the fun."

"If Qasim didn't have need of you," the man growled through a heavy accent, "I'd be killing you right now. Very slow. Very painful."

In a swift and vicious movement, the man flicked his wooden pole up. Loud as a firecracker, it slapped against the bottom of Jack's bare foot.

Stars exploded in Jack's eyes. He didn't want to give the man the small victory of hearing him cry out, but he couldn't help himself and screamed at the top of his lungs. The tears welling in his eyes and rolling down his cheeks were impossible to stop.

Still, he refused to relent. Speaking with contempt he taunted, "Go ahead! Hit me again! Now that I'm tied up and can't fight back, you're safe."

The man glared up at him. Jack glowered back and spat, "Coward!"

The mop handle flew up again, smacking the sole of the other foot. Jack screamed.

The man spun away and limped toward the door leading out of the work area.

"Hey?" Jack called putting all his might into keeping his voice steady. "Where you going? We were just getting to know each other!"

"If I stay here I'll kill you, Qasim's orders or no. Then, he'll kill me. Better I go smoke."

"Well that didn't work out like I planned," Jack said to himself after the door shut behind his guard. Muttering to his now vanished guard, "You were supposed to get so mad you knocked me off this stupid pole."

He hung limp, though it burned into his shoulders, and focused on gathering his composure.

"But I'm alone," he said, still talking aloud to himself. "Come on, Jack! Think! Make the most of it!"

Before anything else could happen, he had to get out of hanging on a pole like yesterday's laundry. Straining his neck to the left and right Jack surveyed the problem in greater detail.

Two lengths of chain, bolted to metal girders in the ceiling, hung down on his left and right. The pole, at either end, had U-shaped brackets welded to it. Large S-hooks were threaded through both the ends of the chain and the U-brackets. In the name of efficiency, somebody took a pair of pliers and clamped the openings of the S-hooks shut.

Pressing his hand hard into his torso, Jack raised himself as high as he could. With a sudden thrust of his legs up toward his chest, he tried to throw himself up into the air.

He flew up just over a foot, then crashed back down. The chains clanged. His shoulders wrenched behind him and Jack thought they were going to rip off his body. One of the S-hooks looked like it may have opened a fraction, but not enough for Jack to be sure. The other looked no different.

The door leading from the offices to the work area burst open.

"What is going on in here?" Jack's guard demanded limping over to inspect his prisoner.

Jack wriggled on his pole. "Believe it or not, this isn't the most comfortable position to be in."

The guard grinned with sadistic happiness.

"You could let me down for a second," Jack suggested. "Maybe let me use the bathroom?"

"Wet your pants," the man sneered.

Jack narrowed his eye into angry slits. "If I knew for sure you would be the one Batesh would make mop it up, I would."

The guard turned away and stumped back the way he came, muttering foul curses in his native language.

"Smoke one for me!" Jack yelled at him as the door closed.

Jack began sliding down the pole toward the hook he thought opened by inching his arm across the bar then dragging his body after it. Making progress was slow, painful work that shaved skin off his arms and back, but it put more weight on that one hook.

Cringing against the pain he knew was coming, Jack threw himself into the air again. He wasn't disappointed. If anything, it hurt worse now that he was off center, but the hook definitely opened more.

Not caring about the pain, urged on by his success, Jack hurled himself up with all his strength. With a mighty crash, his weight fell across the pole. The hook sheared in half.

As the end of the pole dropped Jack found himself sliding off like a chicken off a spit. The U-bracket sliced into his side and twisted the other end of the pole against that end's S-hook so violently it, too, ripped in half.

Clanging like a church bell, the pole clattered to the ground next to Jack.

Within seconds the office door was torn open. "If you can't keep quiet I'll make you quiet!" the man yelled.

He froze in the doorway staring at Jack, who was struggling to rise up off the floor. Moving as fast as his damaged leg allowed, he came for Jack, brandishing his mop handle.

Jack lunged at the table where Batesh had laid out his torturers tools and grabbed the heavy mallet. With his hands still tied together, he had to hold it with both hands.

With a series of limps and hops, the guard closed in. He swung the mop handle like a baseball bat.

Jack lifted the hammer to block the blow. The stick went underneath the head of the hammer and slammed against Jack's fingers. If it weren't for the two-handed grip he was forced to maintain, he would have dropped his weapon.

Jack twisted a quarter of a turn and lashed out with a side kick aimed at the man's bad leg. He managed a glancing blow but, on top of the damage he'd caused earlier, the feeble hit was enough. The man crumpled to the floor.

Jack swung the tiny mallet like a sledge hammer. It caught the man square on the jaw and he flipped onto his back where he lay unconscious.

Pitching the hammer away from him, Jack raced back the table and snatched up the saw. Falling onto his rear end, he squeezed the saw, teeth up, between his knees and began moving his wrists over the blade in piston-like motions. Several times he nicked his own flesh. The chords were drenched with his blood, but Jack didn't stop. He was almost free!

The sounds of car doors opening and slamming hit his ears and made him stop his work. His heart lunged into his throat and made him hold his breath. Batesh and his thugs had returned.

CHAPTER 22

Jack became reckless in his efforts. Rope. Flesh. It didn't matter what was being cut. He had to get free!

The instant his bonds snapped, Jack scrambled out to the center of the room where his coat, socks and boots were piled. He scooped them up into his bloody arms and dove into an enormous heap of discarded curtains and scrap fabric behind large metal barrels marked "Industrial Cleaning Solvent. Highly Flammable."

As he was pulling on his boots, a commotion started roaring out of the offices.

"You betrayed us!" Batesh was screaming in English.

"It wasn't us," an American voice answered just as angry. "One of your people had to of talked!"

Jack scanned the workroom even as he listened. Escape was much more important than whatever was going on in there.

The first thing he saw was that street access for the work room was provided by three large garage doors where trucks pulled in and out. Heavy chains and padlocks on those doors eliminated them from being potential exits. That left going out the office, which was filled with enemies, or the windows, which were high up, close to the ceiling. The only way to reach them would be by positioning the aluminum ladder Batesh used beneath one of them. Jack knew that the instant he began to move that contraption the noise would alert his captors.

He needed a distraction.

"No! No! No, my friend!" he heard Batesh yelling. "Your FBI was there waiting for us. They knew we were coming. You! You sold us out to them!"

Jack asked himself if their argument would be enough to cover him. He decided it wasn't. The ladder would be so crazy-loud that Batesh couldn't help but hear it, no matter how heated his argument became.

He ran to the workbench and took a quick inventory. There had to be something here he could use!

Screw drivers. Glue guns. Various pieces of wire. String. An assortment of batteries, nuts, and bolts.

"THINK!" he snapped at himself.

He turned and scanned the room. His gaze fell on the barrels marked "Highly Flammable," and knew what he was going to do.

He snatched a 9-volt battery off the workbench and pressed it to his tongue. Dead.

Grabbing another he performed the same test. A jolt of electricity buzzed through his mouth. He did the same thing twice more and found he had three charged batteries.

Racing over to the pile of cloth, he pried the lid off one drum of solvent and tipped it over, making sure the liquid was spilling out onto the pile. He opened the remaining barrels. Acidic fumes burned in his nose and eyes.

Back at the workbench, he took three lengths of copper wire and wrapped it around each battery's positive and negative terminals, overloading the battery. With a triumphant smile, he felt the wires begin to grow hot.

Being careful not to break the connections he'd made on the batteries, he laid the heating copper wires against the chemical doused trash. It started to smoke.

Reclaiming the mallet to use for battering the window open, he donned his coat and began moving the wailing ladder.

The heap of rags began to smolder.

As he expected, the sound of the ladder's movements alerted Batesh and his men. They began pouring into the workroom. Jack was the first thing they caught sight of and bounded after him.

Jack scrambled up the ladder, two terrorists at his heels.

He pounded the glass out of the window like a maniac.

They were almost upon him.

Leaping out toward the window, he gave the ladder a mighty shove, attempting to knock it over. He failed and one of the men had him by the boot.

The workroom erupted with heat and fire. The cloth burst into flames, which ignited the fumes from the solvent. A massive explosion of chemicals did what Jack couldn't and the aluminum staircase teetered before crashing to the floor.

It also blew Jack the rest of the way out of the window. He fell twelve feet to the frozen ground outside and landed with a sickening thump. His head was reeling, his ears ringing. Making it to his feet he managed a few steps before falling back to his knees.

He was free, but spent. He had to move, but his body refused to budge.

Peter scooped him into his arms. "I got you, buddy. Let's get outta here!"

Dazed, Jack smiled up at him. "Where did you come from?"

"We can catch up later," Peter snapped. "Right now, we need to run! Come on Jack! Get up!"

They stumbled away from the shop as more flames billowed out the windows. Fire engines could be heard in the distance and Jack was thankful for them. Just like Jack, Batesh and his men had to escape capture which meant they couldn't waste time searching for him.

Aware that he was being carried by Peter more than being assisted, Jack pushed his legs as hard as he could. The farther away he got from Batesh's clutches, the better and more energized he felt. The night was still bitterly cold and the wind howled like a pack of werewolves but, compared to being beaten and the very real prospect of being tortured to death, the chill felt more invigorating than defeating.

Peter led him through meandering streets and into a broad street neighborhood where the houses were all well cared for. Stopping at a chain-link fence surrounding a manicured lawn, Peter whispered, "Think you can hop it?"

"I'd have to be a lot worse off than this not to be able to hop a five-foot fence," Jack quipped, keeping his voice just as low as Peter's. "But why are we going in there?"

Peter pointed to a child's play house nestled in a back corner of the yard. "That's where we agreed to rendezvous. Phil and Collin took up positions to cover our getaway in case we needed help."

A firetruck siren whined in the distance. Peter smiled. "But you saw to that on your own. How did you manage it?"

"I'll explain when the others get here," Jack said, hating telling the same story over and over just because not everyone was present the first time.

They crossed the yard sticking to shadows. Entering the little dollhouse, Peter chuckled, "It ain't much, but it's home. For now."

Jack settled down onto the floor and leaned against the rough plywood. Now out of the wind, it felt almost cozy to sit and rest and not be terrified.

The sound of boots thumping into the snow outside made Jack react. He leapt up, feet apart, hands raised and ready to fight.

"That'd be Phil and Collin," Peter reassured him, eyeing Jack with concern.

"Oh, Jack," Phil cried, throwing her arms around him the instant she laid eyes on him.

Jack eyed the other two, his face twisted in an awkward grin. "If you plan on hugging me too, do it now and get it over with."

"I'm good," Collin said. His trademark deadpan tone and expression felt like a warm blanket on a cold night. Peter raised his hands and, smiling, waved the suggestion off as well.

Phil broke her embrace with Jack and gave him a playful shove in the chest before wiping her eyes with the fingertips of her gloves. "Jerk," she chuckled.

"Oh yeah," Jack drawled. His voice lacked its usual mischievous lilt, but at least he tried.

They spent the next several minutes relating their adventures.

Phil, Collin and Peter ran far enough to be sure they weren't being followed. Using the Find-My-Phone trick, they tracked Batesh and his men to the industrial building. They reconnoitered the area and were desperate in their attempt to come up with a rescue plan when the whole place exploded.

That's where Jack took over and explained how he managed to escape. Collin was impressed with his use of overloaded batteries to start a fire. Praise from Collin was uncommon. Jack didn't know how to take it.

Avoiding it all together, he told them what he'd overheard about the botched meeting where the FBI showed up.

"What I don't get," Peter said, "is why were they at the motel when they had a hideout on the other side of town?"

"Who knows," Collin said. "My guess would be that they didn't want to draw attention to the industrial building by having loads of them hanging around."

Phil smiled proudly. "Well they've got all the attention they can handle, now. Jack saw to that!"

Jack sat silently. First Collin, now Phil was bragging about him. Yesterday it would have made him feel full of himself. Today, his sister was dead and he was beat-up and exhausted. Feeling he didn't deserve kindness, their compliments made him uncomfortable.

"What do we do next?" asked Peter.

Jack struggled to get words past his dry and constricted throat. He rasped, "We go to the police. That was the plan and we stick to it. Besides, now that we know the FBI is on it, it'll be an easier story to sell."

"Guys?" Collin called, breaking the moment. "You'd better come see this."

Huddling around him, he tilted his phone's screen so all could see. "Tell us what we're looking at," Jack ordered.

"They've stopped," Collin said.

"We can all see that, doofus. Stopped where?" snapped Peter.

"Best as I can tell," Collin shifted his weight uncomfortably, "they are at Phil's place."

"At my house?"

Phil shuddered and pinched the collar of her coat tight around her neck. "What for?"

"You can bet nothing good," Peter said.

Phil's face took on a blank, pensive stare. "There'll be nobody home. Mom'll be out with some bozo or other."

"You should call her," Jack suggested.

"No point," Phil whispered. "When she goes out at night, I think she forgets I'm alive. She won't answer."

Her words stung Peter and Collin into silence. Jack, more aware of what Phil's home life was like, said softly, "We'd better get to the police station as fast as we can."

"Why don't we just call the police?" Peter asked.

"Remember what happened the last time I called? By the time we get through to them, get them to take us seriously, explain everything that's happened, we'd have already made it to the station."

Collin interrupted. "They're on the move again."

Peter shouted, "They're up to something! We've got to…"

"What we've got to do is shut up and move!" Jack yelled.

Lights flashed on at the house. "Hey! Who's out there?" a man screamed from the back porch.

Taking off at a run they hurdled the fence and tore down the street.

Sleet began falling in earnest. These were no pretty dancing snowflakes. Needles of ice pricked their exposed skin. Clumps of slush congealed over their shoulders and on their heads.

The streetlights did little more than make a pale white dent in the blizzard. The roads were empty. When cars did pass, they careened down the streets at awkward angles. For some reason, the drivers found it necessary to wail their horns at them.

Having cleared three of the five blocks between where they were and the police station, Collin began yelling at them to stop. They gathered around him and rested their hands on bended knees, panting steam into the frozen night.

"What is it?" asked Phil. She was angry. "You can't tire out on us now. Not now!"

"It's not that," Collin said between puffs. Catching his breath, he finished his report. "They've stopped again."

Jack stiffened. "Where."

Collin looked at Peter who was pacing with his hands locked on top of his head. "Your place."

Peter's hands fell limp to his sides. "My…What?…NO!"

He began stomping his boots into the slush. "No. No! NO!" A flood of profanity flew out of him. He stopped.

"Let me get this straight," he said as if he still didn't understand. "They first went to Phil's. Then to my house? Is that it?"

"Not exactly," Collin said. He swallowed hard still looking at Peter. "They stopped at my house before yours."

Phil wheeled around to face Jack. "You know where they're going next."

Jack filled the air with his own filthy words. Of course he knew.

"Call them!" shouted Phil.

"And tell them what? That their daughter has been murdered and the killers are on their way to the house? They'll never believe it! By the time I convince them to leave home, Batesh will already be there!"

"But Jack," argued Collin, "you've got to try!"

As much as it hurt Jack not to make that call, it would waste time they didn't have to lose and accomplish nothing.

"No. Move!" he shouted.

They ran faster than they ever had. Each one of them, at some point, slipped and fell hard onto the frozen concrete. Ignoring the pain, the one who had fallen scrambled to their feet and caught up to the others. They didn't slow their pace until they slid to a stop on the corner diagonally across from the big, boxy police station.

"Where now?" Jack wheezed at Collin. The half sentence was all his burnt-out lungs could manage.

To his relief, he saw that Collin understood he was asking for an update on Batesh's position and huffed back, "Your place."

"Let's go," Jack said taking a step off the curb.

His phone rang.

He looked at the others. Carefully, as if it might blow up in his hand, Jack eased his phone out of his pocket.

Looking at the screen, the Caller-ID read MOM.

He slid the answer bar sideways and pressed the button placing the phone on speaker. "Hello?"

"Hello again, Jack. You know, of course, who this is?"

"Batesh," Jack growled.

Phil, Collin, and Peter turned to stone. They were so scared of what Batesh was going to say that they didn't so much as dare breathing.

"And you know where I am, don't you?"

"Yes."

"Of course you do. See, I wondered how you found us at the motel. We searched and discovered your little toy. Very ingenious."

"What do you want," Jack demanded.

All the cloying courtesy drained out of Batesh's voice. "What I have always wanted," he snarled. "Kalila. You will bring her to me. Here. At your home. Jack? You will bring her to me or your parent's will die."

"No! You can't! Kelly...Kalila... she's gone. She left with her mother before we arrived at the motel."

"I hope that is not true, Jack. Because if you do not arrive within the hour, with Kalila, Mommy and Daddy die. Do you understand?"

"No! It is true. She's gone."

"Then you had better get her back! Hadn't you?"

"I...I can't."

"Shall I start killing now, then? Save some time?"

"NO! I'll...I'll find her. But you have got to give me more time."

The silence ran on so long Jack began to wonder if he had dropped the call. Then Batesh spoke again and all his sickening patronizing was back.

"Very well, Jack. Very well. I will give you another hour. But know, I am a very punctual man. Do you understand?"

"Yes," Jack said. He started to cross the street.

"And one more thing," Batesh said.

Jack pictured a grin of cruel pleasure slithering onto Batesh's evil face.

"If you take one more step toward that police station, I'll slit your parents' throats just like your sister's. Then, I'll have all the mommies and daddies of your little friends throats slashed, too."

"How can he..." Peter started before Phil punched him in the gut.

"Ah, which of your friends was that?" Batesh cooed.

Jack didn't answer.

"Come, come, come. Which one? Tell them to speak."

Jack looked at Peter and shook his head no.

"Answer!" screamed Batesh. "One parent alive is all I need. Answer or I will kill the spare immediately!"

"Peter! This is Peter!"

The mocking civility was back. "Oh, what a good child. You see, Peter, that is what you are. A child. A child who is pretending to play a man's game. We, on the other hand are professionals. It was nothing for us to hack into such a small and backward police department's computers. Their building's cameras are now our eyes. Their radios are our ears."

Phil cursed.

"Tut, tut, tut. No need to speak like that. Now, let me try again. You are, Philomela? Yes?"

Phil said nothing.

In icy tones Batesh repeated himself. "Yes?"

"Yes! Yes, you son of a...," Phil snapped her mouth shut. In quiet resignation she whispered, "Yes."

"Good!" Batesh laughed. "Very good. Now, you had better get moving. Two hours, then I start cutting. Anybody but you arrives, I start shooting."

Batesh hung up.

"Collin," Jack asked, already knowing the answer. "Is what he's saying possible?"

Collin thought for a moment. "This is small-town Kansas, Jack, not DC or Chicago. If they've got a decent hacker on their team, I'd have to say yeah, it's possible."

CHAPTER 23

"We have got to do something. Come up with a plan," Jack said. The panic in his voice was clear for all his friends to hear. He tried to smooth it out, but couldn't control it.

"Jack," Phil said softly, "maybe we should still go to the police. Tell them what has been happening. I mean, for all we know Batesh is just guessing at where we are."

Jack's mind swam in confusion. Self-doubt, his worst enemy, had its talons skewered into him deeply. The more he thought about his role in everything that was happening to him and his friends, the more catatonic he became. As if flicked by a light switch, that paralyzing terror popped into being white hot anger.

"We can't," Jack exploded. "Even if Batesh is guessing, by the time we get the police to take us seriously, convince them that we are not making this stuff up, which they'll have to verify with some kind of evidence; by the time they get their act together and get S.W.A.T teams mobilized; by the time the feds get brought up to speed, our time will be up. Mom and Dad will be..."

He couldn't finish that sentence and let out an exasperated growl.

"But we have evidence," Peter blurted out. "We have a dead body. All we got to do is lead them to it and..."

"That body is not some 'it'! She is...was...my sister!" yelled Jack.

Peter squirmed, blushing at his own insensitivity. "I know, Jack. I just meant that we do have proof. The police won't be able to blow us off. Not with evidence like that."

Collin spoke up. "But that'll take time, Peter. Time Batesh didn't give us. He might be a lot of things, but stupid isn't one of them. He has to know we'd consider going to the cops no matter what he said, so he fixed things to make time work against us."

"Phil?" Jack asked. Her opinion was always the most important to him.

She swore in reply. She swore using words they seldom, if ever, heard fall from her lips, pacing back and forth with her fists beating the air.

Regaining her self-control, she stoppered her torrent of foul words. "The smartest thing for us to do is go to the police but if we do, everyone's parents are guaranteed to die. The dumbest thing we could do is to try and mount a rescue on our own. Most likely we will all die in the attempt but, however thin, it's the only chance of saving any of our parents' lives."

"Exactly," Jack said as if that ended the debate.

"Jack," Phil said cautiously. "The chance of our succeeding is practically zero."

"I'll take practically zero over a guaranteed zero any day," he answered in cold desperation.

As far as he was concerned he had no choice, he had to try and save his parents even if it cost him his own life. But what about their lives?

No. That price was too high to pay.

"Look," Jack said, "there's no reason we can't do both. I don't have a choice. I have got to save my parents if I can. You three do have a choice. Go to the police. Get them moving. Maybe if they know what I'm about to try they will move faster. Or maybe I can slow Batesh down."

Their glum expressions turned hard.

"No way," Collin said.

"Not going to happen," added Peter.

"Besides," Collin said, "Batesh's clowns are at all of our houses, too. Even if the cops storm one house, bad things will happen at the others. We're all in the same boat."

Phil didn't say anything. She didn't have to. The look on her face made him feel like an idiot for even suggesting they abandon him.

"I have to try," Jack said lowering his eyes in apology for where he was about to lead them.

He knew trying to talk them out of coming with him was useless. He also knew it would be the death of all of them.

"I've already lost Grace. I'm going to lose Mom and Dad, too. I can feel it. Losing all of you?" He swallowed hard, trying to get rid of the lump in his throat. It wouldn't go away and he couldn't manage speaking around it.

The decision was made in silent agreement. They were either all going to the police or they were all going on a rescue mission. No third option existed.

"I have no choice," Jack repeated softly. Apologetically.

For a brief instant he considered changing his mind, leading them to the police no matter what the consequences.

Then the memory of Grace dying as he held her in his arms, the sound of her last breath, burst into his mind. He felt sick. How could he abandon his parents to the same fate she suffered?

The conflict between love for his family and love for his friends locked him up like a computer running bad code.

Phil came to his rescue. "So that's that."

"Yeah," agreed Collin, "but we can't just show up with our hands in our pockets. We need weapons if we are going to do this."

"I know where some guns might be, but I don't know how we could get them," Peter said looking at his snow boots as if regretting speaking at all.

Everyone stared at him astounded.

"Where?" asked Jack with renewed intensity.

Peter's words were a life preserver. Jack wanted to act, not feel. Peter's knowledge of where the tools could be found to take action against those who had wounded him so deep gave him something immediate to grab on to. It gave him relief from the suffering and horror of the past several hours and from being terrified over what the future might bring.

Any action was better than taking no action at all. Even if the action he took was the wrong thing to do, it had to be better than standing around feeling worthless.

Now they needed weapons. That was the next hurdle. Putting all his focus on getting past that immediate problem left no room for fear or regret. Jack dedicated himself to the moment. Now was all that existed for him.

"Well…" Peter hesitated, not looking at any of them and keeping his eyes down.

"Go on," encouraged Phil.

"So, Jenny's brothers. Rumor is, and it's only a rumor, but…Jenny's brothers. Somehow they got their hands on some of those weapons that went missing in South America some time back."

"I remember reading about that," Collin said. "Losing those guns was quite a scandal for the U. S."

Peter went on, ignoring Collin's current-events-trivia. "Jenny's brothers are selling them on the street to the newcomers in town. I don't know where they get them."

"Do you think they keep them at their house?" Jack asked.

"I think so," Peter said. "I was over at her house and managed to see that their door was fitted with a padlock. It's locked up tight whenever they are not there."

"You were at their house?" Phil asked.

Peter blushed and grinned.

Jack bristled. "Now's not the time for gossip, Phil."

"Anytime is good for gossip," Phil shot back, "but that isn't what I was getting at.

"Peter, you said Jenny doesn't get along with her brothers. How do you think they feel about her?"

Peter's eyes narrowed and his head cocked to one side as he considered that question. "It's weird. They want nothing to do with her. They insult her. Threaten her about keeping out of their business. Stuff like that.

"But the other day, they cornered me on my way to morning swim practice. Told me that if I didn't treat Jenny right they'd take care of me. That I'd disappear and no one would ever find me."

"They threatened to kill you?" Collin asked in shock.

"Yeah!" Peter sneered dismissively, as if being threatened with murder was as common as breakfast. "All gangster-like."

"So they do care about her," Phil said to no one in particular. "And your being at their house wouldn't be all that unusual." Her eyebrows knit together for a moment as she made a humming sound.

"What's going on inside that head of yours?" asked Jack.

"I've got an idea. It's a very bad idea and needs fleshing out. And Peter? I'm sorry."

"Sorry for what?" asked Peter.

"When you hear my idea, you'll know."

Feeling the pressure of time, Jack snapped, "Out with it!"

After listening to Phil's strategy, Peter hissed out a single, filthy word.

"I'm sorry," she whispered again.

"No," Peter said as his body slumped. "It's a good play. As good as any. We need to get armed fast and I don't see any other way to do it."

"If that's the way we go," Collin said in his most emotionless tones, "we should do it fast. At their house. Smash-and-grab."

"The best we can hope for is that Jenny's brothers are out. Then all we have to do is bust into their room and take whatever we want. If they are home, I have a trick in mind. It's a huge bluff and if they call it, we are done. We'll need to stop at the office supply store one block over, first."

As they made their way there, Collin elaborated on his idea. He wasn't kidding when he said it was a huge bluff. The more Jack heard, the less he liked it. It did have one appealing point. Collin's approach would be less violent than what they'd otherwise have to do.

Jack pondered Collin's assessment. The best case would be that no one would be home. Then they could break in, steal what they needed, and leg it. Luck hadn't been that kind to him lately and he doubted it was going to change for this.

His fallback was the original plan; break in, overpower Jenny's brothers, then take what they wanted, and bolt. That plan could get messy quick. It would be loud, aggressive, and brutal, none of which he had time for, given what was at stake.

If this hair-brained scheme of Collin's worked, all that might be avoided. Then again it might not. Deep down, he suspected they'd have to resort to violence.

His brain was so filled with Collin's outlandish scheme that he was oblivious to the progress he made towards the store until they arrived. As if dropped from the sky, he found himself standing outside, using the building as shelter against the icy wind.

"Phil?" Jack said after Peter and Collin went inside to grab what they needed. His voice was as cold and grim as the weather.

Her words steamed in the winter night's chill. "I know, Jack," she whispered.

She was rolling her head from side to side, loosening up her neck muscles. Her eyes were locked onto a frozen lump of filth which had dislodged itself from under some car's wheel well. She had reached the same conclusion as he and was gearing her mind up for a fight.

He left her to it.

"Did you get what you needed?" Jack asked when Collin and Peter returned.

"Yep," said Collin, holding up a fat cylinder which looked like an ordinary pen. "We didn't have enough money for it though."

"Nobody saw us," objected Peter in a rush, as if that made their theft acceptable.

"The cameras saw us," Collin said. "but I don't think anyone was watching. When those tapes get reviewed, we're busted."

Peter laughed that possibility off. "Nobody's gonna watch that video unless something major happens at the store, not petty shop-lifting."

Collin hissed out an exasperated sigh. He explained the situation to Peter as if he were speaking to a toddler. "After tonight, our movements are going to be traced back. Every step of the way back. We are busted. It's just a matter of time."

Peter shrugged and grinned. He had the ability to put ugly situations out of his mind, even when he knew they were coming straight for him like a mother grizzly defending her cubs. Of course, once he was in the thick of things he suffered, same as anyone would. However, once the mauling was over, he could put it out of mind like it never happened. Jack envied him.

"What's wrong with her?" Peter asked, inclining his head toward Phil and breaking Jack's train of thought. She had kept her distance after their return and her focus remained on the icy sludge ball.

"What do you think is going to happen if this plan doesn't work?" Jack asked, letting the annoyance he felt over Peter's lack of foresight, the very thing he was just envious of, sound loud and clear in his voice.

"It'll work," Peter said.

"But if it doesn't?" Jack insisted.

Peter cocked his head and peered at Phil out of the corner of his eyes. He exhaled out his nose forcing steam to shoot out his nostrils like a cartoon bull. Jack nodded his head approvingly. Peter got the message and started putting his own mind into fight mode.

"We better get moving," Collin said. It hit Jack hard that Collin knew of the potential for violence in his plan from the very beginning. He was letting the rest of them cotton on in their own good time.

Trudging through the wintery mix of sleet, ice, and snow, they made their way to Jenny's house. Every passing car, every bump in the night, startled Jack. Fear and guilt filled him with the paranoid sense that the entire town knew that he and his friends were up to something. He kept his teeth clamped together, struggling to keep his fear and doubt invisible to the others.

Their target left a couple of blocks to cover, but to Jack it seemed to be a journey of a thousand miles. He kept looking at the clock on his phone, amazed at how slow time seemed to be passing. It felt like they had been walking for hours. The truth was, only a handful minutes had passed.

All the things that could go wrong with this plan, which summed up to a great many, weighed heavy on him. The tension had him dripping with sweat despite the freezing temperature. A bitter taste rose from the back of his throat and scorched his tongue. Not so much butterflies as pterodactyls were racing around in his guts.

An excited rush of words barreled out of Jack's mouth as soon as they arrived. "Collin, this op was your idea, so you get the job of making it happen. Take position somewhere out of sight. Wait for my signal then…well…we'll see if this crazy plan of yours and Phil's works."

Collin nodded in stoic agreement.

"Phil? I want you visible. Across the street. Under that streetlamp. You're the cavalry. If Peter and I need help, you come running. If they make a dash for Collin and manage to get past us you've got to stop them."

"Right," she said grimly. With a slow and purposeful stride, she went to assume her post. She didn't need to hear anything more and Jack knew he could count on her to do whatever needed to be done. Her self-confidence paired with his unquestioning trust in her bolstered his dismal outlook.

"Peter? You get the worst of it. Jenny knows you, so you have to be the one to lure her out of the house. Then, get her to call her brothers out if they are home. I'm still hoping they're not.

If they aren't there, all three of us will go get what we came for. If they are home, I'll go inside and force them to hand over the weapons."

"Alone?" asked Peter.

"Yes. Alone. You'll need to keep Jenny under control and an eye out for her parents."

"Her parents never get home until after ten. It's eight thirty now," Peter said. "I think I should go with you. What if they try something?"

"That's why you can't come. They need to believe Jenny is in danger the whole time. We need them to weigh everything they do against that threat."

"Gotcha, Jack. I'll keep things under control outside."

Jack grunted his approval.

"Let's get this over with," he said.

Collin trotted off and hid behind a tree trunk coated in thick ice. He chose a spot far enough away from Phil so that anyone looking at her would not see him while at the same time was close enough to her to ensure that she would be able to cut off anyone leaving the house and going for him.

Seeing that he was settled into position, Jack led Peter across the road and climbed onto the porch. Reaching into the porch lamp, he unscrewed the light bulb and set it into a towel covered flower box beneath a large window.

"This sucks," Peter muttered after Jack rang the doorbell.

Jack withdrew into the deeper shadows of the porch. "I know. I'm sorry."

From behind the door, Jenny's voice challenged them.

"Jenny?" Peter called back. His voice cracked. He coughed to clear his throat. Not sounding much steadier he said, "It's me. Peter? I need to talk to you. It's kinda important. Can you grab your coat and come out onto the porch for a sec?"

Deadbolts clicked. A chain lock rattled. The door made a sucking noise as Jenny pulled it open, one arm already inside her white down jacket. She looked confused but not unhappy to see Peter.

"What's up, Pete?" she asked pleasantly.

"Yeah," someone called from inside, "What's up...Lover-Boy?"

The brothers were home. Jack swallowed against making an audible groan.

"Shut up, jerks," Jenny yelled over her shoulder. Two voices erupted in laughter. "And grow up while you're at it!" She yanked the door shut.

"Okay, Pete, what's this all about?" she asked less happy than before, still miffed at her brothers.

"You know my friend, Jack? From school?" Peter asked.

Jack stepped out of the shadows into what dim light reached the porch from the street. His heavy snow boots scrapped over the porch boards. Startled, Jenny spun round and edged close against Peter.

CHAPTER 24

"What's going on, Pete?" Jenny asked, keeping her suspicious gaze clamped onto Jack.

He didn't give Peter a chance to respond. If he could spare him any further pain over betraying Jenny, he would. His hard, cold eyes bored straight back into Jenny's. "I need to talk to your brothers."

"No!" Jenny said loudly. "Peter? No! You know I don't have anything to do with whatever those two are into. Now, I want both of you to leave."

"We can't," Peter said. The regret sounding in his voice was obvious.

"Yes, you can, Peter," Jenny pleaded.

The tension on the porch felt like sand trapped in the waistband of Jack's pants. Jenny felt it too. Tears were pooling in her eyes. "Peter! Please! Don't do whatever this is."

"We have to," Jack said. His voice held none of the remorse Peter's was so thick with. "I need to talk to them. Now."

"Who do you think you are?" Jenny blasted at Jack. Her eyes flashed and her face flushed purple. She took a threatening step toward Jack, but Peter threw an arm into her path. Shocked and hurt, she stared at him.

Jack answered, as if her distress was meaningless. "I'm the guy who is going to talk to your brothers. Either you call them out here, now, or I will."

Jenny turned back toward him. Her expression of pain was replaced by one of loathing. She was blaming him for this, not Peter. Jack was fine with that.

Turning she shoved open the door. "Tom? Bill? I need you out here."

Perhaps it was the word 'need.' Maybe it was the clear sound of distress in her voice. Whatever the case, her call triggered an instant response from inside and her brothers bounded to the door.

Peter failed to mention the boys were twins. Jack felt he should have known that already, living in a town as small as theirs. Now wasn't the time to waste thinking about it.

They were lean and lanky boys in their early twenties. Neither was able to grow a proper beard but they both had scruffy attempts bristling under their noses and out of their chins. Patches of soft fuzz dotted their cheeks. They shared Jenny's frizzy blond curls except theirs were less well kempt and greasy.

Tough and scrappy looking, Jack could see them putting up a difficult fight if things went wrong. It was a fight he was confident he would win and that was all that mattered.

"What's going on out here?" the first one out the door asked as the other skulked alongside. Both were puffed up and ready to start throwing punches.

"We need more weapons. Rumor is that you are the two in town to talk to," Jack said without preamble.

He hadn't raised his voice. He didn't need to. Sounding harsh and stern, his words were leaden with authority, expecting his demands to be followed. The brothers were unnerved, but recovered quickly.

"Get lost," one said with a sneer.

"Not going to happen."

The other took a menacing step forward. Before he could take another, the first hooked his hand into the crook of his brother's elbow, pulling him back. "Just what do you mean, more weapons?"

"We've just the one," Jack said casually, as if discussing his favorite hamburger. "It's nice though. Came all tricked out. Bipod. Extended capacity magazines. Even has a laser sight."

Jack raised his hand and waved. The two brothers jerked their heads around until they caught sight of Phil.

"That your shooter?" one asked. "I don't see no gun."

"No. That's just extra help if we need it. But I don't think we will. Do you?" Jack pointed to a small red dot that appeared on one of the porch pillars. Like a nasty spider, the dot crawled over the pillar and across the winter protected porch furniture.

The twin's eyes were glued to it as it made slow progress. It passed over Peter and came to rest over Jenny's left breast. She gasped and tried to duck away. Peter threw his arm around her and held her in place.

Tom and Bill looked at Peter in disbelief. Their expressions, when they turned back to face Jack, were filled with pure hatred. He was in charge. He was to blame. He would be the one to pay.

"We are going to kill you," one said. The other nodded in agreement.

"Get in line," Jack said dismissively.

They bristled and shifted weight from foot to foot but, looking back at the red bead drawn on their sister, did nothing.

Jack began speaking calmly, as if hostage taking was part of his everyday routine. "The three of us are going to wherever it is you've stashed the guns. I don't think I need to tell you what will happen if either of you get stupid?"

Tom and Bill sputtered, but said nothing intelligible. Jack took that to mean they understood. He gestured, indicating they were to lead the way inside. To his amazement, they did. So far, the plan was working.

Jack was surprised to see just how ordinary the house looked. He wasn't sure what he expected to find inside, but bright colors, clean and polished furniture, and well-dusted knickknacks were not it. The boys, however, shared the third-floor attic that had been converted into a bedroom and the more stairs they climbed, the more the cheerfulness of house faded, becoming dingy and sinister.

Reaching the top of the second flight of stairs they went single file down a narrow and dim-lit hall. It terminated at their bedroom door which, just as Peter had described, was fitted with a heavy padlock. The brothers halted.

"Open it," Jack insisted.

"I don't have the key," Bill said. Dangerous sarcasm dropped off his voice.

"Me neither," Tom said nastily. "What you gonna do now?"

They turned on Jack menacingly. Without hesitation, Jack pivoted on his toes. Cocking his knee, he lashed out with a lightning-fast side kick.

His booted foot rammed into Tom's chest. He tumbled back into Bill and both slammed against the door. The wood made a terrible cracking noise but the door held.

Working like a trampoline, the door rebounded the twins back toward Jack. Staggering, trying to keep their balance, they clawed at the wallpaper, tearing strips off with their fingernails as they fell.

Jack cracked off a second kick into Tom. The force of his blow caused an abrupt change in the direction Tom was falling. For a second time, Tom smashed into Bill as he careened away from Jack and into the door.

The wooden door splintered as they crashed through it. A jagged chunk of it tore away and hung at an awkward angle on the padlock's latch. What remained intact creaked open. The twins lay in a tangle of arms and legs on the floor.

"You all right, Jack?" Peter yelled from below.

"I'm fine. Keep watch. If I'm not down in five minutes…" Jack let the sentence finish itself.

"I understand," Peter said.

Jack rounded on the brothers. "That was stupid. Now you have five minutes. It will take me much longer than that to tear this place apart looking for wherever it is you have the guns stashed. But know this: No matter how things go from here on, I've no intention of calling off my shooter until I have them."

Tom crawled across the floor and propped himself against the far wall, clutching his chest and gasping for air.

"Looks like it's all on you," Jack said to the other brother.

Fuming with anger and disgust, Bill lurched across the room and, reaching under one of the beds, pulled out a solid wood footlocker. He fiddled with the combination lock for a moment then jerked it down. With a violent twist, he wrenched the lock off the box and threw the lid back before going to stand next to his brother. "There, jerk! See for yourself!"

Jack came up beside him and peered into the empty chest. He had to grit his teeth to keep from throwing up. "You think this is some kind of joke?" he snarled, knowing it was all too real.

Tom grumbled something nasty. The effort made him start coughing.

Jack reached into the empty box, feeling for a false bottom. There was none.

"They're gone," the wounded twin wheezed.

"Gone where?"

Bill laughed at him. "What do you think we are? A department store with some kind of customer loyalty program? We sold them. Don't know to who. Don't care. All that mattered was that they paid."

Tom, still on the floor clutching his ribs, glared at Jack. "So now you know. Let Jenny go and get out of our house."

"Why didn't you just tell me you didn't have them anymore?"

"Like you'd have believed us," Bill said.

He was right. Jack wouldn't have believed them.

"Downstairs. Now!" Jack ordered.

As soon as Jack's feet cleared the bottom step, Peter was shouting questions from the porch.

"Get in here and find something to tie these idiots up with," was all Jack said.

Peter dashed into the kitchen.

Just as quick, Jenny ran to her wounded brother's side. "What did you do to him?"

As if suddenly remembering where he was, Jack said, "Cracked ribs."

Peter came back, carrying a plastic bag full of zip-ties.

"Bathroom," Jack ordered.

Peter ushered the twins, along with Jenny, into the master bathroom. Tom and Bill were trussed with their hands behind their backs and ankles tight together.

Peter and Jenny were standing side by side but somehow they looked miles apart, as if impassable mountains stood between them. Peter stood slouching and looked pathetic. Jenny was mad enough to crush diamonds between her teeth.

"Jenny," Peter pleaded, "I'm so sorry. As soon as I can, I promise, I'll explain everything."

A sudden, loud slap rang out.

"Yeah, sis!" Bill cheered.

An angry red handprint was beginning to welt on Peter's cheek. Tears shimmered in the corners of his eyes and Jack knew it wasn't from being hit. Peter would never get his chance to explain. Their relationship was dead — another casualty in this war with Batesh.

Collin and Phil arrived just as Peter finished zip-tying Jenny's hands behind her back.

"This was not part of the plan," Collin said from the bathroom doorway.

Jack's lips pressed into a thin line. "It was a bust. No weapons here. Back to the living room. We need to regroup."

Phil and Collin left. Peter gave Jenny a sorrowful and pleading look before he, too, exited the bathroom.

As Jack turned to leave, Bill called out, "We are going to kill you for this. You know that, right?"

Jack's head fell as he turned, keeping his eyes on his feet. "I don't honestly think my friends and I are going to live to see tomorrow. If we do, we will all be in jail."

Jack had to take a moment to collect himself. In his mind, he'd known death was the only way his entanglement with Batesh would end. Saying it out loud somehow made it even more real.

"Believe it or not," he began again, now looking at them, "we all like Jenny. If we somehow manage to survive, as a favor to her, we'll keep our mouths shut about you idiots selling weapons to God knows who. You can use that time to disappear or you can stick around and see what happens. Up to you. But hanging around just to kill us? That'd be stupid. We're already dead."

Jack shut the door behind him and made his way back to the living room.

His friends were sitting in stunned silence on the couch. As soon as she saw him, Phil leapt up and began talking in a rush. "Jack! In less than an hour Batesh is going to kill our parents! We need a new plan!"

"I know, Phil!"

His body ached. The cuts on his back were scabbing to his undershirt and every time he moved they tore open and began bleeding all over again. Every step hurt from where Batesh's man spanked the soles of his feet, but he couldn't keep from pacing. "Options," he demanded as he walked. "Police?"

"No time," Phil said.

"Batesh has the police wired. He'd know the second they respond," Collin added.

"And our parents die sooner," Phil added.

"We have to fight!" Peter shouted. "I won't just roll over and quit on my parents!"

"We've nothing to fight with," Phil said.

Jack's head cocked to the side. "What did you just say?"

Phil stared at him. "I said we've nothing to fight with."

"That's true," Jack said. He nodded his head and pinched his lower lip, returning to his pacing. "Nothing to fight with."

Jack's body grew straight and tall. "That's true ... but they don't know it."

"What are you thinking?" Collin asked.

Jack, more thinking out loud than having an actual plan, started talking. "If we try to get help, our parents die. Guaranteed.

"We can't attack because we've nothing to attack with. But what if ... what if we make such a commotion they think we're attacking them. What if we make them think the entire US Army is attacking them?"

Collin's head nodded. "I see where you're going with this."

"So do I," Phil said, her head bobbing. "Straight into the cemetery."

"It's either that or agree to letting all our parents die," Peter shot back.

"Then let's do it," Phil said.

"Tear this place apart!" Jack ordered. "Find anything that'll make Batesh believe he's being overrun. If we can force him to retreat, we just might save our families."

His friends scattered. Jack sat on the couch and pulled out his phone to work on his part of the plan.

Without knowing why, his mind raced back to what Kelly's mother had said before they parted. "No one wants this life."

After all that's happened, do I still want it?

He knew that he did, but his reasons had changed. Before, he'd been attracted to the heroic glamour he'd seen in the movies. The adventure. The excitement. All fantasy!

He began to see another side he hadn't considered before. As long as people like Oliver and Kelly needed protection from men like Paul Ackerman and Qasim Batesh, he would stand up for them. It came down to picking a side, and he chose Grace's.

It no longer mattered that he had no idea what he was doing. Given all that had happened, he couldn't imagine anyone, no matter how well trained, knowing what to do next. All his heroes? He decided they made it up as they went along. What mattered was that they at least tried to do what was right, and so would he. Even if it meant dying, he was going to do all he could to try and save lives.

He still doubted his capabilities — wondered if he were the right person for the job. But if not him, then who?

He watched his three friends as they darted through the house. It struck Jack hard when he thought about how they all looked to him for leadership. For the first time, he understood what that meant. It wasn't about fame, glory, adventure, excitement, or heroics. It wasn't about always knowing what the right thing to do was, either. Being in charge was about giving all he had to give for *their* sake. Leadership was a debt he owed to the friends who put enough faith in him to follow him, no matter what.

Jack had no misgivings over any of them coming out of this alive. That was no longer the point. Phil, Collin, and Peter were going to follow him because, like him, they knew Batesh had to be stopped and, right here, right now, they were the ones in a position to do it. If they failed, others would get their shot. This chance was theirs and he was going for it, all or nothing.

The first thing he had to do was shore up what he knew to be a terrible plan. Closing his eyes, he pictured the street he grew up on. The neighbors. Their yards. He had no misgivings over what he was about to do. He was going to turn his street into a war zone. Thinking about it, his hatred for Batesh burned deeper still into his soul.

"Score!" Peter chortled, bringing Jack back to himself. "Look what the idiot-twins had in their closet."

Jack grinned at the box of fireworks in Peter's arms.

On cue, Phil came back from the garage carrying a crate of beer bottles. "Molotov Cocktails. A classic!" She shot Jack a sarcastic look of accusation. "What have you been doing, Jack?"

"I've been making us a soundtrack: sirens, gunfire, a few explosions. I could only get a fifteen minute loop but, if Batesh doesn't bolt well under fifteen minutes, length won't matter."

"Jack," she exclaimed, "you're going to have to sneak in and turn on the stereo system before you can pair your phone."

He looked hard at her. "Not me. I'll be knocking on the front door, keeping Batesh and his men distracted."

Her eyebrows knit in confusion. When it dawned on her what he was asking of her, she smiled a wicked grin. "Sweet!"

They were interrupted by a sudden stink coming from the kitchen. Shuffling in, they discovered Collin at work on the stove.

"Whatcha doing there, buddy?" Peter asked.

Collin studied the mess he was cooking. "Jenny's mom is a big gardener. She had loads of potassium nitrate in the garage. Heat that with some sugar until it is the consistency of peanut butter and it has all the makings for smoke bombs. Somebody go grab as many toilet paper tubes as you can find."

Peter

BriNLee

CHAPTER 25

Jack studied the house across the street. Over the driveway hung a basketball hoop. An ice-covered birdbath stood in the front yard. Soft yellow light glowed through lace curtains hanging in the kitchen window. This was Jack's house and everything seemed normal.

Except, it wasn't his house. Not anymore. And things were so far from normal that Jack struggled to believe the past several hours were real.

The reality was that he and his friends were hiding behind a neighbor's hedge. They weren't playing some kid's game, but were planning the daring rescue of hostages being held by bloodthirsty terrorists. Terrorists who were holed up inside that cute little house across the street. The reality was that his mom and dad, along with the parents of all his friends, were the hostages and would be dead before morning. So would he. So would his friends.

Armed with nothing but deception and malice, Jack felt like a disease infecting everything that was good and decent about his neighborhood. Like Batesh, Jack was an abomination.

Attempting to cast off these gloomy thoughts, Jack allowed a shudder to rattle through him. Feeling sorry for himself didn't change the fact that he had a job to do. Self-pity wouldn't free his parents. It couldn't bring Grace back to life.

Lurking in the shadows, covered in cold nervous sweat, he clenched his bare hand around an M80 Firecracker stuffed tennis-ball. His fingers stung from exposure to the winter cold. Squeezing and loosening his grip on the ball kept blood pumping into his hand and prevented it from becoming too stiff. With his friends beside him, Jack was preparing his mind for the assault on that little house across the street.

His house, he reminded himself, but it was such a big lie it hurt to tell, even to himself.

Collin and Peter likewise gripped and re-gripped their gear. Their steamy breath danced in the feeble street light that was trickling in through the leaf-bare hedge. The air was wicked cold. Despite that, Jack watched a bead of anxious sweat roll down Collin's temple and around his face.

Phil alone seemed at ease. She was the farthest away from him, sitting cross-legged in the frozen mulch of the flowerbed they were hiding in. Her position was a tight fit and she had to tuck her knees over her snow booted feet which were pegged behind the bushes' stems. Holding her cellphone in her lap, she looked like a normal teenage girl hanging out with friends.

"You better get out there, Jack," she said while staring through branches at Jack's front door.

"I know," Jack groaned. "It's time. I'll try and stall as best I can. Tell them Kelly has agreed to give herself up once our parents are safe.

"I doubt they'll buy it. Batesh said he will kill all of our parents if we don't hand Kelly over at this meeting. Since we're not doing that, I don't expect this to go well. When I hear the noise begin, I'll charge the house. Remember, the goal is to make them think they are being attacked. Try to get them to retreat. After that … ?"

He didn't honestly believe there would be anything after that, but he went on, "Whatever happens, don't worry about me. It's our parents we have to save.

"Once Phil gets inside, keep an ear out for the fake assault soundtrack. Start setting off the smoke bombs and fireworks. Peter, that's your signal to crash in from the basement. Make it loud. I'll be rushing in through the front. Phil and Collin will have to watch the stairs leading to the second-floor. Do your best to keep pinned down anyone you see coming down.

I'm hoping the first-floor will be too busy with me to notice the rest of you."

"You and me both," Peter whispered.

"Jack," Collin said, "can you send me that audio file?"

"What for?"

"I was just thinking, it might be helpful to have it playing outside as well as in."

Jack's eyebrows drew together in confusion. "How you going to make that happen?"

"I hacked your smart-door not long after your dad installed it."

Phil snorted. "Why am I not surprised?"

"You hacked Jack's doorbell?" Peter repeated.

Collin adjusted his shoulders. It was as close Jack had ever seen him come to showing remorse.

"I hacked all of yours," Collin admitted, then added, "I did mine first, if that makes any difference."

Jack's phone rang in his hand.

Batesh's voice oozed out from the speaker. "Where are you, Jack? Maybe you think I won't kill your parents? Maybe I kill Daddy now, just to show you."

"No! I'm here!" Jack shouted.

"I am looking. I don't see you. I think you're lying."

"No, I am here. I just don't want to get shot the moment you do see me. Turn the porch light on and off a few times. I'll count them and tell you how many times you did it."

"You want to play games? I'll play a game. If you lose, Daddy dies."

Jack's front porch lamp began to pulsate on and off. His heart was thundering so hard in his chest it hurt. The pain made him gasp. The arctic air felt like a knife being plunged into his lungs. Terrified he would miss-count he whispered the numbers aloud.

"Eight," Jack bleated when Batesh demanded his answer.

Batesh kept quiet.

The silence made Jack squirm. That was Batesh's intention — to cause him anguish and suffering; to put him off balance and force him to make a rash mistake. It was psychological torture.

"C'mon. C'mon!" Jack growled looking at his phone making sure he hadn't somehow dropped the call.

"You need to come out so I can see you. And Kalila. I want to see her as well," Batesh said.

Jack didn't answer. It wasn't much, but not giving Batesh the joy of hearing the stress in his voice was the only psychological counter-measure Jack had to play. Hanging up on Batesh, he hastily sent Collin the audio file.

Just as they had planned, Jack jammed earbuds into his ears. He then crept like a thief out from behind the cover of the hedge. Crouching low and keeping to the blackest of shadows, he made his way two houses down before stepping into sight.

Grim and determined, he crossed the street, surrendering to his fate. As he made his way up the sidewalk he fell into the smooth gait of indifference. The heartless cruelty of the past several hours and the conviction that saving his parents was impossible left him numb. A heavy wet snow began falling. He didn't care. He expected to die and didn't care. He wanted this night to be over and soon, it would be.

The memory of Grace dying in his arms kept him company as he walked. Over and over, it played like a video stuck on a permanent loop, projecting onto a screen somewhere just behind his eyes. That horrible image was bright and vivid and clear, and no matter what his eyes took in, that footage refused to be dislodged.

Tears were turning to slush under his eyelids, blurring his vision. He hated Batesh for so many reasons, not the least of which was for those tears.

Sadness and hatred became one big, jumbled mess inside Jack.

Yes, he expected to die tonight. But before he did, he was going to kill Qasim Batesh. He was going to kill him for Grace. He was going to kill him for his parents. He was going to kill Qasim Batesh for all the suffering he caused the world.

Jack's feet turned down the snow-covered walk leading to his front porch. The memory of being a small boy scrawling pathetic chalk drawings on the cement flashed through his mind. He missed that kid as he glared at two terrorists standing on his porch desecrating it with their malice. They smirked at him, relishing in his obvious suffering.

Startled when his phone rang, Jack jerked to a stop.

The terrorists laughed.

The thought of having to hear Batesh's voice again was nauseating. He felt bile building up behind his throat. Answering the call, he forced himself not to throw up.

"Where is Kalila?" Batesh demanded.

Jack kept his mouth shut.

Batesh's voice roared out of his earbuds, "Take your filthy hands out of your pockets and answer my questions. Where is Kalila?"

Jack clenched his teeth so hard his teeth popped. He slipped his left hand out of his pocket, being careful not to accidentally drop his lighter. Slowly, he withdrew his right, leaving the loaded tennis ball inside.

The men on the porch jerked into action, producing concealed handguns and pinning him in their sights. A spate of Arabic burst forth from the house. The men didn't relax, but they didn't shoot him either.

"What game are you playing now, boy?" Batesh bellowed into Jack's earbuds. "Do Mommy and Daddy mean so little to you that you would have me kill them now?"

"How do I know you haven't killed them already?" asked Jack. "For all I know they're dead and you are just waiting for me to deliver Kelly before you kill me, too."

The earbuds were silent. Either Batesh was considering how to reassure him that his parents were still alive, even if they weren't, or he was inside killing them right now in the depth of that silence. Jack had no way of knowing and that ignorance was searing him like a torturer's firebrand.

Batesh laughed. "I will allow you to come as far as the door. From there you can see Mommy and Daddy. But, after you see them, you will have two minutes to produce Kalila or I swear to you they will die."

"If they do, I promise you'll never see Kelly again."

Jack's brain scrambled for his next move. He had no way of knowing whether his mom and dad were still alive or if this was a trap. If they were still alive, their survival depended on what he did next. The weight of that knowledge was soul crushing.

One thing at a time, his brain scolded.

Jack had no good answers for what to do next. A desperate lie was the best he could come up with - one point for Batesh if he saw through it and win for himself if he pulled it off..

"My friends have guns, too. They will shoot anyone who comes near me," Jack said.

"Friends?" roared Batesh. "Friends? You were supposed to come alone. You and Kalila."

Score for Jack.

Forcing himself to appear at ease, Jack stretched a sardonic smile onto his face saying, "If you thought my friends were the kind to just let me walk in here alone, you're a fool."

Laughter trickled into Jack's ears. "Such brave little children," Batesh said. "Go on. Play your games and I? I will play mine. You think I am the fool? Let us see who surprises whom, yes? Play your game, boy. Come, see Mommy and Daddy."

A sinking terror consumed Jack. He had no idea what Batesh was talking about but it filled him with dread. For better or worse, the dye was cast and Jack felt certain he had got something horribly wrong.

He made his way towards his front porch on legs heavy as lead. The men standing there glared at him hatefully. If they could have it their way, he would have been shot as soon as he showed himself.

He stopped and stood on the first of three steps leading to the porch. His front door creaked open until Jack had an unrestricted view of the inside. Blinking against the brightness, Jack began to burn the scene into memory.

Three men could be seen inside, their faces covered. In the dining room, well away from the front door, Jack spotted his mom and dad. They were both blindfolded and gagged. Tied to chairs, their heads were pulled back by cruel bonds to expose their necks. He could see their labored breathing and their squirming against the discomfort of their positions.

Jack's brain spiked with a pain like brain-freeze; like he sucked down too much frozen slushy all at once. It wasn't what he was looking at that caused his pain. It was what he didn't see. Phil's mom? Collin's and Peter's parents? They weren't there.

Jack forced himself to focus on the man holding a long, cruel looking dagger.

Qasim Batesh!

He was tall and thin wearing what appeared to be a military jacket two sizes too big. His jeans were worn and faded and just as baggy as the coat. Around his neck was a red, blue and white scarf the ends of which were tucked aristocratically into the neck of the jacket.

Everything about him looked evil. His eyes, close to hidden beneath bushy black brows, were slits of hatred. Jack couldn't tell if the hook to his nose was due to its being broken or if that was its natural curve. Nothing natural could have caused its awkward, jagged pull to the right. Though thinning, Batesh wore his hair long and pulled behind his head into a ponytail that looked rat-gnawed. Running down the side of his face were deep and bloody scratch marks.

"I hope those hurt like hell," Jack snarled.

Batesh's hand went to his cheek. He smiled at Jack, exposing crooked and yellow teeth. "Mommy didn't take news of your sister's death well. But you see? In the end, she has become most cooperative. And now...I have her. And because I have her, I have you."

Batesh's thick lips pulled a grin of pure evil. "Want to see what I mean? About having you?" he taunted.

Grabbing Jack's parents by their restraints, he gave each a rough shaking. They both squealed in pain past wads of cloth that had been rammed into their mouths and secured with duct tape.

Behind Batesh, slinking through the kitchen, Jack caught just a glimpse of Phil.

"That's enough," Jack shouted, climbing to the second step, making sure all eyes were on him.

Like the sound of a sinister rattlesnake, the firearms belonging to the two who guarded the door rattled their warning of metallic clicks as they snapped up, targeting him. Another rash move on his part and this rescue attempt would die, along with himself and his parents, right here on the front porch.

"You wanted to be sure they were still alive," Batesh said flashing another smug leer. "See?" He jerked his captives a second time forcing more painful whimpers out of them. "They are. If you want them to stay that way, you will produce Kalila. Now!"

Jack had no choice but to turn and walk away. Immune to the cold, his shoulders drooping, he made his way back toward the street. He felt miserable. Useless. Defeated. Resigned to dying and not caring if he did.

He pulled the tennis ball out of one pocket, the lighter out of the other, and stood with his back to the house. His feet wouldn't move. It was time to act and he couldn't bring himself to do it.

Stalling the inevitable, he called over his shoulder to the house, "Let my parents go. I'll do whatever you want, just let them go."

Batesh's patience had run out. "Enough!" he shouted. "Bring Kalila to me now!"

"Why?" he shouted back. "So you can kill my parents and then me just as soon as you have her?"

"I will kill you and your parents now, if you don't do as I say."

Smoke filled the inside of the house. Sirens roared. Voices yelling and gunfire ringing out blasted into Jack's ears. The men on the porch dove inside the house. Batesh was shouting orders in Arabic.

Screaming so harsh and loud Jack could taste blood in his throat, he lit the M80's fuse and hurled the ball inside the house just as the door was closing. Legs pumping wildly, he sprinted toward the porch, but he was too slow. The door was shut and locked.

Springing back the way he came, he howled as, with a massive heave, he pulled the birdbath's bowl off its pedestal. Scarcely keeping his balance, he stumbled back to the door and fell against it, letting all the concrete's weight fall on the doorknob.

Sparks and flame of every color whizzed all around him as he fell through the shattered doorway. Peter's fireworks were putting on an amazing display. Lying on the floor, Jack lit one of his own smoke bombs then, another M80. Angry voices were screaming inside. Batesh's men began to return fire, aiming outside the house, forgetting about Jack who could only pray his neighbors had the good sense to take cover once the shots started ringing out.

He rolled to his right and sprang to his feet, but Batesh was just as quick. A blue puff of smoke erupted in front of Jack. White-hot pain erupted just above his left knee. No longer able to support his weight, Jack crumpled to the floor.

Looking up, he saw Batesh shouting orders to the men inside the house. Pressing a finger against his ear, Batesh shrieked orders into his Bluetooth. Behind Jack, what remained of the front door was being splintered by rapid gunfire. Roman candles and massive explosives meant to light up the open sky burst in the small space of Jack's living room. Fires were starting everywhere. His ears filled with recorded sounds of sirens, soldiers giving orders, and explosions.

Somewhere in the city, a far more enormous explosion thundered, sending shockwaves through the neighborhood. The whole house rocked as if an earthquake stuck it.

Time stopped.

Bullets once more starting flying in greater numbers. An all-out firefight erupted inside Jack's home.

Struggling to his knees, Jack scanned for his parents, but his eyes burned from all the smoke. Hobbling to his feet he did his best to race to where he remembered seeing them.

Anguish and rage consumed him. Diving toward the fireplace he snatched up the poker. He turned left and right, swinging at anything and nothing. Like a spinning snow demon, the pain in his leg forgotten, he rammed the point into a black shadow and was rewarded to hear a man scream in pain. Realizing how exposed he was, he took cover behind a recliner. Searching for more dark shapes, he hurled himself at them, swinging his poker. Inch by inch, he made his way to where his parents sat trussed up in their chairs.

A second explosion, followed by a third, rattled the house so violently that Jack was knocked to the floor. He had no idea what those explosions were, aside from the fact that they were evil. No good could come from them.

From where he lay on the floor, Jack looked around. For the first time since entering his house he took time to assess the hopeless situation he had pulled his friends into.

CHAPTER 26

The living room sounded as if it were filled with angry bees. So many bullets flying that the air was thick with them. The whizzing, fizzing, buzz they made added to the sense of infestation.

Jack rolled three times to his right, taking cover behind the couch. Each time his left leg hit the floor, he received a shocking jolt of pain and each time it surprised him. His mind was pinned to gruesome imaginings of men with scarves covering their faces dragging wicked blades across his parents' throats, just as they had done to Grace's. No other information penetrated.

His parents were already dead. He knew it in every cell of his body. But he had to be sure. If, by any chance, they were still alive, he would rescue them.

Ignoring the pain in his leg, he clawed up off of the floor and onto the couch. Like a toddler playing peek-a-boo, he popped his head over the back.

At the far end of the room he saw two kitchen chairs, now knocked to the floor, his motionless parents bound to them. The front of their bodies were stained dark red, as if buckets of paint had been poured over them. Their heads lay at such awkward angles that it made everything about them seem wrong.

Bullets began pelting the couch but Jack remained frozen.

A sudden jerk on his jacket's hem sent him tumbling behind what little cover the couch provided. The back of his head smacked against the floor.

Dazed, he saw Peter huddled next to him.

"Are you trying to get yourself killed?" Peter shouted at him.

"My parents. My parents."

Waiting for a lull in the fire, Peter jabbed his head out past the arm of the couch and quickly pulled it back, hurling his body well away from where it had been.

A spray of bullets ripped up the carpet and a corner of the couch tore away. More than a few pierced the fabric, stuffing, and wood, passing dangerously close to them.

"Jack," Peter said shaking him by his coat lapels. "We have got to get out of here."

More bullets struck the couch, many pushing through to their side.

"Jack!" Peter was yelling now. "We've got to MOVE!"

Jack felt himself being thrown face down onto the carpet. Beside him, Peter was crawling, sacrificing the use of one hand in order to drag him along beside him.

Three blinding flashes of light followed by thunderous bangs burst in the living room. Jack's ears were ringing and his eyes saw nothing but green, yellow, and blue spots. Beside him, Peter had rolled onto his back and laid there rocking from side to side, his own eyes buried in the crook of his elbow.

New voices, cool and coordinated, began yelling back and forth to each other from the direction of the front door.

"We're in!"

"Lay down suppressive fire!"

The black blurs Jack saw streaming into his house began firing their weapons towards the positions Batesh and his men had taken up. The air was thick with smoke and their muzzle flashes spread in a blur, like headlights in the fog. The terrorists began targeting those flashes.

Jack took advantage of that change in tactics to drag Peter back to the meager cover provided by the couch. They were far safer there than they would be crawling toward the new arrivals' firing line.

Over the other shouts and gunfire, Jack heard a steady stream of excited Arabic words. Batesh was giving orders, too. He was still alive.

The sound of smashing glass and wood rang out. The terrorist's lethal rain of bullets thinned, but remained heavy enough to make movement toward their position a fool's errand. Muffled gunfire told Jack that the firefight was shifting to his backyard.

Making a rash move, Jack popped his head around the corner of the couch. As he suspected, Batesh and one other remained in the house. Judging from the sounds of smashing glass he guessed that the rest had split up and were fleeing out any exit they could make.

Silhouetted in the demolished back door, Batesh glared at him. He took two menacing steps in Jack's direction before his man grabbed his arm and began shoving him out of the door.

Batesh tore free, his arm flying up. A handgun was pointed at Jack but Batesh didn't take time to aim and the bullet flew wide. Jack saw Batesh's hand squeeze a second time but the gun failed to fire. He was out of rounds.

With a sneer, he pressed a finger against his Bluetooth earpiece giving more orders. Then casually, full of intentional defiance and bravado, Batesh swaggered out of the devastation, following the last of his men. The cold brutality of that evil calm set Jack on fire with rage.

Ignoring the protests of his wounded leg, Jack vaulted from behind the couch. He ran to find cover behind the wall separating the kitchen from the rest of the house. Making two darting glances into the kitchen, he saw that it had been evacuated.

Behind him were shouts of "Living room secure!" and "Dining room clear!"

He heard Phil's voice screaming, "Jack! Where are you?"

"I'm here with Peter. We're not hurt," Jack yelled back.

"Stay where you are," a gruff voice barked. "We will make our way to you."

"You, over there," another angry voice called out through the gun smoke and dust, "lock your fingers behind your head."

"Hey!" Collin shouted back. "I'm one of the good guys."

In tones strained with nervous tension the angry voice yelled at Collin again. "Hands behind your head. Now! DO IT NOW!"

"Collin!" Jack shouted in panic, "These guys don't know friend from foe. Do what he says. Phil! Peter! Do the same. Stay still and let them come to you."

"Who is that giving orders?" the gruff man demanded.

"My name is Jack Straw. This is my house. Who are you?"

"Homeland Security. Is this house wired to blow like the others?"

"Others? What others? Were those explosions houses?"

"I need you to focus, kid. Is this house rigged to explode?"

Jack's mind bogged down in the mud of too many possibilities. *Houses? Whose houses? Who else has died?*

"Talk to me kid!" the man insisted.

"I...I...No. I don't think so."

"So, you don't know for sure," the man said less aggressively. He was now standing over Jack, glaring down at him, wearing full assault armor while his face was covered by a balaclava.

The man reached down and, grabbing a fist full of jacket, hoisted Jack to his feet. He was being hauled back out of the house, lifted just enough onto his toes by the man's grip to keep him off balance.

No amount of force could prevent Jack from breaking loose when they reached the spot where his parents' bodies were, looking even more gruesome in the post battle devastation.

"Hey! Cut it out, Kid. What's wrong with you?" his captor barked.

Jack squirmed and tugged against the man's hold. "They're my parents. Let me go! I've got to get them out of here!"

"Kid! Settle down. My people will get them out once we know explosives haven't been planted."

Jack gave a rebellious heave, splitting his coat zipper apart. In an instant he slithered out of it, leaving the man holding an empty bundle of cloth. Racing to his parents, he threw himself onto his knees beside them. Their hideous state jolted the harsh truth into him. They were dead. Beyond help. Nothing he could do would bring them back.

Blind rage exploded inside him.

Before the Homeland Security officer could grab him, Jack sprang to his feet and flew through the kitchen. He leapt over the two steps leading into the back yard with such force he had to dive into a forward roll to keep from breaking his ankles. His injured leg hurled obscenities at him. Ignoring both his pain and the Homeland Security officers inside the house yelling at him to come back, he pelted into the darkness after Batesh.

Jack vaulted over his back fence and darted through the yard of the house behind his. Without a hint of stealth, he burst out of the gate and ran into the street yelling for Batesh, calling him a coward and challenging him to stop and face him.

He got his wish.

Qasim Batesh crawled out of the black shadows like a cockroach and stood in the middle of the street, washed by the glow of a streetlamp. The rest of his vile accomplices had abandoned him to save their own skins.

"They must have fled to the next street over," Jack heard the Homeland Security forces shout as they followed his rash pursuit.

He didn't have the luxury to stand motionless, seething at Batesh. The police, Homeland Security, National Guard, and no telling who else would soon be swarming the street searching for the terrorists. He had to finish Batesh off now or he would never get the chance.

Voicing a savage roar, Jack charged the man.

Batesh stood waiting, an ugly, hateful sneer playing across his face.

Having no intention of giving Batesh the opportunity to hurl taunts, Jack pushed off the ground with all his might, launching himself and twisting in the air so that his feet slammed across Batesh's chest.

Both landed on the ground with a thud. Jack rolled out of his fall, the pain in his leg spurring him on now. Batesh, taken by surprise, landed on his back, the breath knocked out of him.

Seizing the opportunity, Jack rushed in and aimed a viscous kick at the man's head.

Batesh managed to block it.

Jack's second kick was likewise blocked and this time Batesh snaked a powerful hand around his leg and applied pressure at an awkward angle behind his knee. Jack corkscrewed face first into the pavement.

Batesh scrambled to his knees, still pinning Jack to the ground. Eyes filled with murderous hatred bored into Jack's own as a fist smashed into his cheek.

Batesh's face disappeared behind starbursts erupting in Jack's eyes. Another blow like that and the fight would be over and Jack, dead.

As Batesh pulled his fist back to strike the winning blow, Jack managed to squeeze his other leg between them and landed a powerful thrust of his heel beneath Batesh's chin.

Batesh flipped onto his back and rolled to his feet. Jack flung his legs over his head and back-rolled, standing to again square off against Batesh. Just as he regained his feet he was forced to twist like a matador, dodging Batesh as he lunged toward him.

Jack was able to avoid the wild hook-punch Batesh aimed at his head but not the follow-up kick which Batesh targeted for the bullet hole in his thigh.

Jack screamed in agony, stumbling back, but refusing to collapse.

Batesh pressed his advantage with a jab that popped Jack on the nose.

Despite tear filled eyes, Jack was able to bob his head out of the way of a second jab. His anger and hatred had taken him as far as they could. He was spent. Panting, suffering, he knew he was going to lose this fight.

Batesh reared back, preparing to throw a powerful haymaker.

Jack threw his arm up, but forced it to remain relaxed. When Batesh's arm struck his, Jack bent his elbow, pushing upwards so that the blow was redirected over his head. Moving fast to the side, grabbing the terrorist's wrist, he twisted the arm over and locked it into that position with his own elbow. Hopping into the air, he directed all his weight down into the killer's elbow joint.

Their combined weight was too much for Batesh to maintain. When the two hit the ground Jack rolled hard over Batesh's back, using all the force of their fall to wrench Batesh's elbow in a direction the joint was never designed to bend. It separated with a sickening crunch.

Jack staggered to his feet. Batesh screamed with pain as he attempted to do the same, but hindered by a now dislocated elbow, he was a fraction of a second slower. A savage kick between the legs sent Batesh back to the ground gasping for air.

Swaying from pain and loss of blood, Jack had to force himself back in to finish Batesh off. He grabbed a handful of Batesh's beard, pulling his chin up, exposing the man's neck just as his parents' necks had been exposed.

Jack lined up the knife blade of his hand against his enemies Adam's apple. He had once crushed two cement paving stones with this blow in the dojo. Batesh's throat didn't stand a chance.

Lifting his hand even with his ear, Jack took a deep breath in through his throbbing and bloody nose. He let it hiss out his mouth.

Batesh grinned up at him with a face just as bloody as Jack's. "Better this than back to prison."

Inhaling a second time, Jack felt himself settle into a relaxed calm. When the blow fell with his next exhale, all his weight would come crashing down on Batesh's windpipe.

Jack screamed. His hand bolted downward.

Jack was thrown into the air. Hitting the ground hard, he lay on his back gulping for breath. Men in assault gear were everywhere. Four were wrestling Batesh into handcuffs. Others were clearing the area with strategic precision.

The voice he had first heard in his house said, "Sorry, kid. We need him alive."

"No!" Jack screamed in rage.

He staggered to his feet. The world lurched as sharp and hard as any carnival ride. His head was dizzy. With Herculean effort he took a step forward but his wounded leg roared with searing pain. It collapsed under him. Anguish burst out of every cell in his body. Jack pitched headlong toward the ground. Black unconsciousness overtook him before he slammed to the pavement.

CHAPTER 27

Jack's eyelids fluttered open. Too heavy to lift, he lolled his head left, then right, across a starchy pillow. The movement made him dizzy.

As if looking through a dense fog, he was aware that people were there with him — people he felt he should know. The fact he didn't have a clue who they were made him anxious. He squirmed and scrabbled but hands reached out of the fog to restrain him.

His tongue felt thick and his mouth dry. Unintelligible noises came out of this mouth in rasping wheezes. Words refused to come out at all. His eyes slammed up to the top of his head and he was unconscious again.

When he next awoke, he was more alert, but only slightly. Pulling his tongue off from where it was glued to the roof of his mouth, it made an arid, peeling noise. Licking his lips felt like kissing sandpaper.

Kelly materialized beside him. She shook a styrofoam cup and picked out an ice chip with her fingers.

"Suck on that," she whispered as she slid the chip past his parched lips. Dipping a paper towel into the melted ice water, she dabbed at them as he worked the chip around his mouth like a lozenge.

Something terrible had happened, but he couldn't remember what. He didn't want to remember. Kelly's gentle care set his mind at ease. The ice-cold trickle down his throat felt wonderful. Far less violently, unconsciousness folded itself around him.

Cruel memory returned while he was asleep.

"No!" he screamed as he bolted upright in his hospital bed.

Kelly lunged out of the chair she was in and prevented him from leaping onto the floor. "You're safe," she cooed. "Don't try to get up."

He settled just as a nurse bustled in. Jack saw that she was the old-school sort: scrubs crisp, hair pulled back into a tight bun, with a stern face and a no-nonsense demeanor.

Her eyes were another story. A deep and sorrowful look of pity flashed through them, but it lasted mere seconds. By the time she made it to his bedside, her eyes were hard and she was all business.

Jack turned back to Kelly. Her red-rimmed eyes were puffy and dull. Her nose was raw. She had been crying.

"Gracie died in my arms," he said in a deadman's voice.

New tears welled in Kelly's eyes. "Yes."

It wasn't a dream.

The nurse cleared her throat. Jack suspected she made the noise more to keep her emotions in check as opposed to drawing attention to herself.

"You've been through quite an ordeal, Mr. Straw," she said. "While I can't imagine the strain you must be feeling, you need to try and remain calm."

Mr. Straw? That was always his father, not him. But his father was dead. Maybe he was Mr. Straw, now. There was no one else left alive it could be.

The nurse checked the bag of fluid hanging on a pole beside his head. She fiddled with the bandage on his arm hiding a harpoon sized needle. With systematic efficiency, she inspected all his dressings while attempting to distract him by giving instructions on how to raise and lower the bed and the operation of the television remote.

Jack heard her voice, but the words flew past in an unintelligible hum. She left as brusquely as she had come, leaving him alone with Kelly.

"I am so sorry, Jack," she said, crying in earnest now. "I can't believe any of this is real. Except, of course, it is real, isn't it. It all happened so fast! I couldn't stop it."

She buried her face in her hands.

Jack wasn't impressed. To his ears her words sounded rehearsed. Besides, she should have guessed what might happen. She should have gone to the real authorities and not put her trust in a bunch of kids. It all added up to her betraying Grace and that, he could never forgive.

His anger flared when he thought of it. "I knew this whole friendship thing you pretended to have with Grace was an act. You never cared for her. You used her just so you could get close to me and my friends and now she is dead."

As soon as the accusation left his mouth, he knew it was ridiculous. Nonetheless, it hit its mark.

Kelly took a step away from him. She grabbed the bed's guardrail to steady herself. Eyes wide and mouth hanging open, she looked like she'd been slapped.

A disgusting sense of satisfaction swarmed over him as he settled back against his pillows. It tainted his triumph and left him feeling like a worm.

"You never liked Grace, did you Jack?" Kelly said.

"What did you just say?" Jack growled, jerking up and twisting to face her.

Pain exploded in his ribs. The violence of his anger caused an immediate headache to spool up inside his skull. Shooting stars crossed his vision. He clenched his teeth against crying out and settled back into his bed.

"Oh, you loved her," Kelly said hastily, still choosing her words very, very carefully. "Loved her more than either of you realized, until it was too late. But liked her? I don't think so."

"Get out," growled Jack.

"I can't," Kelly said. "Not yet."

"Then I'll call that nurse back in and she will throw you out," Jack said fumbling for the right button to press.

She laid a soft hand over his. Her touch felt like a spring breeze blowing across his skin. She wasn't trying to stop him from calling the nurse. Her hand, so light on his, was pleading with him not to.

"After I leave," she said, "you will never see me again. Homeland Security and the FBI are creating new lives for us. I have no idea where I'll be or even who I'll be. So, before I go, there are some things I need to tell you about Grace."

Jack pulled his hand out from under hers. He wanted her gone, but also wanted to hear what she had to say about his sister.

Kelly sat back down in the chair. She pinched her lower lip, her eyes staring at nothing. He knew she was thinking over what she was about to say and wanted to yell at her to get on with it. Clenching his fist around a bundle of sheet, he waited her out.

"First off," she said shakily, "you are wrong about me and Grace. She was my friend. I loved her."

"You were nothing alike," Jack sneered. "You had nothing in common."

"We were very much alike. Your sister, Jack? She felt things so deeply. So intensely. Just like I do.

"When Grace and I first met, we were both still little. Mom had just brought us to America and I felt so alone. So scared. I looked different. I talked different. Back then, I had a noticeable accent. I stood out. Didn't fit in at a time when being different meant being feared and hated. Grace was kind to me.

"As the years passed she began to put up snooty defenses against sympathizing so much with everyone. It wounded her so badly. In the end, I was the only one she could open up to and be herself."

"She could have always talked to me," Jack protested. A sick feeling in his stomach told him that was another lie.

Kelly smiled. "She loved you, Jack. She was always bragging about her kid brother. But she never understood you. The things you were into, the plans she knew you had for your life. They confused her. They frightened her. That's why she kept you at a distance."

"I never did anything to hurt her," Jack objected. "She had no reason to be frightened of me."

"She wasn't physically afraid of you. Not ever! She was afraid what would happen if she opened her feelings to you. You and your friends? She thought you all were so strong. Much stronger than she could ever be. She was afraid of what you would think of her if you found out she was so emotionally weak. At least, that's how she saw herself."

"That's crazy," Jack said. "It would have brought us closer, not driven us farther apart."

"That's what I kept telling her," Kelly said. A sad, nostalgic smile flickered across her face. It didn't last. "She wouldn't listen. You and your friends just kept getting stronger. You intimidated her."

"Great! Our lousy relationship was all my fault! Thanks for telling me that, Kelly." Jack spat sourly.

"No!" said Kelly. She was stern and adamant. "Not your fault. Not her fault. You were two people who were complete opposites of each other. You also happened to be brother and sister. It's no more complicated than that."

Jack didn't like that answer. He didn't like a single thing Kelly was saying.

"Is that it? Is that all you have to say?"

"No. There is one more thing." Kelly paused, thinking. "I wasn't going to tell you. I changed my mind because I know you will figure it out sooner or later, and I want to be here when you do."

"What?" Jack was getting impatient. He wanted her to leave him alone.

"Months ago, I realized what was going to happen back home. It got scared and told Grace my secret. She insisted we talk to my mother about it. Mother was furious. She made us promise we wouldn't tell anyone. Mom believed we were safe. Off the radar."

"She was wrong," Jack snarled.

"She was wrong," agreed Kelly. "Still, Grace and I trusted her judgment. What else could we do? But I was still terrified. Grace wanted to help! Jack, it was Grace's idea I cozy up to you and your friends."

Kelly's words sped up as she tried to justify Grace's actions. "She was always bragging about how special you were. How you were going to do great things with your life. Your friends, too.

"'Just flirt with him a little,' Grace said. 'He'll feel flattered and want to protect you.' She thought of you as being some kind of a knight in shining armor."

Jack's words were venomous. "So, my own sister set me up. That makes me feel so much better. Thanks, Kelly."

Kelly snapped to her feet, her face pale. "No! Oh, no Jack! She never intended to betray you. It wasn't supposed to be like that. She thought all I needed was a security blanket. A crutch. If she knew what was going to happen she never would have let me anywhere near you!"

"If that's all you have to say, I want you to leave," Jack said coldly.

"Jack! This is why I had to be the one to tell you. I had to explain! Explain for Grace. I can understand you hating me but please, not Grace," Kelly pleaded. "Never Grace. She thought it would all be harmless."

"Leave," Jack insisted.

"Try to understand," Kelly said, uncontrollable tears streaming down her face. "Grace never dreamed what would happen. No one did!"

Jack had heard enough. He pressed the call button.

Kelly stopped arguing Grace's case. She wiped away tears that were flowing down her face.

The prickly nurse came in. Before she could get a word out, Jack told her he wanted to be alone but Kelly was refusing to leave. Kelly hung her head and gathered her things. She walked out without looking back. The nurse followed close behind.

As soon as the door snapped shut Jack heard Kelly lose it. He tried covering his ears with his pillow but the sounds of her agonized sobs refused to be blocked out.

"Come, come, child," he heard the nurse say. "You can't just lie on the floor bawling. That young man has been through an astonishingly cruel ordeal. And so have you, from what I gather. Let's get you a nice cup of hot chocolate and find someplace you and I can talk."

Jack was relieved to hear Kelly's sobs soften. As he listened to the pair shuffle down the corridor he was grateful the nurse wasn't so thorny after all.

He had been wrong about that nurse. *What if I'm wrong about Kelly? And Grace?*

Time meant nothing to Jack. Whatever was going on in the outside world didn't concern him. His existence consisted of bad hospital food, gowns that never seemed to cover his backside, and a steady stream of doctors and nurses who poked and prodded and asked stupid questions like, "How are we feeling today?"

Jack found the 'we' part the most aggravating. We. As if they were sharing the misery.

"Let's find out," he unloaded on a team of doctors and interns. "I feel like I've been shot. Like my family has been murdered and I'm an orphan. Like the same thing has happened to my three best friends and they are now orphans, too. And, oh yeah, I feel like every bit of that is my fault. How do you flippin' feel?"

He was out of patience with them all. All, that is, except the stern looking Nurse Coltrane. She didn't bother him like the others did because she never asked him stupid questions. She gave him orders.

"Sit up."

"Swallow these."

"Under the tongue."

One afternoon, as Nurse Coltrane was bustling out, a man barged in and dropped a white, grease stained, paper sack onto his tray-table and set a sweaty waxed cup with a straw poking out the top next to it.

He wasn't a tall man but Jack could tell he was powerful despite most of his body being hidden beneath an expensive looking sport coat. He had yellow streaks in his otherwise tawny hair that matched the gold necklace just visible beneath his starched white dress shirt. A lighter yellow stubble grew out of his cheeks that looked more like he forgot to shave for a couple of days instead of being an actual beard.

After depositing the bag, the man jammed his hands into the pockets of his pressed dress slacks and stared at him with the bluest eyes Jack had ever seen while smiling at him with perfect teeth.

"What the heck is this?" Jack asked grumpily.

"Burger. Fries. Chocolate malt," the stranger said as he glided over to sit in the room's only chair. Lifting his right foot and resting it on the opposite knee Jack noticed three more things. First, the guy was wearing old-man loafers, complete with their signature tassel. Second, he had a gold ankle bracelet identical to the one around his neck. Finally, the guy forgot to put on his socks this morning.

"And you are…?" Jack asked unpleasantly.

"Simon."

"Simon the doctor? Simon the social worker? Simon the poisoner?" Jack gave the paper sack a loud thump with his fingertips.

"Just Simon."

Jack persisted. "Okay. So is that Simon Something, or Something Simon?"

"Well, you can call me Mr. Simon, if it makes you feel better. I know kiddos like to do things like that."

Jack bit his tongue to keep from saying something nasty about being called a kiddo.

The room started filling with the smell of delicious fast food. Jack's stomach lurched and gurgled, urging him to eat. He ignored it.

Simon did not. "Better dig in before that malt melts. It's been in the car all the way from across town. Best little burger shack in the state is," Simon paused and made finger guns with his hands and, aiming at Jack's hospital window barked, "Boom. Boom. Boom. Right across town."

"What I meant," Jack said gritting his teeth in order to maintain his cool, "was what do you do around here and what has it got to do with me? And why are you bringing me burgers?"

"Let's take those in order. I don't do anything around here. I'm not associated with the hospital. Next, you and your little buddies have been assigned to me so I've got everything to do with you. At least for a while, anyway. As for the burger? Well, let's just say I'm a nice guy."

Simon flashed his pearl white teeth again.

Working on a hunch that Simon was the one with all the answers, Jack asked, "So where's Batesh?"

Simon patronized him with a smile. "In a hole somewhere that doesn't have a name."

That answer was very unsatisfying. "And that's all you know? Useless!"

"I know you were a bit of a tool to Kelly."

"She deserved it," Jack grumped.

"Did she?"

"What was that?" Jack demanded.

"She and her family were in the wind. All that they had to do was to keep going. We'd have never found them.

"Instead, Kelly and her mother stopped and called in on a phone they knew full well would be traced. How do you think Homeland Security arrived at your house before you and your plucky friends managed to get yourselves killed?"

Jack didn't want to talk about Kelly or that night. He gave up on trying to get information out of Simon. It was too much like playing chess with Collin; hard work and he was only going to lose.

More as a distraction, he began pulling food out of the sack and started nibbling. Before he realized how hungry he was, Simon interrupted his wolfing down of the burger.

"Careful, sport. Don't go biting off more than you can chew."

Jack glared at him. He didn't know if that was supposed to be a joke over the way he was eating or a snide comment about what he had put himself and his friends through.

Simon ignored the glare. "After all," he said with a grin, "you've been eating that hospital trash for going on two weeks now. Real food might take some getting used to."

"Two weeks?" Jack sputtered around the handful of French fries he'd rammed into his mouth out of spite.

"Yep. That's a long time to be laying around goofing off. Well, the vacation's over, sport. I'm here to make sure you are up to starting physical therapy and other," Simon tapped the side of his head, "therapies."

"What other therapies," Jack asked.

"I thought I made that pretty clear," Simon said. "Individual counseling first. Grief and loss stuff. Then, you and your pals will begin group sessions."

"How are they? My friends? No one here will tell me anything," Jack said.

"Of course not. Doctor/patient confidentiality," Simon said as if Jack should have figured that out on his own.

"But you could have told them it was okay. You said you were in charge of us," Jack objected.

"I could have," Simon said. He offered no explanation as to why he didn't.

"They are all fine," he went on. "Phil was the worst hit but simple grazes and flesh wounds. The real miracle is that any of you are still alive.

"Anyway... She was in the hospital, too. Three floors down. She's out now."

Jack closed his eyes. In his mind he heard the three explosions. He now knew what they were, but he had to ask. He had to be sure.

"She's back home with her mom?"

"Jack," Simon said and for the first time looked sincere in his sympathy, "Phil's mom was killed, too."

Jack dug the heel of his palm into his eye before the pooling tears rolled out, allowing Simon to see them.

"They want to come visit," Simon said, giving Jack the courtesy of turning away to stare out the window.

"I don't want to see them," Jack answered so quiet he doubted Simon could hear him. He stared at his half-eaten hamburger, his appetite gone.

Simon hoisted himself out of the chair and adjusted his sport coat, preparing to leave. "You'll feel different after you have had your noggin tidied up a bit."

"I'm not going to therapy. And I'm certainly not going to group counseling with all of them," Jack proclaimed.

Simon laughed at him as he walked out the door.

"What's so funny," Jack demanded to know.

"You said that like you have a choice. See ya, sport!"

CHAPTER 28

After a week of Jack's stubborn refusal to cooperate in counseling, Simon had him released from the hospital. It happened in a whirlwind. Simon showed up before breakfast, wheeled him down to a big black SUV and lifted him into the back seat.

"Where are we going?" Jack ventured to ask.

"You'll see when we get there," Simon said.

Jack didn't try talking again.

After a twisting drive past frozen trees with picturesque snow-covered homes beyond them, they pulled onto a long peat drive at the end of which stood an enormous mansion.

Simon got out, unloaded the wheelchair onto a raw-wood, newly constructed walkway with ramps leading inside, all without saying a word.

"You going to tell me where we are?" Jack asked after struggling to get into his wheelchair. Simon didn't offer to help.

"Safe house," Simon said, moving toward the door.

Jack rolled after him, his wheels struggling for traction on patches of ice.

"I thought safe houses were supposed to be inconspicuous," he said. "This stands out just a bit, don't you think?"

"Some of the people we have to keep safe are accustomed to a certain quality of life," Simon explained.

Jack laughed, "You think I am accustomed to this?"

"It was available," Simon said with a shrug. "This place was supposed to hold four kids but you screwed that up when you refused counseling and therapy, so it's just you."

"Why not bring them here and send me somewhere else. They'd love it here," Jack objected. It hurt him to think that he was still ruining his friends' lives again.

"Whole house has been outfitted to accommodate someone with special needs. Too late to undo all that work and redo it elsewhere," Simon said.

The house was just as beautiful inside. Jack was awestruck. "Are the others in a nice place like this?"

Simon's answer was harsh. "You want to find out what's going on with them, ask them. If you can't bring yourself to do that, deal with not knowing. Now, I've work to get to."

"You're leaving me here alone?" Jack asked, regretting it as soon as the words left his mouth. He sounded like a frightened and whiny child.

"That was your choice, sport."

Being left alone was far better than being in Simon's company. Rolling his chair past the grand staircase that filled the entryway, he came to a living room decked out with a baby grand piano and luxurious furniture.

Jack rolled himself over to sit in front of massive windows. He stared out at a garden that snow made it look like it had been decorated with white frosting.

"I suppose you think you're going to sit there moping around all morning?" a stern voice said from behind him.

Jack's face twitched into a smile. Nurse Coltrane stood in the doorway, stuffy as ever, her fists planted on her hips.

"What am I supposed to be doing?" Jack asked, relieved.

The idea of thinking for himself was detestable. He longed to be told what to do, not smugly, like Simon, but assigned tasks he was expected to complete then left alone to get them done.

"You *are* a boy of school age," Coltrane said sharply. "You can start by catching up on all the work you got yourself behind on. You'll find your books in the library. You passed it on your way in here."

"I remember," Jack said.

"Good," Coltrane answered. "Your assignments and a schedule are on the desk. Lunch is in an hour and a half."

"Yes, ma'am," Jack drawled obediently.

The library was, in keeping with the rest of the house, beautiful. Jack liked it because the room was an octagon and not an ordinary square room. The ceiling was covered in the same cherry wood the bookshelves were constructed from. Jack couldn't help thinking how happy Collin would be in a room like this. With Collin, Peter, and Phil heavy on his mind, he rolled himself in front of the fireplace and wept.

Pulling himself together, Jack surrendered his mind to the distraction of schoolwork. Over lunch, Jack made it clear he wanted nothing to do with Christmas. Nurse Coltrane commented that she wasn't surprised by this, given what he had gone through and promised to provide him a schedule that would pull him through the holidays.

On Christmas Morning, Jack awoke to find Simon sitting in his room. "Come to give me a present?" Jack asked sarcastically.

"Depends on your point of view, sport," Simon said.

"What is that supposed to mean?"

Laughter erupted from the floor below. Phil, Peter, and Collin were there. Jack locked eyes with Simon whose eyebrows rose, taunting him with the unspoken question, *What are you going to do now, sport?"*

Giving Simon the dirtiest look he could muster, Jack pushed himself out of bed, dressed, snatched up his cane, and stumped out of his room. Not stopping, he went out the library's patio doors and retreated into the snow-covered garden.

The fresh-fallen snow crunched and squeaked as he marched fuming and swearing across the garden, leaving a trail of shoe prints and cane-poked holes behind him. He continued to storm away from the mansion until he reached a gazebo where he stood glaring at the slushy pond.

Phil sidled up alongside him.

He knew she was coming. From the moment she exited the mansion he was aware of her following him. He didn't turn. He didn't greet her. He allowed her to come up behind him and take position next to him without acknowledging her at all.

A jacket was being draped over his shoulders. He didn't want it. He didn't want her there with him. He didn't want anything to do with the way things had turned out for them all, but the universe didn't seem to care about what he wanted.

The two stood in silence, leaning against the gazebo's rail watching the pond freeze over. She would have to speak first because Jack was determined to not be the one who did.

It wasn't the gallant thing to do. It wasn't the bravest. Jack felt neither gallant nor brave. His shame smothered everything else. Under his leadership people he loved died. His friends, trusting in his abilities, followed him and the ones they loved died, too. He was done with leading.

"You are being stupid. You know that, right?" Phil said, as if reading his thoughts.

"If you say so."

"Well, I do."

His temper, always so very close to the surface these days, erupted on her.

"That's great, Phil. That's just great. I made myself and my friends orphans all because some girl was flirting with me and turned my head. But, hey! Philomela says I'm just being stupid so, you know, I should just let it go!"

"Jack," she said surprisingly gentle given the bile he had just spewed at her, "none of this has anything to do with Kelly. Think about it. Reconstruct the whole thing. Say it wasn't Kelly. Just for a moment pretend it was a guy. Any guy. And say this guy came to you and told you the same story Kelly told you. Would you have turned your back on him? Walked away? When things went so very, very wrong…"

Her voice quivered and she had to pause.

Swallowing hard against her grief she continued, "…would you have given up and stopped?"

"Maybe," Jack lied.

She nudged him with her shoulder. "It's me rock-head. You can try and sell that trash to the shrinks we all have to see, but not to me. I know you better than that."

"You think you know me?" he said dangerously.

"Yeah," she said without hesitation, "I do. Sometimes better than you know yourself. Grace did too. More than you gave her credit for."

Jack turned on her, seething with rage. "You don't know anything!" he yelled.

Exasperated, she shoved herself off the railing. Cupping her mouth with her hands she called out to the empty, frozen grounds as if she were the captain of a ship, "Red alert! Teenage boy having feelings! Take cover immediately!"

Turning back to Jack she said, "You get hurt and that's the remedy you come up with? Throw a tantrum?"

Phil shook her head in dismay as she reclaimed her spot at the railing. "Boys!"

"How am I supposed to act? Tell me Phil! Because I don't know. I never know. You said you know me, but you don't. Neither did Grace. None of you do!

"I'm always lost. Always confused. Never sure of anything, but everyone keeps expecting me to know."

"The only person who expects that out of you, Jack, is you," she whispered.

"Then why does everyone keep turning to me?" he snapped. "I'm sick of it!"

"We follow you because even though you might not know what to do, you always figure something out. More often than not, it turns out all right in the end because you can see the big picture."

"Yeah? Well it didn't turn out alright this time? Did it?"

"Maybe not. Then again, maybe it did."

Jack was stunned. "In what universe is any of this okay?"

"Not in yours," she said testily. "You know? The one where Jack Straw can save everybody as long as he can keep being perfect?

"But where the rest of us live, Jack? Where people aren't perfect. Where it was obvious from the start people were going to die and nothing you or anybody else could have done would prevent it? In that universe? Things could have been a lot worse."

Jack felt like a fool.

They both turned to face the lake. Phil threaded her arm through his and bumped the side of his head with hers. She was being kind to him and he was being a jerk. Her kindness worked on his anger like water on a fire.

"Are you able to listen without exploding, Jack?"

"Sure," he said flatly.

She gave a feeble chuckle and tightened her grip on his arm.

He allowed it.

"Remember that joke you all made? About me and Anne?"

"Yeah," he drawled not seeing where she was going but feeling too uncomfortable to interrupt by asking questions.

She sighed out her frustration with him.

"Phil?" Jack said, feeling she expected him to say something. "Are you trying to tell me you really do like girls or that I hurt your feelings?"

She pulled away and slugged him in his arm. Hard!

"Hurt feelings then," he said rubbing what would definitely become a bruise. "Look…"

"No! You look! Shut up, Jack, and let me explain.

"You and I. We have been friends since we were six. We are way too close for hurt feelings. At least not hurt in the sense most would understand."

"Not in any sort of sense I understand, either," he groaned.

"Shut. Up."

Phil waited, as if daring him to say something. When he didn't, she started again. "My feelings weren't hurt in any painful sort of way. I was more…confused."

Phil paused to think about what she wanted to say as if she were explaining it to herself just as much as she was to him.

"You all know I spent the first part of the school year going out with Bobby. I liked him enough to make out with him. The weird thing is, I love you way more than I liked Bobby, but the thought of making out with you is, well, kinda gross."

"Nice," Jack hissed.

Phil ignored him. "The reason I felt confused was because I know I'm so much more than just 'one of the guys' to all of you. But, in that moment, I also knew that I would never be a maybe-someday-girlfriend to any of you, either."

Jack was lost. "Oh my gosh, Phil. Just spit it out!"

She shouted at him in frustration. "Don't you see? We're family, Jack. I'm just as much your sister as Grace. Peter and Collin? They're our brothers. We have been like that forever, we just never named it. We never needed to because we all had real families of our own. Now that we've lost those families, we can't afford to go on silently accepting it."

Jack looked at Phil. He felt the same way about her and knew the others did, too. Saying it out loud was the new and strange part. The problem was, he already had a sister. Calling Phil his sister felt like betraying Grace.

But Grace is gone, he told himself. *I'm still here. I can't go on alone and I don't think Grace'd want me to.*

"Do you really think it can be that easy? That we can just say it and that'll make it true?" he said aloud.

"Easy?" she scoffed. "There's nothing easy about any of this, Jack! But we've already done the hard part."

"And what part is that?"

Phil smiled. "We've accepted that getting on each other's nerves comes with the territory and we've decided we don't care. All of us are angry, Jack. We're hurting. But we are all still here, together. We love each other too much to let anything drive us apart."

"Have you talked to the others about this?"

"Unless you're on board, there's no point. If we are going to become one hot mess of a family, you have got to be the one to pull us together. It's what you've always done. That's your gift."

Jack's face turned grim. *Great! I've to play leader again.*

He tried to hide his fear behind sarcasm. "Are you trying to tell me that, in this new family we are creating, I'm supposed to be Dad?"

Phil pursed her lips tightly. "You'll get your answer to that the first time you try and send me to my room, Jack Straw."

Jack chuckled a little but otherwise kept silent. He felt Phil shiver and for the first time it dawned on him just how cold the winter air was. He didn't care. He would stand there till spring if Phil needed him to.

Standing next to Phil, hearing her talk to him in the same way she had always done filled him with relief. In a flash he realized what he had been so afraid of all this time.

Yes, he blamed himself for everything, but that he could bear. His real fear was that his friends would blame him, too. He was terrified they would reject him, so he rejected them first. As always, she had him pegged. He *was* being stupid.

He was here. She was here. Peter and Collin? Here! And none of them hated him. Phil was giving him the one thing he needed most and expected least. Forgiveness.

"I'm glad they aren't splitting us up," she said eventually, not noticing or, more likely ignoring the tear rolling across Jack's cheek. "You know they planned on sending us to different boarding schools?"

He breathed in and out heavy and loud. His ribs still hurt but he ignored the pain. He wasn't going to let her, or anyone else, see him wince.

"I told them it was a bad idea," he said. His voice was as icy as the weather surrounding them.

"I did, too," Phil agreed. "In the end, Simon told me it wasn't going to happen, for safety reasons. I mean I was glad we weren't being shipped off or anything but still, I could have killed Simon! 'Haven't we proven we can take care of ourselves?' I yelled at him."

"What'd Simon say?" asked Jack, imagining the look on Simon's face as he tried to cope with an enraged Phil.

"He said I misunderstood the situation. According to him, their game theorists and statisticians had worked it all out. It wasn't our safety they were worried about. It was the schools' they'd planned on sending us to. Apparently, there's a thirty percent chance that any place we are sent would be turned into rubble."

Jack gave his first genuine laugh since their ordeal began.

"They'll want to keep us together. It's in their best interests," he said.

"What makes you say that?"

"We aren't just kids anymore. Not to them. We are assets now. Field-tested. They'll find a use for us, sooner rather than later."

Phil shivered. Jack wasn't sure if her shudder was caused by the cold or by what he told her. A comfortable silence settled over them.

"I'm going back inside," Phil said as she pushed herself off the railing. "It's cold out here."

"I'll be along in a bit," Jack said. "I need to think. Clear my head."

Phil turned to leave.

"Phil?" he called to her, but kept facing the lake.

She stopped but didn't turn.

"Grace would be proud to call you 'sister'."

THE END

ABOUT THE AUTHOR

Shawn's debut novel, *Leigh Howard and The Ghosts Of Simmons-Pierce Manor* was Amazon's #1 Bestseller worldwide, and the #1 Bestseller in the YA Thriller/Mystery genre. The book, and the story of how it was discovered is a Tik-Tok sensation. Shawn appeared on The Today Show, was interviewed on NewsNation, InsideEdition, various FoxNews outlets, and has been featured on local, national, and international television, news, and radio programs.

Before taking up writing, Shawn served as a paratrooper, a social worker, and an engineer. He was a stay-at-home dad who home schooled his two children. His experience in the infantry as well as working several years in pediatric mental health helps him bring operational and psychological realism to Jack's story.

OTHER TITLES BY SHAWN M. WARNER

NOTE FROM SHAWN M. WARNER

Word-of-mouth is crucial for any author to succeed. If you enjoyed *First Mission*, please leave a review online—anywhere you are able. Even if it's just a sentence or two. It would make all the difference and would be very much appreciated.

Thanks!
Shawn M. Warner

We hope you enjoyed reading this title from:

BLACK ROSE writing™

www.blackrosewriting.com

Subscribe to our mailing list – *The Rosevine* – and receive **FREE** books, daily deals, and stay current with news about upcoming releases and our hottest authors.
Scan the QR code below to sign up.

Already a subscriber? Please accept a sincere thank you for being a fan of Black Rose Writing authors.

View other Black Rose Writing titles at
www.blackrosewriting.com/books and use promo code
PRINT to receive a **20% discount** when purchasing.

9 781685 134280